D0122142

The
FRIEND
SCHEME

Cale Dietrich

FEIWEL AND FRIENDS

New York

To Helen

A Feiwel and Friends Book
An imprint of Macmillan Publishing Group, LLC
120 Broadway, New York, NY 10271

Our books may be purchased in bulk for promotional, educational, or business use. Please
contact your local bookseller or the Macmillan Corporate and Premium Sales Department
at (800) 221-7945 ext. 5442 or by email at MacmillanSpecialMarkets@macmillan.com.

Library of Congress Control Number: 2019948804
ISBN 978-1-250-18699-7 (hardcover) / ISBN 978-1-250-18700-0 (ebook)
Book design by Eileen Gilshian Fannell

Feiwel and Friends logo designed by Filomena Tuosto

First Edition, 2020
1 2 3 4 5 6 7 8 9 10

Fiercereads.com

PART ONE

CHAPTER ONE

I NEVER WANTED TO BE A CRIMINAL.

I don't want this, I don't want to be here. The current *here* is the back seat of a burner car, in this case a shitty black Ford. My brother, Luke, is beside me, staring at his phone, smiling. His mind is clearly elsewhere.

My father is driving, and beside him is my uncle Tony.

Outside, the Atlantic coastline streaks by, in all its neon glory. Golden lights, glittering buildings, million-dollar sports cars. It's like Florida forgot it's a swamp for a second. Hordes of well-dressed people are out partying, but we speed past them.

I cross my arms. Everyone else in the car wants this life. They want power and glory, to drive fast cars and wear expensive suits and hook up with pretty girls.

They want to kill, too. For power. For family.

Or maybe they don't *want* to. But they're at least okay with it.

I'm not interested. In any of it.

Outside the window on Luke's side, the ocean stretches out, reflecting the Technicolor city lights, the neon blazing against the dark sky. This town truly is designed to be seen past sunset. During the day, it looks gaudy, like a bad theme park. At night, though, it turns into something kind of magical. It's a playground for adults, where you can get pretty much anything you want . . . as long as you're hot or rich enough.

We stop at a red light. A group of guys in tank tops and designer jeans crosses the street. We're in Donovan territory now, so those boys belong to them, even if they don't know it.

"It's time," says Dad, looking up at us through the rearview mirror. "Masks on."

Shit.

I didn't bring a mask.

Luke remembered his—of course he did—and pulls it on. It's a black ski mask, leaving only his eyes and mouth exposed. Dad and Tony put theirs on, too. I can't help but think this is them in their natural state of being. Miller criminals. One of two plagues on the city. There's us, and the Donovans, and we're both as bad as each other.

At least that's what the cops say.

"Hey, Dad," I say.

"What?"

"There's a small chance I forgot my mask."

His silence is intense alongside the classical music he plays in the car. Beethoven, maybe? I don't know, and I don't know why he does it. Maybe he wants to add a little class to our grim task. Like classical music somehow makes us sophisticated, better than other criminals.

I wipe my sweaty palms on my slacks. I don't even need to look at him to know how disappointed he must be. I'm already such a failure in so many ways. I'm no Luke, for starters. On top of that I'm too soft, too careless, too lacking in family devotion . . .

He has no idea I left my mask on purpose.

I'm a good actor. I can sell it.

He has no idea who I really am.

"You *what*?"

"Are you sure it's not in your bag?" asks Luke. "Come on, we've been planning this for weeks."

I make a show of going through my backpack. I see books, a school sweater, and my tablet. But no mask.

"I'm sorry," I say. "It's not here. I must've left it at home or something."

"I told you," says Tony. "He's not ready."

"He is," says Dad. "He's just distracted. Probably chasing some girl. That's it, right, champ?"

I shrug.

"See?" says Dad. "Don't get me started on the dumb shit you did when you were seventeen. Donna was the only thing you ever thought about."

Tony chuckles. "She sure was."

Dad looks at me through the rearview mirror. His murderous expression tells me everything I need to know. I get it. I've let him down, yet again. He lightened the mood to save face in front of Tony, but I'm nowhere near off the hook. I swear I've tried to be good at this stuff. I'm just not as *in* this as they are. The Millers hate the Donovans with everything they have.

Me?

I'd never admit this to the others, but I've never really hated them. I know I should, because of what they did to my family.

We used to be the closest of allies. The Millers controlled our territory unopposed since the twenties, making millions off the illegal alcohol trade. And right by our side were the Donovans. Things were good, fortunes were made, and little blood was spilled. But then the fifties came around, and the patriarch of the Donovan family wanted to get involved in narcotics. Our patriarch, my great-great-grandfather, said no, not wanting to pump poison into the area, or risk destabilizing their relationship with law enforcement.

The Donovans betrayed my family, broke off, and built their own empire off narcotics. Now they control nearly half the city.

So, yeah. Donovans and Millers aren't friends at the best of times.

Last year, it got even more personal, though.

They murdered my grandfather. They shot him as he was leaving a supermarket of all places. Right in the street. He died on the curb, with bullet holes in his back. It was the spark I think both families had been waiting a long time for, and once long-simmering tensions finally erupted, the city went to war.

When it's done, only one family will rule.

"You can stay in the car," says Dad. "It's too late to go back. We do this tonight."

"All right," I say. "If you think that's best."

"No, Matt, I don't think that's best. I wish you'd remembered your damn mask."

"It was a mistake, okay?"

"Just . . . don't do it again. I've got enough on my plate right now, I shouldn't have to manage you, too."

I can't help but think, *Isn't that your job? Seeing as you're, you know, my dad.*

Dad pulls over, stopping down the street from the restaurant that's a favorite meeting place for the Donovans. *Sofia's.* It's 11:00 p.m., so it's closed. At least that's a good thing. My family won't be burning anyone alive tonight. This is about taking something away from the other side. Making a statement.

It's the way things are done.

"You sure this is a good idea?" asks Luke. He's gone pale. "We could try again tomorrow."

"No, we do this tonight," says Dad. "They won't see him, the windows are blacked out."

"Are you sure about that?" asks Tony.

"I just said I am."

"There are probably security cameras up and down the street. Lie low, Matt. Just in case."

Dad grips the steering wheel tight. I undo my seat belt and slide down the seat.

The three of them climb out of the car and go around to the back. I hear the trunk open. They reappear a few moments later, each one of them holding a Molotov cocktail. These aren't the ones used in street warfare, though, these are the best of the best: thick bottles filled with powerful incendiary chemicals.

Dad holds up a lighter, and soon, the ends of each one burn bright.

And there they are, my family. Doing what they're supposed to. I know there's the stuff to make a fourth Molotov in the trunk, but obviously that's not happening tonight.

I'm glad I "forgot" my mask. Dad being mad at me sucks, sure, but I don't want any real part of what's about to go down. Even though I'm here. Despite my best efforts to distance myself from this, I'm still an accessory.

All at once, the three of them hurl their Molotovs toward the restaurant's large front window. Luke misses and hits the wall. There's a huge fireball, smoke and sparks. Dad's and Tony's aim is true, and their bottles go crashing through the glass.

The three of them stand there for a moment, watching, as the fire spreads inside. It happens so fast, and soon, the whole place is alight. Torrents of black smoke stream out the windows. The trio calmly walks back to the car and climbs in. I pull my seat belt on as Dad plants his foot on the gas.

As we speed away, I watch the restaurant burn through the rear-view mirror.

The scariest part is knowing the night isn't over.

* * *

A cheer breaks out as soon as we step inside the bar.

I slink to the back of the crowded room and stand in the darkness. Tony goes up to my aunt first and kisses her on the cheek. Dad goes up to Grandma and starts talking to her in a low voice. She glances at me, and my blood goes cold. I really hope they aren't talking about me and about what I did.

Or, more accurately, about what I failed to do.

Once we were sure we weren't being followed, Dad drove us out of the city, to a meeting spot on a quiet stretch of road. An associate met us there, waiting inside Dad's black bulletproof Mercedes. We swapped vehicles, then the four of us drove straight here. It's a bar called Jimmy's, and it's a hangout for the city's Miller-affiliated criminals. It's sort of a home base for us.

I pull down on the cuff of my sleeve. Dad's been meaning to take me shopping for a new suit, but he hasn't found the time yet. He's been too busy with war stuff.

Luke makes his way over to me. His suit fits him well, sitting snugly against his broad chest. He's been working out even more than normal lately, and he's freaking jacked now. Dad's so proud. With his new body, and his hair slicked back, my brother looks way older than nineteen. His face is thin, with high cheekbones and a strong jawline, and his eyes radiate an intensity that always seems kind of desperate. It's like whatever it is he wants, he wants it *really* bad, and he's willing to do anything to get it. He reminds me of a jackal sometimes. Starving. Unpredictable. Deadly if needed.

Honestly, he looks right at home here. He'd be a golden boy, if my family were into that sort of thing.

My life would be a lot easier if Luke wasn't so good at the family business.

"What was that?" asks Luke.

"What was what?"

"Your mask."

I shrug. "You know me, airheaded as usual."

He rolls his eyes. "Come *on*. I know you left it on purpose."

How does he know?

"I . . ."

But then he smiles. "I'm just messing with you." His grin is toothy. Doesn't feel right. Like he's doing it for show. He swats my shoulder. "For real, though, don't be so stupid next time, 'kay? I can't be the smart one *and* the good-looking one."

I give him the middle finger. He's both, and he knows it.

He's right, there *is* going to be a next time. And I can't use this same trick again. One way or another, I'm going to end up as a soldier in this war. Now that I'm seventeen, I'm considered ready to fight. To put my life on the line.

I'm expected to kill.

As far as I know, Luke hasn't killed anyone yet. But he's ready for it. He's told me he's looking forward to putting "one of those Donovan bastards in the ground."

I believe him.

"I'm gonna get a drink," says Luke, walking backward. "Want anything?"

"I'm good, thanks."

"Suit yourself."

He spins and walks away, wading through the crowd.

The bar is dimly lit, filled with men in dark suits and women in dark dresses, talking and drinking in low voices. A bunch of them are my family, uncles and aunties and cousins, along with members of families we're allied to. I'd say about half are blood relatives. Dad has two younger brothers, and they all got married young and got to work filling out the family.

I push that thought away and scan the room. There are red latticed windows at the back, above the booths, and there are candles in red glass holders on each of the tables. All this combined gives the whole place a somewhat eerie glow.

Despite my best efforts to be invisible, Dad's youngest brother, Vince, spots me and makes his way over. He stops and sizes me up. He's a sort of big dude, the kind of guy who was fit in his twenties but has since let it slide. He's double the size of my dad, who's thin, like me.

Uncle Vince is our family's best torturer. It's said he's managed to crack even the hardest criminals in the city with his switchblade. Left in a room alone with him, anyone would give up their darkest secrets.

"Well, well, well, if it isn't Little Matty," he says, grinning. "What are you doing hiding back here?"

"Nothing," I say. "And don't call me little."

He chuckles. "That's fair, I guess you're not so short anymore. When'd that happen?"

Adults are borderline obsessed with pointing out my growth spurts to me. It's like they think I don't already know I'm finally getting taller. I never know how I'm supposed to answer questions about my body, even though I get asked about it *so* much. It's like they've never realized most guys get taller and stronger. Or maybe they're just weirded out that the nickname *Little Matty* doesn't fit so well anymore.

Lord save me if my voice cracks around them. I'll never hear the end of it.

Vince keeps staring at me. I hate it. I wonder if he's thinking about my weight. People love talking about that, too. Apparently I'm too skinny, and it's something people take pearl-clutching levels of offense to. Especially because Luke is so big now.

"It's a good thing you're here, with your dad. Hanging around here will teach you a lot, trust me."

I force myself not to raise an eyebrow. "If you say so."

"You look thin. You been eating enough?"

Blank. Stare.

"Like a horse."

"Good. You should come by my gym and start lifting. Tall is good, but strong is better; don't let anyone tell you otherwise. Unless you're okay with the rumors."

"What rumors?"

"That you're, you know . . ."

Oh. *Those* rumors.

"I'm not gay," I say. "Not that I care what anyone thinks."

"Good, good, didn't think you were, but you know how the family talks. So, you got a girlfriend yet? Handsome lad like you must be fightin' 'em off, eh?"

"Not really." I clap him on the shoulder. "Listen, sorry, man, really need to hit the bathroom. Talk later?"

He grins. "She must be a pretty one if she's making you blush like that. Be careful, girls like that will only break ya heart."

"Here's hoping I get so lucky."

He laughs and then finally lets me slide past.

On my way to the bathroom, I walk past Barbie Barker, who runs a bunch of secret brothels, only for the wealthiest local citizens. She's in her fifties, and her light brown hair is cut into a wavy bob. She's dressed in a black suit, with sparkly material on the lapels.

Her booth is nearly full, as she's surrounded by a group of pretty young women, along with a few pretty young men. I'm guessing they work for her, which means . . . you know. They're on offer tonight. They're all stunning. Luke goes up to Barbie, stands up straight, and starts talking to her. She lowers her glasses and smiles at him. In that second, he looks like a pretty boy for sale, blending into the crowd, not a Miller man. I wonder if that's what he wants: to not be one of the power players by birth, if only for a second.

I accidentally make eye contact with one of her male companions. He looks me up and down.

Shit.

I step inside the bathroom, and walk into one of the dark wooden stalls. I lock the door behind me, then sit down on the closed toilet seat. I feel light-headed and sick to my stomach.

I can't hide in here for long, so I need to make every second of peace count. I pinch one nostril closed, breathe in deep, then let go and exhale. It helps a little, but not enough. I can't get the sight of the burning restaurant, along with Dad's look of disdain through the rearview, out of my head. And then there's the fact that my family has been talking about me.

It's a pretty killer trio.

I wait for as long as I can, and then I step outside.

And find I'm not alone in the bathroom.

Washing his hands is a guy I haven't seen before. He's wearing a dark blue shirt tucked into gray slacks and nice black shoes. His dusty brown hair is short, cut in military fashion. The top two buttons of his shirt are undone, showing off some pale skin.

He has the kind of body you notice.

I ignore him and start washing up.

"Rough night?" he asks.

"Huh?"

"You look like you've been through it," he says, turning to face me. He's drying his hands with a paper towel. I notice his posture, too; it's weirdly great.

Dead straight.

I shrug and turn off the tap.

"I'm Jason, by the way," he says.

He looks young, maybe around my age. It's not super uncommon for the sons and daughters of mob players to show up here: They like to get us indoctrinated early. So much illegal stuff happens here; underage drinking is the least of their concerns.

"Matt," I say. "I'd shake your hand, but you know . . ."

I raise my wet hands.

"Don't worry about it," he says, and he smiles. "Hey, this might be a long shot, but are you up for sneaking out of here?"

His smile makes my heart beat faster. This boy, whoever he is, has a great freaking smile. It feels almost dangerous. He should warn a guy before smiling at him like that.

"What?" I say.

He steps closer, and his shoes click on the tiles. "Look, I can tell you'd rather be somewhere else right now. And conveniently, that's what I want, too. I know a diner down the road. If you're game?"

I eye him warily. Who suggests something like that? Who is this guy? But he's right. I *would* rather be somewhere else right now.

And fine, I'll admit it. He's absurdly hot.

"Sure," I say. "Let's do it."

CHAPTER TWO

JASON AND I ARE WALKING DOWN A QUIET ALLEY.

It feels a little like this stretch of the city belongs to us.

I'm not sure if anyone else would want it, though. It smells like trash, and the walls are covered in graffiti. I look up. The moon's out, and I can hear the ocean. I feel a little unsafe, but weirdly I kind of like that. At the end of the alleyway, across a road, is a diner, called Sunshine Diner. Its signage is blue neon.

I look across, at the tall hot guy keeping pace beside me. It doesn't feel real, that I'm doing this.

"What?" he asks.

"Huh?"

"You just looked at me weird. What's up?"

We pass by a blue dumpster.

"Nothing, dude," I say.

He raises both eyebrows.

"Okay," I say. "I'm just sort of pinching myself that I'm doing this. I should be back at the bar."

"Why?"

"My dad, I guess. You know how it is."

He must, if he was at the bar.

He stops walking, and I do as well. He turns to face me. Beside me is a metal chain-link gate, leading into a small yard. It's overgrown. Above me, there are thick black power cables, connecting power poles that run down the alley.

I feel a little pressed in.

"Let's make a deal," he says. "How about we don't talk about our families? We can just be us, not our last names. How does that sound?"

I wasn't expecting that. It sounds amazing.

But I'm Matt Miller. All anyone really cares about is my family. I don't recognize Jason, but I hardly pay attention when I'm forced to be at the bar. I'm guessing he's the son of one of the families we're allied with. Or maybe he's one of Barbie Barker's rent boys. He's hot enough for it.

Wait, what if he *is* one of her rent boys?

I decide it doesn't matter. I couldn't afford it anyway. I hope he isn't, though. For a lot of reasons.

"Sure," I say. "Why not?"

He grins. "Sweet."

We start walking again.

"So you like this place?" I ask, pointing at the diner. It doesn't look like much. It puts the *suss* in *suspect*. Also, it's right next to a gas station, which for some reason feels really damning to me. Like it's going to be especially cheap and fast, even for a diner.

"I do."

We reach the front door, and Jason opens it for me. A bell chimes. The place is massive, with pink booths and faded wooden paneling. At the back is a mural, sky blue, with a slightly wonky palm tree painted on it.

It's a whole lot of *why?*

Jason leads me to a booth in the back and sits down. I sit opposite him. This place smells like coffee and sugar. The local hit-music station is playing on the radio.

The menu in front of me is freaking huge. I flip it over and see there are just as many options on the other side. There's something available called the "sunrise special" that includes both eggs and pineapple. I almost gag at the thought.

The bell above the door chimes again, and two cops walk in. They sit down at the counter. The server smiles like she knows them and pours them each a mug of coffee.

Okay, so this isn't the kind of place I'm supposed to be in.

Why am I here? What am I doing?

"Do you do this a lot?" I ask.

"Do what?"

"Ask random guys you meet in bathrooms to diners?"

He laughs. "You're the first."

"So why me?"

We're interrupted by the server. The menu is so huge I haven't even decided what I want.

"What can I get you boys?"

"Um," I say, as I desperately scan the menu. "I . . ."

"Two double cheeseburgers, and two chocolate thick shakes, and a large waffle fries," says Jason, then he looks at me. "You happy with that?"

"Um, yeah."

The server walks away.

"You looked freaked, so I ordered for you," he says. "Hope that's cool."

Weirdly, I don't find it annoying.

"Thanks."

So, I'm here. With this strange, attractive boy.

Because really, oh my God. This boy. He's bananas hot. He's got this sort of military vibe about him, with his strong jawline and short haircut, and well-built body. Also, his eyes are fascinating. At a distance, they look light brown, but up close, they're almost green. Plus, he's clean-shaven, and his skin is blemish-free. He's a perfect, all-American boy.

He probably even gets along with his dad.

Anyway.

I can totally see him as one of those West Point guys whose whole life is about perfection and military service. Maybe that's why he's so buff.

But we met in a criminal bar, so I know if he is a soldier, he's not a lawful one.

I wonder if he's killed any Donovans.

I hope not. He's way too pretty to be a killer.

"So, man," he says. He stretches out, putting one arm on the back of the booth. "What's your deal?"

"What do you mean?"

"Like, what do you like? What are your hobbies?"

Why would he ask me to do this? What does he want from me?

"Listen," I say. "Before you ask about my hobbies, I'm going to need a better idea of what's going on here."

He tilts his head to the side, and his lips twitch up a little. Oh great, I'm amusing him.

"We're getting food," he says.

"Yeah, but . . . why?"

"Why what?"

"Why'd you ask me to come here?"

"Because I thought you'd say yes."

I feel my eyebrows narrow. It was an impulse. "That's not an answer."

"Sure it is," he says. He leans forward and rests his hands on the table. "You're here, aren't you? Don't overthink it. Let's just have a good time, get to know each other a little. So . . . your hobbies. What do you like?"

I guess he has a point. I do tend to overthink things a lot, and it's never worked out so great for me.

"Um." I rack my brain. "I like movies."

He nods. "Oh yeah, what kinds?"

"Any, really. I like superhero ones, but I'm kind of sick of them being the only ones out there."

"Aw, man, I love superhero movies! I see them day one, every time."

Shit, that's cool.

"I didn't say they were *bad*; I like them as much as the next guy. I just . . . I wish there was other stuff, too. Like, the only things with big budgets these days are those. I miss movies like *Alien* and *Terminator* or whatever."

"So big-budget, but new?"

"Exactly!"

"That's fair, I miss those, too. Or the thought of them. All right, you like movies, what else?"

I shrug. "I dunno, I like normal stuff. How about you?"

"Movies, TV. I read a bit, play baseball on Fridays. Oh, and I like games a lot."

"Oh, wait, me too," I say. "On the gaming, not the baseball, obviously."

I gesture at my thin arms.

"Really?" he says. He looks at my body for a second. "What games do you like?"

The server returns and places the food down in front of us. It looks great. I squirt out some ketchup and try one of the waffle fries. Way good. I lift the burger and take a bite, and oh, damn.

It's amazing.

"I like fantasy RPGs the best," I say, still chewing. And, oh my God, this burger is officially too good for this place.

His eyes light up. "Dude, me too! Fantasy RPGs take over my life whenever I get one. This might be embarrassing to admit, but I put four hundred hours into the *Skyrim* remaster."

It's kind of alarming how cool I find that. I'm not sure everyone would think it's cool, but I seriously think it's amazing.

"That's not embarrassing at all. What class do you play as?"

"I have two characters. One is a rogue; the other is a wizard. How about you?"

"I swear I'm not copying you, but I always play as one of those two."

"Yeah, because they're the best. Who wants to be a knight?"

"Not me, that's for sure."

I feel a little fluttering in my stomach. I'm sitting across from a hot guy who plays video games. Eating a great burger. This so isn't how I was expecting the night to go.

And I wouldn't change a single thing.

* * *

The bell chimes as the door to the diner closes behind us, and I get a waft of gasoline from the gas station. *Glorious.* Jason stretches, cracking his back into place. I find myself kind of marveling at the way his muscles move under his shirt.

Seriously, damn, boy.

"So where to?" he asks.

"Huh?"

"Where do you wanna go now?"

I frown. "Back to Jimmy's?"

This was fun, but I feel a creeping dread about it. If Dad noticed I was missing, I don't know what I'd tell him. I can't say the truth, which is that I met a random guy in the bathroom and decided to leave with him because I thought he was gorgeous.

There are the rumors about me. I don't know what Jason's deal is, and what he likes, but I feel hanging out one-on-one with a boy like him might add some fuel to that particular fire. I don't feel bad about being gay, I don't even really care about it. It's just what I am; boys have always done it for me. I like deep voices and short haircuts and big arms.

I especially like how boys look when they take off their shirts.

I just don't want anyone to know yet. I suspect they'll make a big deal out of it, which I don't want. It's none of their business. Me liking guys is my thing. It's not like anyone's trying super hard to date me, so for now, it doesn't even matter.

"You don't want to hit the beach or something?" he asks. "The water's nice this time of night."

"I can't," I say. "Dad will freak."

He nods. "Fair."

"Won't your parents? Who are they, by the way?"

"We had a deal. No family talk tonight. Just us, being our own men, remember?"

"Oh, right."

I get kind of a kick out of him calling me a man.

Still. I want to poke further about who this boy is, but a deal is a deal. We walk in silence, until we reach the back door of the bar.

"That was fun," says Jason. "I get told I'm hard to read a lot, so I figured I'd just say it. I had fun."

I nod. "I had fun, too."

He tucks his hands into his pockets. "Maybe we could do it again sometime, then? Would you like that?"

I would. Very much. I'm not ready for this to be over. But maybe this should be a one-time thing. A welcome one, but I have a feeling hanging around Jason is a bad idea for me.

Am I being presumptuous? I don't think this is a gay thing. It's probably just a friend thing.

Or maybe not?

"Well, maybe next time you see me in the bathroom, you could ask," I say.

So now I know flirting isn't a gift of mine. Great.

He laughs. "I'll keep an eye out. Well, I'm off. Later."

"You're not coming back in?"

"Nah, I'm going to head home."

"Okay, well, nice meeting you or whatever."

"It was nice meeting you, too, Matt. Or whatever."

Our eye contact lasts a little too long, and then he spins and walks away. I push open the door of the bar. I laugh, at the ridiculousness of this whole thing. I start coming up with a lie I can use if anyone asks where I went.

What can I say? I wanted some air?

I go in and see Luke. He's talking to a family friend of ours, Cassidy, giving her all his attention. She's in a short black dress and heels with red bottoms. Her hand is on his chest, sliding through the gap in the material of his shirt. Dad is nowhere to be seen, which means he's probably upstairs. That's where the serious business is done.

Huh.

I don't think anyone even noticed I left. That means I got away with it.

CHAPTER THREE

I'M LAYING OUT BY OUR POOL, LOUNGING ON A DECK CHAIR.

I haven't stopped thinking about what happened last night.

I met Jason . . . whateverhislastnameis. And I know it might be stupid, because we just went to a crappy diner to get a surprisingly un-crappy burger. And shakes. And waffle fries.

But it felt kind of special to me, like we just sort of . . . clicked.

I don't know.

I've tried to find him online, but so far, nobody I'm friends with knows anyone named Jason. Which makes me think maybe he doesn't use social media much. He gave the impression he was a sort of busy guy, so maybe he's got too much going on to keep up a social media presence.

Which feels like nonsense, even to me.

Hot guys like him *love* social media.

Where else would they post thirst traps? Why even work out if you're not going to post shirtless photos?

I just need to look harder.

I sit up and unlock my phone. I load my cousin Ethan's Facebook and search his friends for anyone called Jason. He has one, and my heart kind of soars, but then when I click through, I see it's not him. Unless he looks really different in person. I . . .

The gate to the pool opens, and Luke steps inside. He's holding a towel and is wearing black trunks.

He throws the towel onto the deck chair beside me and then pulls his shirt off over his head. He fixes his hair, adjusts his trunks, then thumps down. He puts his arms behind his head, stretching out.

He's so defined; it's so unfair. I know he works out almost every day and tracks his calories and macros, so I'd probably look more like him if I paid more attention to it. Still, it feels so damn unfair that he has a sculpted torso, complete with a defined six-pack, and I don't.

It's just rude.

We look so alike in every other way. We both have black hair, and both got Dad's brown eyes and thick eyebrows. But being buff makes all his features click together in a way mine don't. I try not to be hard on myself, but he was right about what he said last night. He is the good-looking one.

He pumps out some sunscreen from the tube I have beside me, and slaps it down onto his chest.

"Where'd you go?" he asks.

"Huh?"

"Last night, you disappeared for a while. Where'd you go?"

I don't have a lie planned. I truly thought I'd gotten away with it. I should've expected Luke to notice, though.

"Oh, nowhere exciting. I was craving fries, so I went to the diner down the road."

"By yourself?"

I shrug.

"You're a weird dude, anyone ever tell you that?"

"You did, just now."

He laughs. "Where was my invite? I'm bulking, you know I need all the calories I can get."

He slaps his hard stomach. I have no idea how the whole muscle thing works, that he can eat burgers and stuff and still look like him. It seems to go against everything I've been taught at school about being healthy.

"You were busy."

"Doing what?"

I chew my nail. "You were with Cass, remember?"

"Oh yeah. I almost forgot. So many girls, so little time, you know?"

Obviously, I don't.

"Did you two hook up?" I ask as I put my hands behind my head, so I'm mirroring him. In front of me is my pool, then a small stretch of perfectly kept lawn. Dad makes us cut it on alternating Saturdays. If I forget, Luke reminds me. It looks really short, so I guess he's already done it this morning.

"Even if I did, I wouldn't tell you," he says.

I roll my eyes.

"How 'bout you?" he asks.

"Are you asking if I hooked up with Cass?"

"No. Did you meet any girls?"

"What do you think? Nobody even noticed I was there."

"God, stop being so pathetic. I'm telling you, just find a girl who gives you a happy feeling down there, then give 'em the old Miller smolder. They'll become obsessed with you, for the night, anyway. Trust me."

My brother, folks. I love him. But he's such a douchebag.

"Noted," I say.

I don't know why I said that, because I already know it's not really possible for a girl to give me any sort of feeling down there. Trust me, I've tried. I watched all sorts of videos on the internet, hoping they'd inspire some sort of reaction in me. Like I'd see one girl, the right girl, and everything would click into place. But my attention is always, *always*, drawn to the guys.

I'm just built that way.

I'm done with this conversation, so I turn the volume of my music up, roll over, and face the opposite direction.

* * *

It's Monday, and I'm at school, wishing I had the powers of the Invisible Woman from the Fantastic Four.

Naturally.

The main hallway is bustling, filled with people grabbing stuff from their lockers or heading to class. Guys high-five. Girls whisper things to one another. A teacher yells at a boy who is running somewhere, threatening him with detention if he doesn't slow down.

I'm thinking about Jason again.

I'm still confused.

I'm starting to think he's, like, a ghost or something. Or a figment of my imagination, created out of extreme loneliness. I created a cute gamer guy because he's, like, my dream friend.

Who has *no* social media?

I know it's hard to find someone if you don't know their last name. But still, how can he not be friends with *anyone* I know?

It's probably for the best, though. I'm officially thinking about him too much. Having access to his social media would just push things over the edge. It's sure to be really cute, filled with selfies of him gaming and stuff. And maybe hot. He probably posts thirst traps, and I very much want to see those.

I pull my phone from my pocket, put my earbuds in, and hit play on my current playlist. The top song is "Straight to My Head" by You Me at Six, which is this song I've become weirdly obsessed with lately. It's pretty much the only song I listen to. I turn the volume up way too high to be safe, but whatever. It lifts my mood almost instantly.

God, I love this song.

Up ahead, making their way down the hall toward me, is a group of football jocks. Even though it's hot out, the whole group is wearing matching black-and-white varsity jackets, most unzipped with the sleeves pushed up. Damn, there are so many nice arms in that group. Any one of them could push me around and I'd be sort of a-okay with it.

Like, if they put me in a headlock . . .

They reach me, and one, Zach Lunsford, makes a show of not moving for me.

I duck out of the way at the last second.

"Watch it," he says, growling.

"Sorry."

I reach my locker, spin in my combination, and realize something. He's the first student I've talked to all day.

* * *

Another hour of searching, and I still haven't found Jason.

I do this a lot. I have this weirdly obsessive brain. Whenever something catches my fancy, I latch on to it. I do it with movies and gaming, too. When I like something, I like it *hard*. I dive deep into theory threads on Reddit and watch analysis videos on YouTube, just generally obsess, until I find something else that draws my focus.

This is the first time I've felt this way about another person.

I'm aware I'm being ridiculous. I'm lying on my bed, staring at my phone, thinking about a boy.

I search my room for a distraction. Like, a game I can play, or a movie I can watch to get my mind off this. Beside my desk, which holds my space-gray MacBook Pro, is my bookshelf. It's mostly epic fantasy and YA books, but front and center is my record of *Sam's Town*. I don't own a record player, but Luke got it for me because he knows how much I love that album.

On the dark gray wall above it are a few Polaroids from my real-photography-is-better phase, ugh, and custom art of Spider-Man, Harley Quinn, and Captain Marvel I bought on Etsy.

See, I love superhero movies.

Why'd I tell Jason I don't like them that much?

I'm so weird.

The rest of the space is covered in movie posters. They're all acceptable favorites, like *Mulholland Drive*, *Creature from the Black Lagoon*, and *Jaws*. For obvious reasons I haven't put up a *Love, Simon* poster, even though I love that movie so damn hard. I've watched it maybe ten times.

Nothing distracts me, so I lift my phone and open Grindr.

Grindr always terrifies me, seeing as I'm so not ready to be out, but I'd be lying if I said I didn't like it, too. I've never met anyone on there, but talking to guys is still so exciting. I had to lie about my age to make my account, but that's never really bothered me. The out gay guys at school constantly talk about their app conquests, so, like, I know everyone does it.

I use a shirtless mirror selfie, with my head cropped out. So I don't think anyone would be able to figure out it's me. I scroll the wall of guys, and see there's another shirtless and headless profile five miles away.

His profile name is just "J."

I sit up in bed.

He has only one photo, the shirtless one. He has pale skin, a six-pack, and nice biceps and a smooth chest. I picture him wearing Jason's clothes.

Could it be him?

I open his profile, and message him.

Hey man, what's up?

There's a knock on my door. I jump so much I nearly drop my phone. I close Grindr, and then cover my crotch with my blanket. Just the thought of Jason being on Grindr was enough to make me hard.

Or maybe it was just the shirtless guy.

Yeah, I'll go with that.

"Matt?"

"Yeah?"

The door opens. It's Dad.

"What are you up to?" he asks.

"Nothing."

He crosses my room, and opens my window. Okay, Dad, message received. He then grabs a few dishes I have festering on my desk. It's maybe passive-aggressive, sure, but he's cleaning up after me. I'm not going to complain.

"Have you eaten?" he asks.

"I had a pizza pocket."

"And?"

I glance at the half-empty bottle of Coke Zero Sugar I have on my bedside table. A pizza pocket and no-calorie Coke. Dinner of champions.

"How about you have something not made of chemicals?"

"*Everything* is made of chemicals."

He sighs. "Just have a piece of fruit, that's all I ask. Something that's seen sunlight at least once."

"Okay, fine."

I get out of bed and grab the remaining dishes from my desk. Dad and I walk through our house. Our place is massive, admittedly too big for the three of us. Or, four, if you count Eddie, our dog. Which I totally do.

He's dozing on his spot in the living room right now. He's a German shepherd, and Luke's his favorite. He likes me well enough, but even though he's technically the family dog, he's always sort of felt like Luke's more than he has mine or Dad's. Luke even named him, after Eddie Brock, aka Venom, his favorite character.

I wonder if it'd feel more homey if Mom were still alive, but I guess I'll never know. She died in a car accident when I was three. It was totally random; she was driving to visit her mom, who lives in Tampa. A drunk driver swerved into her lane, and that was it. I don't think Dad's ever gotten over it. I'm pretty sure she was the love of his life. As far as I know, he hasn't even dated since.

I miss her, even though I never really knew her. Her name was Diane. I get told a lot I have her smile, which always makes my heart ache. I feel like she'd get me more than Dad does. But then again, she married him, knowing what he does. So maybe not.

Dad loads the dishwasher as I grab an apple from the fridge. Eddie perks up, growls, then lies back down. I guess someone walked past our place.

"Hey," I say as I toss the apple up and down. "Are we going to go to the bar anytime soon?"

His eyebrows lift up. "You want to go to Jimmy's?"

I get why he's so shocked. I know getting me to do anything family related is normally like pulling teeth. Getting me to do *anything* is like pulling teeth.

"Not really. I'm just, like, curious."

He puts a dishwashing tablet into the slot in the machine and then closes the door.

"I have a meeting there on Saturday. I was going to go by myself. I know Luke has plans, and I didn't think you'd want to."

Wow. Okay.

This is kind of perfect.

I can go to the bar without Luke.

"Can I come?" I ask. "I'm kind of sick of spending all weekend in the house, I'd rather do something."

Dad eyes me warily. But then I guess he decides he doesn't care, and he smiles.

"Sure, Matt. You're more than welcome to come."

CHAPTER FOUR

FOR THE FIRST TIME EVER, I'M EXCITED ABOUT GOING TO the bar.

I even put way more effort into my appearance than normal. I'm wearing my favorite formal clothes, which are dark gray pants and a nice white shirt that actually fits me.

I ironed them, and Dad didn't even need to tell me to. I've tucked the shirt in, and left the top button undone. I've put pomade in my hair and pressed it down, so it looks a little more deliberate than the shaggy mess it usually is.

Right now, I'm in the passenger seat of Dad's car. We reach the bar, and he pulls into the parking lot. Outside, there are a bunch of parked cars and motorbikes, but the street looks mostly empty. It pretty much always does after sundown in this part of town.

The skyline is deep purple. I'd take a photo for my Instagram, if Dad wasn't right here.

He pulls on the hand brake, then turns to face me.

"Are you wearing cologne?" he asks.

I am, in fact. I snuck into his room and stole some of his. I picked Bleu de Chanel. I didn't think he'd notice.

"Yeah, I hope that's cool?"

"It's fine. Don't take this the wrong way, but I think you might've put on too much."

Did I?

Oh God, I did.

I feel totally sick. The whole point of doing this is so I'll smell good. For Jason. And everyone on earth hates people who wear too much cologne or perfume. One of my aunts always wears too much, and it makes me dread being near her. It's like being thwacked in the face with a bouquet of flowers over and over.

"Next time, just use two sprays, one on each wrist, then hold them to your neck for a few seconds," says Dad, showing me how it's done. "That's all you need."

"Noted."

I used literally four times that.

"But I do like the enthusiasm," he says. "You wearing cologne, coming along. It's a good look for you."

I smile weakly. "Thanks."

We get out of the car and go down the street. Around us are low white buildings. A few thin, sad-looking palm trees are dotted around the place, along with power lines, and overflowing dumpsters. We're far enough away from the city that there's no flowing traffic, so the whole place is really still.

The exterior of Jimmy's is nothing special, to be honest. It's just a big off-white rectangle, with the name of the bar in red and green neon on the front. The alley runs down its left, and there's a red pop-out awning above the door. Underneath it is a bouncer, a big guy wearing all black. He has a tattoo of a scorpion snaking up his neck.

He recognizes Dad, so he waves us through.

Inside, I peer around.

My cousin Ethan is playing pool with Vince. They both nod at Dad and ignore me. Cassidy is standing by the jukebox.

I can't see him.

Phew.

I mean, I do want to see him. Just not yet. Not until I've washed the cologne off and Dad's gone upstairs.

"Are you okay to entertain yourself for a few hours?" asks Dad, who is looking at his watch. It's an heirloom Rolex, one handed down to him from his father. If anything happens to Dad, Luke'll get it, for sure.

"Yeah, 'course. Have a good night."

"You too."

He turns to walk up the stairs.

"And, um," I say, calling him back. "I might, like, Uber home. So if I'm gone, like, don't stress."

"That's fine. Just text me your plans."

"Will do."

I know he has no trouble leaving me, because I'm surrounded by family. There's not much trouble I can get into, seeing as half the crowd here are blood relatives. My grandma is even here. She's sitting in a booth with a few of my aunts.

Maybe this plan is dumb.

What will even happen if I do see Jason? I can't leave with him again. If I do, people will talk. I go into the bathroom and half expect him to be standing there, washing his hands, like last time.

But it's empty.

I wash my hands in the sink and then wet a paper towel and wipe the sides of my neck. I scrub a bit, until my skin turns slightly pink. Then I do the same on the back of my wrists. I think that should get rid of most of it. Once I'm done, I look up at my reflection.

What are you doing?

Why are you here?

I leave the bathroom, head to the bar, and sit down on one of the stools. I spin and look around.

He's not here.

Now I feel stupid.

I came here for him. I hate this place, and yet I came here, on the off chance that he might show up again. What else could I do? I couldn't find his social media, and I wasn't just going to let it drop. My stupid brain is too curious about him.

Now I need to spend the night here. By myself. Ugh.

It's times like this that make me wish I liked drinking.

I don't, though. For one, it tastes bad. And two, I hate the thought of not being in total control of myself, especially around my family.

I kick my shoe against the bar. It's made of dark wood and varnished so it's shiny. Like always, bluesy, small-town rock is playing on the speakers. I breathe in, and the air smells like Scotch. And still faintly like Dad's cologne.

Maybe I should just leave. Call it a night, cut my losses.

Maybe . . .

I hear the front door open.

I'm too nervous to look.

Then a dark shape slides into the space beside me.

"Hey, you," Jason says.

My heart starts thudding.

"Oh, hi," I say.

He leans against the bar. "Waiting for someone?"

Um. I mean, yes, I was waiting for him, but I don't want to admit it.

"Um, no, I'm not waiting for anybody. Dad's in a meeting up-stairs. I'm just killing time. You know, the usual."

I glance back at him. He's wearing a gray shirt this time, neatly tucked into black slacks. The top two buttons are undone again, and he's wearing the same shoes as last time. I can't believe I noticed that, but you know.

They're great shoes.

His hair is gently tussled and styled with product.

I glance at Vince. He's busy playing pool.

"Too bad," says Jason. "I was hoping you might be waiting for me."

"I don't do that."

"Do what?"

"Wait for people."

He smirks. "That's smart. I totally came here hoping I'd see you." He taps his knuckles on the bar.

I feel like I've been punched in the gut. It's everything I want to hear. But it feels *so* dangerous. I'm not ready for anyone to know about me yet. Not even a stranger. But this boy . . . he's making me feel all sorts of things.

He's turned his body to the side now, so he's fully facing me. My stare goes down his neck, to the smooth skin visible between the halves of his shirt. It's so captivating. I imagine brushing my fingers along it, then immediately push the thought away.

"Wanna sneak out again?" he asks.

Hell yes.

But I feel like I shouldn't. People might see.

He leans closer. I feel like I can't move. Like I'm rooted to the spot, all my focus on him. I can smell his cologne, which is perfect, and the mint on his breath. His lips are nicely arched and look really soft.

It makes me think about kissing.

He leans down and whispers in my ear: "Outside, five minutes."

He pats my chest, his hand lingering against me for a second, and then walks away.

Okay, fuck.

I turn, and watch as he leaves the bar. Then I scan the crowd.

Nobody is even looking my way. Everyone is too wrapped up in their own conversations, their own drama. Vince sinks a ball and then grins. It looks like a close game, and Ethan's face is set in concentration.

Nobody saw him touch me.

Let me process this. The boy who hasn't left my brain in over a week wants to see me again. Outside.

I crack my neck, and then the bartender notices me. I don't want anything, but I don't want it to seem like I was here just to get Jason's attention.

"What can I getcha?" he asks.

"Er, just a Coke?"

He frowns, like that's weird, but pours me one. It costs five dollars. FIVE DOLLARS FOR A COKE. And that's a Miller price.

So stupid.

I sip it slowly. It's ice-cold, so it's actually pretty delicious. But still, five dollars. I wait a while, just thinking. Has it been five minutes yet? I doubt it. I think he asked me to wait so people don't think we left, like, together.

I finish my Coke and put the glass down on the bar. The ice rattles.

I stand and find my legs are shaking. I cross the room as quickly as I can, keeping my stare down so I don't accidentally catch anyone's eye, and then step outside. It's humid out here, like an armpit.

Florida can be disgusting.

Jason is leaning against the wall of the alley. It's so dark I can barely see him.

"Hey," he says as he detaches from the wall. "For a second there I didn't think you were coming."

I shrug, managing to look everywhere but at him.

"Don't get me wrong, I'm glad," he says. "I've been looking forward to seeing you all week. I had so much fun with you."

"Oh, um, cool."

He grins at me, then starts walking down the street. I fall into step beside him. We're going away from Sunshine Diner. I'm kind of bummed. I want more of those waffle fries in my life.

"Where are we going?" I ask.

"I love that you asked that," he says. "So trusting, like a little lamb."

I scoff. "I didn't say I'd go *anywhere* with you. I just want to know what the plan is. Don't you want to go to the diner again?"

He shakes his head. "Not tonight."

We reach the parking lot of the bar. I'm a little worried about how well lit it is. I feel like anyone could see me.

I turn and look at the bar. The upstairs windows face the lot.

He stops in front of a small silver Toyota and unlocks it with a fob. Its lights flash orange.

"Um," I say. "I don't know about this."

"About what?"

"I don't think getting in a car with, no offense, pretty much a total stranger, is a good idea."

He tosses his keys up and down. "Why is that?"

"I dunno. I just want to be smart. No offense, but for all I know you could be a murderer."

"I mean, maybe I am," he says, and he grins.

"Hey, please don't joke. I'm actually nervous."

His face drops. "Oh, okay, sorry. Listen, I'm not going to hurt you. Look at me, I promise."

I look into his eyes, searching for any warning signs.

There aren't any.

He seems honest.

But something tells me that murder victims think the same thing before they're killed.

Jason looks hurt that I don't fully trust him. I get that. I would probably be pretty offended if someone implied they thought I might be a murderer.

"Seriously," he says. "You're going to be fine. I'm sorry I joked. I just know somewhere I think you'll like. And to get there, we need to drive. We could go to the diner if you want, but trust me, this would be more fun. You in or you out?"

I should move fast, in case Dad looks out and sees me.

I get in the car.

CHAPTER FIVE

LUCKILY, JASON IS A GOOD DRIVER.

Or, he's at least competent. He's not, like, swerving all over the road and nearly hitting people, and he's obeyed every road rule I've noticed. He stops at yellow lights, is all I'm saying. It makes me feel a little better about being here.

Despite my nerves, I'm actually having a good time. This section of the city is really pretty, the perfect place for a night drive. We're surrounded by gleaming skyscrapers and clean, pleasant streets. To my left is a portable traffic sign that reads, ENJOY THE BEACH, KEEP YOUR DRINKS INSIDE in big orange letters.

And it makes me think of something.

"Hey," I say. "How old are you even?"

"How old do you think I am?"

"I have no idea."

He smiles. "I turned eighteen last month. You?"

I nod. "Seventeen."

"Yeah? You look older."

I don't know what to think about that. He doesn't say it like an insult, but . . .

"I mean that in a good way!" he says. "I don't mean that you look old or anything. You just look . . . you know. Older."

"Oh, cool," I say. "Thanks."

"No worries." He chews his lip. "So . . . what music do you like?"

My music tastes aren't exactly cool. And I care about being cool right now.

I can't even remember the last time I cared about something like this.

"I like alt rock," I say. "But stuff that's more on the pop side of things."

"Sorry, dude, that makes zero sense to me."

My cheeks are burning. The car is dark, though, so I don't think he can tell.

At least I hope he can't tell.

We've reached the main strip of the beach now, where the most famous hotels are. This whole street is deigned in this cool, art deco style. People are everywhere. I'm guessing most of them are tourists.

"The Killers are my favorite, but I also really like You Me at Six. That sort of thing."

He grabs his phone from the slot on the dash and hands it to me. "Play something. Password is four thousand and one."

His phone is the newest model of iPhone, in a clear plastic case. It's really clean, not a smudgy mess like mine. I have the latest model, too, I just never really clean it.

I feel like I've been handed a holy grail.

I could find out his last name with this thing.

He hasn't mentioned it, so I assumed our no–last–names thing is continuing. I just get a vibe from him that he doesn't want to talk about his. Still, with his phone, he wouldn't need to tell me.

I could find it out all on my own.

But he's watching me warily. If I snoop, he'll know.

Maybe he's realized that he's made an impulsive mistake. He

looks a little pale and keeps glancing my way. It might be usual they-have-my-phone anxiety, but it could also be more.

And I don't want him to distrust me. I unlock his phone and open the Spotify app. So no funny business. I search for *Sam's Town* and play the title track. Then I lock his phone and put it back on the dash.

Matt Miller: fully trustworthy.

"What's this?" he asks as the music starts playing. There's an unmissable quiver in his voice. I get it, I hate it when people look at my phone, too.

"'Sam's Town.' It's from my favorite album."

I feel weirdly anxious.

I hope he likes it.

He must. It's a slam dunk of a song.

The vocals start, and he smiles. He starts bobbing his head along to the beat.

"I love this," he says.

"Me too."

Too soon, we reach our destination.

Outside, I can see a stretch of sand illuminated by streetlights on the footpath. There are a few pedestrians out, but the city is still, and the beach is almost totally empty. We've gone past the main hub, so we're in a much quieter section of town. We're still in Miller territory, but only just.

Jason turns off the engine.

It's so quiet.

"Are we even allowed to be here?" I ask.

He shrugs. "It's the beach, why wouldn't we be?"

Nobody else is around. It makes me feel like it's off-limits. There are areas of the beach that are busy at night, but this spot, where he picked, is dark and dead.

"You look a little freaked," he says.

"No, I'm fine," I say.

"Good," he says, and he steps out of the car.

I follow him. The air smells salty here, and I can hear the ocean. I'm not really a big beach guy, but I do kind of like it right now. He goes around to the trunk and opens it. From it, he retrieves two towels. He closes the trunk with a too-strong push.

"You want to go swimming?" I ask.

He nods.

"But like . . ."

"What?"

"Don't sharks hunt at night?"

"Oh, yeah, I guess they do."

"And that doesn't bother you?" I ask.

"Not really. I dare them to eat me."

He raises his eyebrows and then sets off toward the beach.

I jog after him to catch up.

Again, I think: *What am I doing?*

"Seriously," I say.

We reach the sand, and he takes off his shoes. I bend down and start unlacing my shoes.

"Is this safe?" I ask as I kick them off. "I don't want to be stupid. It'd be just my luck to get got by a shark."

"'Get got'?" He chuckles. "You're funny. And you won't; I do it all the time, and they haven't got me yet. If they eat you, I'd almost be offended, like I'm not good enough for them, or something."

"Really?" I say, looking out at the dark water. It stretches on and on. There are a few lights, probably yachts, bobbing out on the water. But that's it. There's nobody else for miles. I can't believe we're so close to the city and yet it feels so empty.

"I mean, you come here a lot?"

He nods. "It's a good place to think. It's the one place I've found that's quiet. Games, and this, those are my escapes."

I wonder what he wants to escape from.

I wonder if he wants to escape his family, like I do.

We reach a spot a few yards from the shore, and Jason stops and throws down the towels.

"No offense," I say. "But my bad luck is seriously a thing, so I might just stay on the shore, if that's cool with you?"

"It's totally fine."

I sit down. Out here, it's undeniably pretty. The moon is nearly full right now, and the waves are gently lapping against the sand. The water looks really dark, nearly black almost.

Across from me, Jason starts unbuttoning his shirt.

Okay.

So.

How do straight guys act around other guys when they take off their shirts? I feel like they'd be totally oblivious. Like how I'd be if I was around a girl in a bra. I'd notice, sure, but it wouldn't be like . . . you know.

Jason finishes unbuttoning his shirt and pulls it off his shoulders.

His body is pale and absolutely freaking gorgeous. His chest is totally smooth, and he's ripped enough that he has a six-pack. It's on the leaner end of abs: I can see some definition, but he's not super bulky.

I'm not sure how I feel about noticing this, but . . . his body is as hot as possible for a body to be to me.

If he cares about being shirtless around me, it doesn't seem to show. The top band of his underwear is even poking out above his belted jeans, which has always been such a big turn-on for me.

This feels weirdly intimate, even though I know he's probably not feeling anything even remotely close to what I am. He plays baseball; he probably strips off around other guys all the time.

Now there's a thought.

"You're seriously not coming in?" he asks.

"Nah."

He shrugs and unbuckles his belt.

I sit down on the sand and then pull out my phone. I don't have any new messages, but I remember I'd told Dad I'd tell him my plans. I start writing a message to him.

Hey, I went home, just FYI.

Nope, that won't work. What if he beats me there?

I give up and decide I'll just deal with it if I get in trouble. I start to feel ill. Vince and Grandma saw me at the bar. So they must know I left. I'll need to come up with some reason why I did, because surely they'll ask.

I'm so stupid.

Jason takes off his slacks and then kicks them over to me. They land on my legs, and I have to push them away.

He laughs.

He's now wearing black boxer briefs, and that's it. He has really nice thighs, too. I guess from baseball.

"Come on," he says as he walks backward. "You won't regret it."

"I'm good."

"Okay, I'll be quick, then we can chat."

He turns and walks toward the water.

I definitely do check out his butt. But only for a second.

And then I'm on my phone, on Grindr, keeping my phone up so he can't see it. It loads, and I see that "J" has finally responded.

Good thanks cutie, how are you?

I start typing out a response.

Great thanks! Got more pics?

He comes online.

And damn.

Jason obviously isn't holding his phone now. Which means "J" isn't him.

I get a new message.

Jerome here ☺

He also sends me a bunch of photos. Not sexy ones, he's clothed in all of them. He's really cute and has even included a photo where he's dressed up as Klaus from *The Umbrella Academy*. But he's definitely not Jason. I type out a response, because even though I don't want to talk to him anymore, I don't want to leave him hanging after he sent photos of himself.

You're cute dude ☺

I know he's going to ask me for pics, which I don't want to send, so I switch to Safari and google shark fatalities. Apparently there were sixty-seven unprovoked attacks last year.

Worldwide.

That's not bad.

Jason is waist-deep in the water now, facing out toward the ocean.

I don't want him to leave.

I stand up and start frantically unbuttoning my shirt. I pull it off and then toss it to the ground. Then I step out of my slacks.

When I'm done, I see that Jason has turned and is watching me. He was probably watching the whole time I was undressing.

Cool. Cool cool cool.

Guarding my crotch so it's at least kind of hidden from his view, I jog down to the water. I step in, and, damn, it's cold.

"It's nice once you're in!" he calls.

"It better be!"

He laughs and then scoops up some water and runs it through his hair. It makes it dark and spiky. The waves are really gentle here. Cursing him, I walk into the water until I reach him. Our bodies, up to our waists, are submerged. The water laps gently against me. I adjust and find he was right. It is nice. It's just so warm out that it's a shock to the system. It's not even cold.

Jason watches me for a second. He's dripping wet.

"Hey, shark bait," he says.

And there we go. Spell broken.

I cross my arms. "Don't call me that."

"But that's what you are! I bet they can already smell you and are on their way as we speak."

"Seriously, stop! I'm trying so hard not to think about it, you have no idea."

He starts humming the *Jaws* theme music.

"Stop!" I say, and I splash him.

He laughs. I laugh, too.

But then it settles. And I realize that I'm here.

But surely he's not gay, too. I mean, he could be. But for some reason I don't think that's what's going on. I guess because he's so attractive, I feel that, even if he is gay, I wouldn't be the kind of guy he'd be into.

I think he just wants to be friends with me. Which I'm so down for.

I don't need to make out with him or anything to have a good time. I really like it here, doing just this. I mean, I'm not totally over the fear of sharks. It's constantly running underneath everything. But other stuff has the focus. Like how the moon is out, and I can see a few stars.

Plus, behind us, the city lights.

"This is nice," he says. "I like hanging out with you. It just feels really easy, you know? Like we don't need to talk just for the sake of it."

"Totally."

"I think that's a sign that we could be good friends. That we just, like, work."

"I think so, too."

He lies back so he's looking up at the stars. I do the same.

Because of pollution, I can't see many. But it's as good as it ever is here. I remember, once, Dad, Luke, and I went on a camping trip to Yosemite, because Dad loves it there. The stars there were next level.

Anyway.

I really don't want to think about Dad right now.

I feel like I'm in the middle of another magical night, doing something I never thought I'd do.

And it's all because of Jason.

* * *

We swim for a while and then walk back up the beach, toward the car, with towels wrapped around our waists. We collect our shoes, and then Jason goes up to the public shower and turns it on. He gestures to me, but I shake my head, so he steps under the spray.

He closes his eyes and dips his head under. His hair gets pressed flat, and water runs down his chest. For someone who games so much, he's clearly found a way to stay in great shape.

Because damn.

I catch myself staring, and I look away. I know this is just a friends thing, but I can't help myself.

He's the first person I've ever talked to who seems to like all the same stuff that I do. Our interests line up really well. Mostly we talked about games, because it's clearly the thing he likes most in the world. He plays big franchises like *World of Warcraft*, *Pokémon*, and *Minecraft*, but also likes indie games like *Factorio*, *Don't Starve*, and *Stardew Valley*.

Currently he's playing the new *God of War* game and loving every second of it.

Once he's done, I shower, and then we both get dressed. I still feel a little salty, though. It's, like, clinging to me.

"Better?' he asks.

"Yeah, much."

"Cool. Want me to drive you home? I need to head out soon, I've got homework."

"Yeah, me too. And, um, is that okay?"

"Yeah, sure is. I don't make offers to do things I don't actually want to do. I feel like that doesn't do anyone any favors, you know?"

"Totally. I'm the same."

I'm so not, though. I constantly bend over backward to try to keep people happy.

We climb into his car. He starts playing the Killers through the speakers.

Just when I think this night couldn't get any more perfect.

Too soon, we reach my place. To be honest, I'm not ready to stop hanging out with him. He turns off the engine, which makes the car feel really still. We're lit by streetlights, and the neon-blue dash of his car.

"Nice place," he says, looking out at my house. I guess it does look pretty cool. It's all one level, and I know it's big. It's white, with terra-cotta roofing, and is surrounded by greenery. The driveway is empty, so I guess Dad and Luke are still out. That's good.

It means nobody is going to ask me where I've been.

"Thanks. Whereabouts do you live, by the way?"

"Gladeview."

"Oh, nice."

That's right on the edge of our territory. We control it, but only just.

I don't want to think about that, though.

"Yeah."

I notice that the night is winding down, and I don't want to chicken out.

"Hey, um," I say.

"Yeah?"

"Could I maybe get your number? Is that okay?"

He grins. "And what exactly would you want with that?"

"You know, just . . . I dunno."

"Shark bait wants my number. How amazing."

"I'm not shark bait! Just tell me: Are you going to give it to me or not?"

For a second I think he isn't.

But then he puts out his hand.

I retrieve my phone, unlock it, and swipe through to my contacts book. I hand it to him, and he starts entering his details. Then he hands it back.

"I was going to ask you, if you didn't," he says. "Just FYI."

"Oh, really?"

He smiles. "Yeah, course."

And oh man. His smile is really cute. I love how it changes the whole way he looks. Normally he looks kind of serious, because his features are so handsome. But when he smiles, he looks a little like a sweetheart. Like the kind of guy who'd earnestly go for school council, or get upset if he gets a bad grade because he doesn't want to disappoint his teacher.

Maybe that's the sort of guy Jason really is. Maybe his macho thing is just an exterior.

I know about that. Too well.

"Um, cool," I say. "That's nice to know."

I feel like this conversation could go further, but I don't know where to take it.

"Well," he says. "Later."

"Yeah, I'll message you."

"Already looking forward to it."

I don't know what to say to that, so I leave the car. I hurry up to my front door, unlock it, and then step inside. Eddie is standing by the door, whimpering and wagging his tail. I scratch between his ears, in the spot I know he likes best, then go to my room. Because Luke isn't home, he follows me.

I text Dad, telling him I got an Uber home. Then I strip down to my underwear and fall backward onto my bed. Eddie jumps up and joins me. I put my hand on his flank and give him the occasional belly scratch.

And then I spend about an hour lying in bed in the dark, just thinking.

It takes me that long to come to the realization.

He entered his details.

Maybe he included a last name?

My heart racing, I check . . .

And see that he left the last-name field totally blank.

CHAPTER SIX

I HAVE JASON'S NUMBER NOW.

And I have no idea what to text him.

I feel like I made yet another mistake when it comes to him. What I should've done is put my number in his phone. Or I should've texted him something like *Hey* as soon as I got *his* number. That way I'd know there's a chance he could message me.

It's on me.

It's been five days, and I still haven't thought of anything.

I want it to be the perfect message. I want to ask him to do something I know he'll say yes to, basically. I'm maybe stressing more than I should, because I know how hard it is for me to make friends.

I'm really scared of messing this up, like I have every other time.

Right now, I'm in Dad's Mercedes, sitting in the passenger seat. He's driving me to get a new suit tailored, because there's this big party coming up at the end of the month. It's a ball for the whole Miller empire, including our allies, so I need a suit that actually fits me. It's such a big deal that Dad has finally slotted in the time for this outing.

Plus, Jason might be at the ball. So I want to look good.

Because maybe I get a bit of a vibe from him. I dunno. Like, sometimes, I feel like he looks at me in a way that doesn't feel exactly platonic. It's too intense for that.

It's not like it matters. Even if he is gay, what I want right now is a friend. It'd be nice to have someone to talk to about that.

If I have the guts to tell him, that is.

As Dad drives, I look out the window. I have headphones in and am on my playlist. It's a sort of dreary day today. It's not raining, but I think it could start at any second. In the distance, I see a fairground. Its candy-colored lights look especially bright against the gray sky.

And that's it.

That's how I'll ask Jason out. To a fair.

But that maybe feels a little too date-y. And I don't want to freak him out. We're becoming friends, that's it. If I were straight, what would I do?

I probably wouldn't ask him to a fair.

Maybe I'd ask him to come over and hang out. We could play some games or something and eat pizza and stuff. That actually sounds like a dream date to me, but you know, it is also I guess what straight dudes would do to hang out. They might also watch sports, but, ew, no.

For some reason asking him to come over and play games feels off, too.

Dad and Luke know I don't have any friends.

They'd pay super-close attention if I had a guy over, because I haven't done it in years. Unless they were out of the house. They do go out most Saturday nights, so most of the time I have the place to myself.

It still doesn't feel totally right, though. Can I really sneak Jason into my house just so we can hang out? I feel like it'd be a lot safer to go somewhere where we're less likely to be seen.

This is the loop I've been stuck in for a long time. Nothing fits perfectly.

I'm still thinking about it when Dad pulls into the parking bay in front of the tailor's. I open a message thread to Jason as I get out of the car.

Hey! Was just wondering if you wanted to come over and play some games this weekend? I have Smash Bros and Mario Kart, and my brother has Mortal Kombat.

I like the rushed nature of it. I think it'll make him think I haven't thought about it as much as I have.

I hit send as Dad and I walk into the building.

* * *

The new suit is black, sleek, and, to be honest, badass. It'll be delivered in two weeks. Dad was kind of pushy with the tailor, making him guarantee it'd be ready in time for the ball. I wish he'd been nicer, but whatever.

As Dad pays, I sit down and check my phone.

Come on . . .

I have a new message.

I unlock my phone.

But what about our deal? If I meet your parents, I'll know who you are.

I feel like he must already. I'm a Miller. We're one of the two most powerful families in the underworld. If he's from a family allied to us, he *must* know who I am. I'm underworld famous. I hate even thinking this, because it feels smug, but I'm sort of a prince, given Dad is our current leader.

I don't mind you knowing who I am. Why do you care so much?

That feels a little too aggressive, though, so I delete it. He obviously does care about this, and I don't want to scare him away. This is also confirmation that our deal is continuing, at least for the time being. I change tack:

Not if they're out of the house. I usually have the place to myself on Saturday nights.

My phone chimes.

Okay. If they're not there, I'm in.

* * *

It's Saturday night, and Luke still hasn't left.

Dad has gone to a meeting at the bar. Apparently something big is going down, something he isn't ready for me to know about yet. All I know about it is Dad told me to be prepared, even though I don't really know what I should be preparing for.

This is typical. He still thinks I'm too young to know everything.

Most of the time, I don't want to know.

Anyway, I checked, and I know Luke is going out with his friends from college, a lot of which are his friends from high school. He's always been popular. I get it; he's a cool guy, but it bothers me that he's figured out how to be likable when it's been so damn hard for me.

Jason is the first person in a long time who seems to like my company.

And he's coming over tonight. But only if Luke isn't here.

Which is why I'm so stressed that my brother hasn't left yet. I swear he doesn't normally take this long. It's, like, comical how slow he's being. He's currently in the shower, singing "Sweet Caroline."

Loudly. And terribly.

My phone buzzes in my pocket.

Has he left yet?

Nope. He's in the shower now. Singing.

Haha! You're not a fan?

He's no Beyoncé.

To be fair, nobody is. And that's promising, right? The showering, not the singing.

Yeah!

Cool. Well, I'm ready to go. Text when your place is free, I'll head over.

This feels so risky. I know from past experience that Dad and Luke don't normally come home until really late, and most of the time I'm asleep by then.

But what if they come home early?

Maybe I should just cancel. Bringing Jason into my house feels like a kind of leap I'm not sure I'm ready for.

But I don't want to cancel. I just don't want to get caught.

If I told Dad and Luke that I was having a friend over, they probably wouldn't care. If they asked how I knew him, I could say school. If I said I met him at the bar, I know they'd ask me what family he's from. And I don't know the answer to that.

Why is he being so weird about which family he's from?

Down the hall, I hear the shower shut off. *Finally.* A few seconds later, Luke walks past. I watch a *BuzzFeed Unsolved* video as I wait. A few moments later, Luke appears in my doorway. He's dressed in his usual attire: a well-fitting black shirt, jeans, and his most expensive pair of dress shoes. Dad got them for him.

"Hey, I'm about to head out," he says.

"Okay, have a good night!"

"You too. Don't get into too much trouble without me, okay?"

"I never do."

I hear the door close. Then I wait. I hear a car pull up by our house, I'm guessing his Uber, because he's planning on drinking. It drives away.

I want to be sure, though, so I go through the house, to the front door. There are glass panels on either side of it, so I look through those, out at the driveway.

The street is empty. Eddie comes up to me. He always sulks whenever Luke leaves. His ears are pressed down, and his tail is hanging limp. I scratch the top of his head, until his tail starts wagging.

"You can keep a secret, can't you, buddy?"

He nuzzles against my leg. I'll take that as a yes.

So I text Jason. My heart is seriously pounding.

Hey, guess what?

What?

He's gone.

The typing bubble appears.

Sweet! I'm on my way.

CHAPTER SEVEN

THERE'S A KNOCK ON THE DOOR.

Oh man.

I'm so not ready for this.

I've changed my outfit maybe ten times. So now my bed is covered in clothes, although everywhere else is clean. I even lit a sandalwood candle to try to make sure my room smells nice.

The outfit I ended up settling for is a You Me at Six band shirt I got from when I saw them live, skinny black jeans, and my Vans.

I think I look good.

I'm not totally confident in my decision to wear a band tee, but I know from trying on almost all my clothes I'm not going to be totally confident in any of them. And I'm out of time. I scoop up all rejected choices and throw them into the closet and shut the door.

Presto, instant clean room.

I jog down to the foyer. Earlier, I scanned the house to make sure there are no obvious signs on display of who Luke and Dad are. I had to hide a few photos in my room, like one from Luke's high school graduation, a few of Mom, and one with my grandparents. I triple-checked and am sure I did a good job. Eddie is jumping up and down, pressing his paws against the door, and I can see a male figure outside. I grab on to Eddie's collar and open the door.

"Hey, hey," says Jason.

Even under the harsh porch light, he looks fantastic. I've never seen him wear casual clothes, but they suit him really well. He's wearing a dark red T-shirt and navy skinny jeans, along with cool Nikes that were probably really expensive. They look kind of extra.

"Hey," I say. "Thanks for coming."

"No, thanks for having me."

Eddie is going wild, like he wants to lick Jason to death.

I mean, I get that.

Jason crouches and starts petting Eddie. "Who's a good boy?"

Eddie sits proudly and lets Jason rub his chest.

"He likes you," I say. "He's normally way more skittish with new people."

"Really? That's, like, the highest compliment possible. I love dogs."

"Me too."

Jason stands. Oh man, Eddie really does like him. He's nudging at his legs, wanting more attention. But now Jason is looking at me.

What's the proper greeting for something like this?

I go for a handshake, and he ignores it, going for a hug instead. And he's a *great* hugger. He's so firm, and yet . . . we kind of sink into each other.

It's perfect.

"Should I take my shoes off?" he asks as we break apart.

"Nah, it's fine."

"Cool."

We walk inside.

"Anyway," I say. "Um, are you hungry?"

He shoves his hands into his pockets. "I am, yeah. Is that all right? I could've eaten before, but I thought . . ."

"Yeah, dude, 'course. I was thinking we could order pizza or something. There's this New York–style place down the road that does honestly the best pizza I've ever had."

"That sounds fucking amazing."

"Great."

I close the door behind him and lead him through the entrance foyer, into the kitchen. I walk around the kitchen island while Jason checks out the place. Eddie brings Jason his favorite toy, a chewed-up rope with a ball on the end of it. Jason tosses it, and Eddie runs off to retrieve it.

"Do you want a drink?" I ask.

I open the fridge and scan the options. There's white wine, but that's Dad's. Luke keeps a couple of bottles of beer on the bottom shelf, because Dad isn't super strict about him drinking. I could offer him one of those, but Jason might not like that. I get the idea he's pretty straight-edge.

Or as straight-edge as someone in our world can be.

"I'm good," he says as he throws the toy again. "Thanks, though."

I close the fridge and turn back. "No problem."

"Nice place, by the way," he says.

I imagine being him, seeing my place for the first time. In front of us is the living room, where there's a brown couch in front of a huge TV. Outside, through a set of glass sliding doors, is the pool. Down one hall is Dad's room. On the other side of the house is a hall that leads to my bedroom and Luke's, plus a bathroom. The floors are stone-colored ceramic tile. They make the whole place feel kind of frosty.

"Thanks. Um, what kind of pizza do you like? We should probably order, like, now, if you're hungry."

I bring up the app on my phone. He moves around and stands

beside me, so close that we're nearly touching. I can smell his cologne now, and it's very nice.

"Pepperoni, obviously," he says.

Honestly, it's the only acceptable answer. I'm glad he said it.

"Cool. How about I get one of those and a garlic bread? We already have Cokes and stuff here."

"Sounds perfect."

I order the food, and the app tells me it'll be delivered in twenty minutes.

"I could show you the pool, if you'd like?" I ask.

He nods, so I take him through the house. Eddie follows behind, with the toy in his mouth. He's so needy.

"I love your TV," says Jason as he takes the toy from Eddie and throws it. "Where do you keep your games?"

"In the drawer."

He slides it open, revealing my stack of games.

"Can I?" he asks.

"Sure."

He rifles through them. "All nice choices, man. You clearly have good taste."

"Thanks. But come on, I'm not done yet."

"Fine, fine, sorry I'm so curious about you."

I don't know what to say to that. But for some reason, I blush.

We go outside and go through the gate, to walk around the pool. It's lit up by underwater lights, which makes it look sort of magical. The whole area is really nice.

It gets a massive smile out of him.

"This is so awesome," he says.

"I'm glad you like it. I hang out here a lot. Like, when I read or listen to a podcast, I sit there."

"I do that, too, actually. Just, at my place."

"You do?"

"Yeah."

"Awesome."

Once we've done a lap, we go back inside. He marvels at everything, including a piece of modern art hanging on the hallway wall. I know it's ridiculously expensive, even though it's pretty much just a single black line on a red background. Dad bought it for himself to celebrate landing a big protection racket deal. We get a lot of our income from that. Businesses pay us to keep them safe . . .

But if they don't pay, they get torched. So really, we're protecting them from ourselves. It's totally messed up, and I hate thinking about it.

"I like this," he says.

"Yeah, me too."

"What do you think it means?"

"Hmm." I put my hand on my chin, and lean back a little, like I'm an art critic. "I think it's about the way men bottle rage, until it all finally erupts, ruining the lives of everyone around them."

"Really?"

"God no, I have no idea."

He laughs, and then we go down the hall.

"Oh, and the bathroom is there, if you, um, need to use it," I say.

"Noted."

"And down there's my brother's room. Don't go in there, it smells like Axe."

"Really?"

"Yeah. Like, all the time. And this one," I say as I walk into my room, "is mine."

I feel really self-conscious. I've put a lot of work into my room. Now it feels stupid.

Like, who has this many movie posters? They feel childish now. Maybe I should've taken them down before I invited him over. Tried to man the place up a little.

"I love this," he says.

I kick at the dark carpet. "Really?"

"Yeah, dude, your room is sick. Have you seen all these movies?"

"Multiple times, yeah."

"That's amazing."

He walks over to the poster I have of *Creature from the Black Lagoon*. He touches it.

"Which one's your favorite?"

"Movie or poster?"

"Either."

"Well, my favorite movie is *Mulholland Drive*. I don't really have a favorite poster."

I walk him over to one of the posters by the door. My *Mulholland Drive* one.

"What's it about?" he asks. "It looks cool."

"It is. It's about this actress . . . actually, you should probably just watch it. It's better to just experience it blind, trust me."

That's how I found it. I heard a lot of discussion about it being good, so I decided to finally watch it. When it ended, I knew right away that I'd just seen my favorite movie.

"There's this great song inspired by it. I could play it, if you want?"

"Sure."

I pull out my phone, and sync it to my Bluetooth speaker. I find the song, and hit play. It's a song called "Mulholland Drive" by the Gaslight Anthem. To me, it feels like how the movie feels. And I love it for that.

The chorus hits. It goes: *Oh that I'd just die if you ever took your love away.*

"Damn, nice," he says, nodding his head along. "I like it. He sounds so desperate."

"Dude, that's exactly why I like it!"

"Nice. You have such cool taste in music; I'm so jealous."

I sit down on my desk chair, and he sits down on the edge of my bed. He kind of lounges, which I really like. It's as if he's already super comfortable here.

"What music do you like?" I ask. "Sorry, that's such a broad question. I'll narrow it down: What's your favorite band?"

"I don't really know. I feel like I haven't come across any I like that much. I like this, though."

"That's exciting," I say. "That means they're still out there, for you to find."

He smiles. "I've never thought about it that way. That *is* pretty exciting."

"In the meantime, though, what do you listen to?"

I have a moment where I realize this is happening. There he is. Sitting on my bed, like he's done this a bunch of times. I have a friend over. This is so cool.

"I usually just listen to the playlists Spotify makes for me," he says. "I'm not really a big music guy." He shrugs. "Sorry. I know you are."

"Hey, don't be sorry. I'm not one of those people who expects people to like everything I like. I hope I don't seem like I am."

"No, you don't. You seem very cool."

He smiles. God, he's so cute.

"I'm glad."

He quirks his head to the side and then pushes up off my bed and goes over to my bookshelf. He scans it.

"*Harry Potter*, nice," he says. "The Game of Thrones series, too."

"Yep."

He taps the top of the shelf and looks around.

"I really do love your room," he says. "It feels like, yours, you know?"

I lean back against my chair. "Yours doesn't?"

"Nope."

"Why?"

"Can't say. It's a family thing."

"Oh, right."

That kind of lingers between us. I get the idea he wants to change the subject pretty badly. For the first time since he got here, he looks uncomfortable.

"Did you want to play some *Smash Bros.*?" I ask.

"Dude, yes! I love *Smash Bros.*!"

"Me too."

We walk back to the living room and sit down on the couch. He sits fairly close to me. Not close enough to touch, but still. I grab the remote from the coffee table and turn on the TV. I feel very aware of the space I'm taking up, and the space between us.

He seems to like getting close to me.

I'm not complaining, but I wish I knew why he was doing it. If he's gay, it'd make sense. But if he's straight and just messing with me . . . I'd hate it.

Jason bounces up and down. I watch him.

"What?" he says. "It's really comfy."

"Okay."

I glance at the front door. I'm kind of freaking out that we could get walked in on at any second by Dad or Luke. And then I'll have to explain why I didn't just say I was having a friend over.

And why we're sitting so close together.

I think my lying will make them think I'm keeping a secret about Jason.

I don't know if it'll make them think I'm gay.

But it might. Because, seriously, he's so close to me right now.

And I'm not stupid. Something is going on here. Right? Or maybe I just really want that to be the case. Ugh. I just wish I knew what he wants.

I load the game and hand him a controller. Our hands touch. It feels deliberate.

But it can't be. If Jason is gay, there's no way he'd be into me. He'd be into someone cool . . . not a guy he found freaking out in a bathroom in an ill-fitting suit. He'd be into someone, like him, who'd charge into the water, not someone who has to google shark attacks before going in. He'd like someone bold and cool. So not me.

The game starts, and we both go to select the same character: Pokémon Trainer.

"Are they your favorite?" he asks.

"Yeah. Yours too?"

"Yep. I can be Lucario, though, I love him almost as much."

It's kind of a deep cut, when it comes to *Super Smash Bros.* and *Pokémon*. I love that. He switches to Lucario.

And then we fight.

∗   ∗   ∗

It takes about an hour for the nerves to completely settle.

Together, Jason and I have demolished an entire pepperoni pizza and two loaves of garlic bread. We also each had a can of Coke Zero Sugar, which I found out he likes as much as I do.

I've lost every single match. He's way too good at this game.

And I don't even care.

I feel full, and happy, and like I've settled into a comfortable groove with him. Like we've been friends for ages and we're just hanging out.

I've wanted something like this for so long. An actual friend.

Right now, we're selecting our characters. For the first time, I pick Link.

"Oh, nice," he says. "I love Link. I had the biggest crush on him when I was a kid."

HOLD UP.

"Um," I say.

"Er, yeah, I'm not exactly straight. Surprise!"

WOW.

"Oh, um, cool," I say.

"That's all you have to say?"

"I mean, yeah. I think it's cool. But, wait, how exactly do you identify?"

His eyes widen a little. "Um, I'm only into guys, or anyone who presents as male. So I usually go by gay, if I *have* to label myself. I don't really like doing that, though. It feels weird."

I focus on the TV. I'm shaking. I lower my controller so he doesn't notice.

"That's awesome," I say. "It's not a big thing for me; I literally don't think of you any different, by the way. But thanks for telling me."

"No problem," he says. "I just thought you should know. I've been trying to bring it up this whole time, actually."

"Really? Why?"

"Let's just say . . . I wanted you to know."

I don't know what to say to that. I think he's flirting with me.

So now I have a hot *gay* dude sitting next to me. And he's looking at me like he's expecting me to tell him about myself.

Or maybe kiss him.

I have so many questions that I can't ask. *Does* he know about me? Is this why he wanted me to know? Does he want me to tell him right now? Does he even know I've never told anyone?

A part of me wants me to come out to him. To just say fuck it and jump in. I think that's what he wants, and his knowing would be kind of awesome.

I think about doing it . . . but then swerve away at the last second.

It's too scary. I'm not ready.

"How was coming out?" I ask. "I've heard it's, like, rough for some people."

He maintains eye contact. "I won't lie, it was scary. And it wasn't great for a while. It was just . . . weird. I came out at fourteen."

"Wait, fourteen? That's so young."

He leans back against the chair. "Eh, I've known pretty much my whole life, so it didn't feel young to me. Anyway, my mom was fine, but Dad was a bit of a dick about it. I think he maybe thinks when I'm older I'll straighten out, like this is some sort of trend I'm following."

I lean back so we're both up against the backrest. Our arms are so close to touching. His hand is resting on the couch. He has really pretty hands, with long, dainty fingers. There's a freckle on his wrist. I wonder what it'd be like to circle it with my fingertips.

I glance up.

He's so handsome.

And now I know he might be an option. Because I'm picking up a vibe that he would make out with me, if I went for it. But is that all he wants? To hook up with me?

I'd actually hate that. I'd rather have a friend.

I don't want this to be a one-and-done type deal. Even if his lips are such a nice shade of pink and look sort of glossy right now. And even if I can see the curve of his muscles through his shirt.

I don't want to be just a conquest for him.

I want to be more than that.

Oh God, I'm so glad nobody can hear my thoughts.

"That's so stupid," I say quietly. I think we've both forgotten about the game. "He should realize it doesn't work like that."

"Yeah, it doesn't. Trust me, I know."

"I'm sorry," I say. "It sucks that your dad makes you feel like that."

He nods. "Thanks for being cool. You can never tell with guys. Girls are pretty much always fine with it, but with guys, it's a total crap-shoot."

"Did you just make a gambling reference? Are you sure you're gay?"

"Shut up!"

He laughs and pushes me. His hand rests on my stomach for a second too long.

"But, yeah, I'm very sure," he says. "Guys just do it for me. They make me feel like I'm, like, on fire. It's that intense."

I glance down. It feels like a barrier has been broken.

That touching each other is okay now.

The moment passes. The walls go back up.

"Wait," I say. "What about your baseball team?"

"I told you I play baseball?"

I nod. I feel a little busted. He only told me once, and I remembered. I'm not sure if that's weird.

I'm sure stuff like that will give away my sexuality. And if he knows about me, then we might make out or something. Which would be great.

But risky.

What if we don't click romantically? That'd be the end of things. And I've never been kissed. Not even once. What if I'm not good at it? Right away, at least.

"Um, yeah," I say. "You did. Or was it basketball?"

"No, you were right the first time. Good memory. But yeah, the team seems fine with it. I think they have to be; they know how much trouble they'd get into if they said anything homophobic." He stares off into the distance, clearly remembering something. "After I came out my coach did a whole speech about how we're a team and how our personal lives shouldn't impact that. I normally don't like being fussed over, but that was pretty great."

I can picture it now. Him, blushing, while his coach grills his team.

"Anyway," he says. "Now that's out there, let's play *Smash Bros.* I mean the game, by the way, in case your mind is in the gutter."

I freeze, my eyes wide.

"I'm just messing with you," he says, and he nudges my leg with his. "No need to freak."

"Sorry. I'm just getting used to it. I don't want to say the wrong thing."

"You're not secretly a homophobe, are you?"

"No."

"Then you've got nothing to worry about."

"Cool."

The game finally starts. It feels like the most intense of all our fights so far. But the whole time, I'm thinking about him having a crush on Link.

The fight ends, with him just winning. It's the closest I've gotten to winning so far.

"Nice work," he says. "You nearly had me."

A fluttery feeling fills my stomach.

Eddie barks, and then runs over to the door. I freeze.

No.

No no no no no.

This can't be happening.

But it is.

Headlights flash in through the windows at the front of the house. Someone's home.

CHAPTER EIGHT

"WHAT'S WRONG?" ASKS JASON.

My mind is racing, trying to come up with a plan to get out of this.

I look at the coffee table, and see the remnants of our hangout. Two empty, but clearly used, glasses are sitting on it. I'll need to hide one of them. And, obviously, think about something to do with the hot tall guy currently sitting beside me.

"Someone's here," I say as I turn off the TV. I stand up and grab one of the cups. "Follow me."

"What?"

"We have our deal," I say. "Unless you want to find out who I am, you need to come with me. Please."

"Oh, shit, okay."

He stands up. He's not moving fast enough, so I take hold of his wrist and run him through the house to my room. I look around. Under the bed won't work, it's too obvious. I have a window, but it has a bolted-in, bulletproof metal fly screen. Nobody is coming in or out of it.

I realize I'm still hanging on to his wrist.

I let go. As I do, I glance at my closet. It's perfect.

Jason crosses his arms and tilts his head up. "Really?"

"I'm so sorry. It won't be for long. I'll think of something, just, hide."

I open the sliding door, and then push aside some of my clothes.

Because Jason is so tall, it's going to be cramped, but it'll have to do.

He frowns.

But then he steps inside, bowing his head to do so. "I hope you appreciate the irony of this. I come out to you, and then you shove me right back in a closet."

He grins.

I wish I could find this amusing, but I'm way too freaked to find anything funny right now.

"I'm really sorry," I whisper. "I thought they wouldn't come home, I swear."

"It's cool, it happens."

I wonder what that means as I slide the door shut. I take a step back and look. He's perfectly hidden.

Okay, phew.

I run back down the hall and dump the cup in the sink, just in time for the door to open. There are still two controllers sitting on the couch. Maybe they won't notice, but it definitely still looks like two people have been playing.

Luke steps inside.

"What's wrong with you?" he says, coming straight up to me. "Why don't you answer your fucking phone?"

"What?"

I guess I haven't checked it in a while, I was too busy with Jason.

I pull my phone out and check. The screen is full of notifications. Ten missed calls from him, along with a bunch of messages. I had it on silent, like I always do. I guess I was so distracted by Jason I never thought to check it.

"I . . ."

Then I notice Luke's eyes are red.

He closes the distance and hugs me tight. I can't even recall the last time he did this. Is this because of Jason? Surely this isn't how he'd be reacting if he knew about what I was doing.

"What's going on?" I ask.

Luke sniffs. Wait, is he crying? I check, and he's only just managing to keep it together.

"It's Dad," he says. "Matt, he's . . ."

"What is it? Just tell me."

"He's been shot."

No. No way.

This must be a prank. A terrible, awful prank.

"He's okay," says Luke. "Well, he's not. He's in surgery now. Apparently that's a good thing, they don't operate on people they don't think have a chance, right? But you know Dad, he's tough, he's not going to . . ."

Die.

That's the end of that sentence.

Holy shit.

"Everyone else is at the hospital," says Luke. "People kept asking why you weren't there, so I came to get you. Let's go."

"Now?"

"Yes, now. Maybe grab a sweater, it's cold inside."

I nod and run back to my room. I close the door behind me. I feel like crying, but I can't. Not until I've dealt with the Jason mess. I hardly even care about it right now, though.

My dad's been shot.

It must've been the Donovans. It doesn't feel real, it's *that* horrible. He's been in the hospital, fighting for his life, and I've been here, with Jason. I open the closet door.

"What's going on?" says Jason. "I heard shouting."

"Nothing, it's fine. Well, it's not. We're about to go out. Just wait, I'll text you when we're out of the house. Go out the front door, lock it behind you. Okay?"

"Sure, but . . ."

I grab my black hoodie from beside him. Jason is watching me, unblinking.

"Is everything okay?" he asks.

"Don't worry about it. This has nothing to do with you, I promise."

"Dude, talk to me."

"It's a family thing, so I shouldn't, right? That's our deal."

His face falls. "Oh, okay. Up to you, man."

I slide the door shut again, then I go back to the living room. Luke's already gone outside. I lock the door behind me, and go down to Luke's car. It's a black Ford Mustang convertible that he got for his eighteenth birthday. It's his pride and joy, along with Eddie.

I climb into the passenger seat and pull on my seat belt.

Luke spins the car out onto the road and then steps on the gas.

We drive in silence. The radio is playing some crappy pop song about generic true love.

Barf.

"Hey," I say.

"Yeah?"

"You might want to slow down."

He was starting to speed. Only just, but I noticed it.

"You're right," he says. "Sorry."

He's clearly messed up. I am, too. But I don't think it's properly hit me yet. My dad is supposed to be untouchable, the strongest one out of all of us.

If they can get him . . .

I know this is his war. After Grandad died, Dad is the one who spearheaded the charge to fight the Donovans. I do know that most of us wanted some form of retaliation. Still, I get a sense sometimes that not everyone is okay with the fact that it's turned into an all-out war.

I hate thinking this, but maybe this will be a sign he needs to stop the fighting.

That would honestly be such a relief.

I can't believe I'm thinking it, though. I should hate the Donovans more than I ever have.

Up ahead, I can see Mercy Hospital. The parking lot is a massive tower, and the words "MERCY" are in dark blue neon on the side. Between the "M" and the "E" is a cross, which feels a little bit over-the-top to me, but whatever.

Luke parks in the closest free spot, and we climb out, and start heading toward the front door. The lot is dark and still. Luke practically jogs across it, and I try to keep up.

To be honest, I can't help but feel slightly responsible for this. Maybe I shouldn't, but I can't help it. I hang out with Jason one time, and then this happens. I know there's no direct link, and I shouldn't feel this way.

But still, I do.

The hospital's walls are cream colored, and the floors are speckled blue. The desk and furnishings are all modern and sleek, which feels promising. Luke broke his arm when he was younger, and the place he went was ancient. This place looks top-notch. It smells clean, like antiseptic spray. It's so strong my nose starts tingling.

Luke takes me down a hallway, and we reach a waiting room.

Inside, most of my family has gathered. We fill almost the entire space. Everyone looks tired and drained. It's Millers only, no allied families.

Everyone glances my way. A few of them sneer at me.

Luke was right. I should've been here right away, as I'm sure Luke was. And yet, I wasn't.

They don't need it, but this is clearly another strike against me.

Luke goes across the room and sits down. I sit beside him.

And we wait.

After a few hours, a doctor finally steps into the waiting room. I've never felt so sick.

We all huddle around the doctor. Luke is closest to her.

"Just tell us," he says. "Is he okay?"

"It was touch-and-go for a second there, but it's looking good," says the doctor. She's in blue scrubs and holding a clipboard. "We managed to get the bullets out and stop the bleeding. He's expected to make a full recovery. Your old man's quite the fighter."

Relief washes over the crowd.

He's going to be okay.

"We'll keep him in an induced coma for the next few days, to give his body some time to heal. You'll be able to sit with him during visiting hours, but for now, I advise you all to go home and get some rest. It's been a long night, but the worst is over."

Vince goes up to her and shakes her hand. As he does, I notice he's handed her a wad of cash.

He wants her to keep this quiet.

I shouldn't be surprised. I know my family has a foothold in most major institutions in the city. If they scratch our back, we'll scratch theirs. Not passing on this information to the police is one of the things they can do.

"Hey, Matt," says Luke.

"Yeah?"

"A word?"

Luke takes me down a hallway to find a quiet spot. We stop beside a vending machine, and he tucks his hands into his armpits. The lights here are so bright my eyes sting.

"I think someone should stay here," he says. "In case something happens."

"Yeah, same."

I think I know where he wants me to go with this.

"You go," I say. "I'll take first watch."

He looks totally wiped out. His hair is messy, and there are angry dark circles under his eyes.

"You sure?" he asks.

"Yeah. Get some rest, dude, you're done."

"Okay, thanks. I'll go sleep, then we'll swap in the morning?"

"Sure."

"Cool, thanks."

We go back to the waiting room. Everyone is in the process of slowly gathering their things to head home. It seems like I'm the only one staying.

That suits me just fine. Luke's company is always welcome, but the others . . .

I'd rather be alone.

I take a seat and watch as everyone leaves. A few of the guys shake my hand as they go, each one crushing my palm with their grip. I also get a few emotionless hugs from my aunts. But that's it.

And then I'm alone.

It's moments like these that my lack of friends hurts the most. I'm just not close enough to anyone to talk to them if I go through something rough. All I can do is pretend I don't feel anything.

I think that's what my family wants from me. To be like Luke, so strong, so okay with everything that happens in this family.

But I'm not.

I'm just not built like that. I could cry right now, but I feel like I can't.

I wait for a while, just thinking about my life and Dad. Mostly I'm just wishing that he will be okay. I'm not ready to lose him. I know we don't see eye to eye on basically anything, but he's still my dad.

I can't lose him.

It makes me think I've been taking him for granted. I know he raised me on his own. And he's never complained about me being so obsessed with movies, and he lets me buy as many as I want. He's been a good father, and I haven't given him any credit for that.

Then I think about Jason. This feels typical. I have one really fun night, and my family swoops in and wrecks it.

Plus, he's gay. I haven't even had time to deal with that revelation.

I still don't know where this is going. It makes at least as much sense as him just randomly seeing me in a bathroom and deciding to be friends with me. People aren't normally super friendly to strangers, unless they want something from them.

I check my phone and see he's messaged me a few times.

Okay, I think the coast is clear. Attempting to break out now.

Eddie just wants to keep playing fetch. Worst guard dog ever. Haha.

I'm outside. I feel like a criminal right now, you have no idea.

MISSION COMPLETE! Wow, that was fun. Thanks again for a good night, I always have such a good time with you.

I find I'm smiling.

He's such a goof. I start typing a message.

I'm glad you made it home okay. ☺

The typing bubble appears right away.

What happened?

What do you mean?

It sounded serious. Is everything okay?

I told you, it's a family thing. Something bad and it sucks. But don't worry, I'll be okay.

The typing bubble appears, then vanishes. Then appears again, only to vanish once more.

Finally, a message comes through.

Where are you now?

Mercy Hospital. Why?

The message appears pretty much straightaway.

I'm on my way.

CHAPTER NINE

HEY, I'M HERE, WHERE ARE YOU?

I stare at my phone for a second, as that sinks in.

I mean, it's not that tough a question to answer. I'm on the rooftop of the hospital. There's an ocean breeze, cutting through the humidity, and I can hear the endless traffic flowing through the streets. It's dark out, but the space is well lit by the buildings around.

I wanted to find somewhere where I could talk to Jason without stressing about being interrupted. I explored for a while and then found an elevator that goes up to the roof. I'm not sure I'm allowed to be up here, but nobody has stopped me yet.

I start typing my response.

On the roof.

My thumb hovers over the send button.

It's really nice that he came. Of course I think that. But isn't this risky as hell? Anyone in my family could show up at any time, and then I'd need to explain why I wasn't in the waiting room, like I said I would be.

And if Jason met anyone, he might be able to figure out that I'm part of this city's first family of crime. Knowing that, he might not want to be friends anymore. I think he thinks I'm like him, from an allied family. I don't think he knows just how deep in this world I am.

It's a risk I'm willing to take, though. Having a friend to talk to right now would be so nice it almost doesn't feel real. I'm so used to bottling up how I feel, but tonight, maybe I don't have to.

I hit send.

I tuck my phone back into my pocket and try to find a place to sit. Obviously there aren't any chairs or anything: but there is the lip of the roof. It's pretty thick; it'll be fine. I go over to the edge and peer down. I can see the street below, which is quiet. I spot a parked silver Alfa Romeo. Luke would love that car.

I push myself up and onto the lip of the roof. I scoot forward, until my legs are hanging in thin air. The cement is cool and rough.

My hands are shaking now. From everything.

My dad got shot.

He nearly died.

It's completely fucked-up.

It makes me think about the Donovans. I picture them and try my best to hate them.

There's Frank Donovan, the current patriarch. He's an overweight man, balding, who always wears a three-piece suit. He has reddish hair and a beard. It's said that he's vicious but not very smart. In this business, though, pure, ballsy aggression often does work. Still, it's his wife, Maria, who's the really dangerous one. She's pretty much the opposite of him: Her hair is dark when his is light, and she's incredibly slim, to the point where she looks ill. She's a scalpel to his hammer, an expert at finding our weak points and exploiting them.

She's ruthless and wants my family dead as much as most of my family wants hers. Not for any personal reason that we know of, other than that she's sick of her family being second-best.

Always being the bridesmaid gets old, apparently.

Then there are all the Donovans we don't know. Part of this game has always been trying to figure out who they are. Once we find a Donovan, we normally try to kill them. They're the same with us.

I hear the sound of sneakers scuffing on gravel and spin.

Jason raises his hand at me. I wave back.

Good timing, too. I was just starting to fall down a rabbit hole thinking about my family and the war. And now I don't have to. That's the beauty of our deal, I guess. It lets us pretend we're normal. It makes me understand why he doesn't want to talk about our families, because I don't want that, either.

With him, I just want to be myself.

He's dressed in the same clothes he was when I last saw him. I guess it hasn't even been that long. A few hours, tops. It feels way longer.

He crosses the roof and sits down beside me. Like at my place, he sits a little closer than I feel he needs to.

"It's high up here," he says as he looks down.

"Yeah."

He smiles and kicks his feet. It's cute. "What made you choose this spot?"

"I didn't want my family to see us, I guess."

"Because of our deal?"

"Yeah." I cross my arms. "I mean, what else would it be?"

A complicated look crosses his features. He almost seems offended.

"You tell me," he says.

I crack my back, and then look out at the city. This is tough. I think he's here to provide emotional support, which is great. But I can't tell him about everything that's happened, because of our deal. And I guess I don't want to.

I don't know what to say.

"Listen," he says. He adjusts his position, so he's facing me a little more. "I know we have our agreement."

"Yeah."

"And I want to keep it going."

"I know, me too. I wasn't going to . . ."

"Good, but you can tell me some things, if you want." His voice is even, and a little slow, like he's being careful with his words. "Just, like, keep it vague. That way it doesn't matter. You can tell me why you're here, just, in a roundabout way. If you want."

"So no personal specifics?"

"Exactly. I mean, you *could* tell me, if you want to."

I chew my lip. "I don't. Sorry."

"Hey, don't be. I figured. Pretend I didn't ask."

"Done. Well. I will say that a family member of mine was hurt pretty bad."

I figure he probably already assumed that, given where I am.

Still, saying it feels good.

"Shit, dude, that's really rough," he says. "I'm sorry."

"Yeah. They're going to be okay, but it was a little scary for a second there. I didn't know . . ."

"Didn't know what?"

Tears fill my eyes. I blink them away. "I didn't know if they were going to make it."

I sniff and look down. There's so much I want to say, but I can't.

Jason puts his hand on my shoulder and squeezes.

"I'm sorry," he says. "Whatever you need, I'm here."

He leaves his hand there, resting against me.

We sit there for a few seconds, watching the city, with his arm on me.

I've never had anyone do this to me before. It's so nice. He doesn't need to say anything more. Just him putting his hand on my shoulder tells me that he cares about me and he's sorry that this really awful thing has happened to me.

He's got my back.

"You don't need to do anything," I say. My voice sounds croaky. "You being here is more than enough. I don't want you to think I'm a burden or anything."

"Dude, what? I'd never. I'm here because we're friends now, right? This is what friends do. They support each other."

My eyes widen.

We're friends now. It's official.

"I wouldn't know," I say. "I've never really had any friends. Good ones, anyway."

"Really? Come on, you've got to be messing with me."

I shake my head. "No good ones. I just don't click with people. I don't know why."

"Well, everyone else is missing out," he says. "I can tell you're a great friend."

I feel like crying, but I smile. He squeezes one last time, and his hand slides off my shoulder.

I miss the contact.

"So," says Jason. "I take it you've had a really shitty day?"

"The shittiest."

"Then it's my duty, as your friend, to cheer you up. That's how it works, by the way. If something shitty happens to me, you need to be there for me. Deal?"

"Of course."

"Okay. Well, to take your mind off it, I want you to tell me about something you really love."

"What?"

"It's a game I like. All you have to do is talk about something you love a lot. I've found it's a really good way to get to know someone, in a deeper way."

"Um," I say. I stare up at the night sky and think. "Okay. So, I really love the movie *Donnie Darko*."

"Oh, nice. Jake Gyllenhaal is in that, right?"

"Yeah. Have you seen it?"

He shakes his head. "What's it about?"

"It's weird. There's this guy, Donnie, and he, like, sees this dude in a bunny costume who tells him the world is going to end in twenty-eight days, six hours, forty-two minutes, and twelve seconds. And it goes from there. When I first found it I watched it literally once every day for a week."

"Are you serious?"

"Yeah. I got kind of obsessed. I just wanted to pick it apart and learn the craft of it. I knew it worked; I wanted to figure out why."

"That's so awesome, man. You're so dedicated; it's really inspiring."

"You're dedicated, too, just, for games. You played *Skyrim* for four *hundred* hours, remember."

"Right. I guess it's similar. Yours is cooler, though."

"I was thinking the same about yours. But okay, your turn. What's something you really love?"

He thinks about it for a second. As he watches the city, I find myself gazing at him.

He truly is so handsome.

Perfect, even.

I mean, he's not. There are slight bags under his eyes, his lips look really dry right now, and he has quite a few moles. He looks perfect for a real person, is what I mean.

I shouldn't take for granted how cool it is that he wants to be friends with me.

He's so different from most of the guys I know who are a part of this world.

I hope he thinks the same thing about me.

"Okay, I've thought of something," he says. "I was going to say *Skyrim*, because that's my favorite game. But you already know I love that. So there are these books called the Bartimaeus trilogy. I read them over and over and over as a kid."

"Dude!" I say. "I've read those!"

He beams. "You have? You're not just saying that?"

"I wouldn't lie to you like that. I love them."

"Me too," he says. "They're my favorite. I love *Harry Potter*, but I kind of like that these are a little less known, you know? It feels like they're mine, in a way. I'm not sure if that's stupid."

An ocean breeze hits us, and his eyelids flutter.

"It's not. I totally get that. It's less fun to love something everyone loves, for some reason."

"For sure," he says. "I can't believe you've read them. We have so much in common; it keeps happening."

"Yeah, it's weird, right?"

I start feeling a little daring.

I mean, he's my friend. He's already come out to me, and he came here, just to support me.

I want to tell him about . . . me.

I'm not expecting more than his friendship. I think he'll be okay with it. As far as I know, there aren't any homophobic gay dudes. That'd be stupid.

I have nothing to lose and a lot to gain.

How do I even do this? What should I say?

I think about starting with *We have something else in common*, but that feels too obvious. This is my first-ever coming-out, but still, I don't want it to sound totally naive.

"Um," I say. "I think I want to tell you something." I stretch my arms out in front of me. "Fuck, I'm really nervous."

"Dude, it's me. Don't be nervous; you can tell me anything. You know that, right?"

I exhale. "Yeah. So you know how I said I like *Donnie Darko*?"

I say each word faster than I normally do. He nods.

"Well, it kind of had a big impact on me. More than I was saying before."

"What do you mean?"

"When I was watching it, I sort of realized . . ."

I look into his eyes.

"Oh," he says. "Are you saying you think Jake Gyllenhaal is totally hot?"

I nod.

It's all I can do. I'm too scared to vocally confirm it. It's enough, though. The job is done. I, Matt Miller, have officially admitted that I can find a guy hot.

"I mean, he is, right?" he says.

I laugh. "Yeah, he is."

I just came out.

That sinks in. He knows about me now.

"Are you surprised?" I ask.

"Honestly, nope."

I laugh. "And here I was, thinking I'm being stealthy."

"It's not that. It's just I don't tend to assume anyone's sexuality. I've found it's too hard to predict, anyway."

I nod again. That checks out.

"What was it about the movie?" he asks.

"I noticed this energy about him. It's, like, I was so drawn to him. For the first time I wanted to see what someone looked like with less clothes on. And I found myself having dreams about him. Not sex ones, just, like, normal dreams. I couldn't stop thinking about him. It was really intense. I've never told anyone about that, it's so embarrassing."

"It's not, I totally get you. It's kind of magic, in a way."

"What do you mean?"

"That another person can make you feel that much."

I mean, agreed.

"And I've totally felt that, too, by the way," he continues. "I had this devastating crush on Sam Winchester from *Supernatural*. I watched all the episodes, just for him."

"Good choice. He's hot."

I've never said those words out loud. *He's hot.*

It's so simple, yet it means so much.

"Yeah," says Jason. "He is. I think those feelings are what makes being gay worth it. Like, it's hard, but who wouldn't chase that feeling, you know?"

"For sure."

He swats my shoulder. "But, hey, now we have another thing in common!"

"Yeah. I guess so."

That lingers between us.

"Have you told anyone?" he asks. "Not about the Jake thing, about your liking guys."

I kick my legs. "Nope. Just you."

"Dude, I'm so honored. And, like, welcome to the family, I guess. I wish I had a rainbow flag I could wave."

"Hey, let's not go overboard." I grin.

He puts his hand on my shoulder again.

"Congrats, Matt," he says. "I know how hard it is, and you did really well. I promise, it does get easier."

"Thanks. That'd be nice."

We sit in comfortable silence. Jason really was right before. We can just be together, and it's not awkward.

"Do you think you'll tell your parents anytime soon?" he asks.

"God no. Baby steps, for now."

He laughs. "Well, that suits me just fine. It can be our secret. But seriously, if you ever have anything you want to get off your chest,

I'm around, okay? Anytime. You could even talk about your family, if you want."

I flinch. "I don't think that's a good idea."

"Oh, why?"

My mind is racing now. This all is just starting to feel a little too perfect. Here I have this gorgeous guy, who seems so interested in me as a person when nobody else has been before.

Something must be up.

"I'd just rather not," I say.

"Oh, dude, don't stress. I get it."

Then again, I think I'm just being paranoid. Dad did raise me that way, after all. I'm probably just scared about being vulnerable. Which is scary for me.

But I think it's worth it.

Jason is worth it.

Someday, maybe soon, we'll be good friends.

I won't keep anything from him.

CHAPTER TEN

My LIFE FEELS SPLIT DOWN THE MIDDLE.

On one side, it's horrible. Dad is in a hospital, still in a coma. Apparently his recovery is going slower than they expected, so they decided to keep him under for a few more days.

I'm grateful his room is private. Apparently that's the best money can pay for here. On his bedside table are a few bouquets of flowers. The machines beside him are constantly whirring and beeping.

When he wakes up, I'll find out if the war is going to end or just get worse.

On the flip side, there's my friendship with Jason.

I came out to him.

I still can't believe I did that.

Now he really knows me, in a way I've never let anyone know me.

My phone lights up on the table beside me.

It's from Jason.

Hey. I have the house to myself all Sunday, my parents are going to some wine-tasting thing. Want to come over?

Wait, his place?

I don't want to talk to him about my family. At least not yet, until I'm completely sure he can be trusted. But still, going to his place feels like a big step in that direction, which I'm not sure about. Even though I like the thought of us being our own men, we aren't. As much as I dislike it sometimes, I'm a Miller.

And he is whoever he is. It makes me doubt if I even can be friends with him if he doesn't know who I really am. We're the sons of criminals. We'll grow up to be fully-fledged members of the under-world. If we even survive that long. At any second, either one of us could be shot and killed by a Donovan. I know that for sure now.

I read his text again.

A part of me thinks I should wait a while before responding. I want him to think I'm, like, busy or something, not just waiting around for him to message me. But he's seen that I've read the message. Which means I can't do that anymore. Once a message has been read, only an asshole doesn't reply. I start typing.

Hey! I'd love that!

Sweet. You could come over at around twelve, if that works for you?

Sounds perfect! ☺

* * *

When I reach Jason's house, I sit out front and gape.

It's a stunning mansion, with white walls, enormous windows, and a few sections of slate gray. The front lawn is massive and per-fectly kept. His family is clearly loaded, which for some reason I wasn't expecting.

He might even have more money than me.

Which is cool. Just . . . unexpected.

I go up to the front door and text him: *Hey, I'm here.*

My phone lights up immediately.

I'll come grab you, give me a sec.

I scroll Instagram on my phone until the door opens. He looks so good, I'm at a loss for words. He's in a black tank and gray shorts and is wearing a silver necklace with a circle pendant.

His arms are exposed. I can't help but notice them. His biceps are nicely muscled.

"Hey, you," he says, and then he hugs me.

It lasts for a while. I like it.

"I can give you a tour of the place, if you want?" he asks as he breaks away from me.

"Sure."

Jason goes back in. I linger outside.

"Want me to take off my shoes?" I ask.

"Don't worry about it."

"Cool."

I go inside.

And damn.

Inside is a beautiful foyer, brightly lit with natural light. The floors are polished timber. Art hangs on the off-white walls, and there's a Greek-looking sculpture in the corner. It's the kind that's missing arms for some reason.

He walks to the next room. It's an open area, a combination of a kitchen, living room, and dining room. It's like mine, but bigger and brighter. The kitchen island is made of speckled white stone. At the far end, there's a huge TV in front of two white leather couches. The whole place is immaculate and smells so nice. It's a warm sort of smell, like vanilla.

Outside, there's the biggest infinity pool I've ever seen. A bunch of inflatable pool toys are floating on the surface, including a unicorn with a rainbow mane. They are at odds with the whole sleek, expensive look of the rest of the place, but I like it. It's surrounded by white sandstone, and there are wooden deck chairs under a blue umbrella.

So he's clearly mega rich.

Seriously, who is he?

His family must have a side gig going. I want to ask what it is, but we have the deal, and I know he'll just remind me of that if I ask.

Jason takes me up a flight of stairs. We walk down a hall with white walls. The whole place is so perfect it almost doesn't look lived in. The first room we pass is obviously a girl's bedroom. It's empty. The blankets on the single bed are pale pink, and a plastic *Minecraft* sword is lying on the floor. Two huge white bookshelves are built into the back wall, arched over the bed frame. They're crammed with books, which makes me smile.

So he has a little sister. That's cool.

I bet they're really close. He seems like the sort of guy who'd be close with his siblings. Like, the best big brother ever.

Jason closes her door.

I wonder where she is, if their parents are at a wine tasting.

We walk down the hall and reach another door.

"And this," he says with a proud flourish of his hands, "is my room."

Oh my God. It's the cleanest boy's bedroom I've ever seen. Not that I've been in many. But still. It feels unnaturally perfect. Everything is expertly organized. And it's so masculine. There are framed posters of all-star baseball players on the walls, some of which are signed. He even has a beanbag that looks like a baseball and a whole shelf devoted to trophies. It's seriously crammed full of them.

There's no gaming stuff, like I was expecting. I thought his room would be like mine, but for games instead of movies.

"What do you think?" he asks as he shifts from one foot to the other.

"I like it." I look around. "It feels way more adult than mine. I like it."

Seriously. He has a king bed with dark gray sheets and navy pillows. It's the kind of bed I imagine an investment banker sleeping in.

"Yeah, but your room feels like yours. This could be anyone's. I had no say in it."

Okay. So his parents are controlling, like my dad.

I glance around. He does have a point about it being anyone's room, as besides the baseball stuff, it looks a little generic. Nice, but maybe a little lacking in personality.

Which sucks, because I really like Jason's personality.

"Well," I say. "You have signed posters, not everyone has that."

"I guess."

He crosses his arms. "So, you wanna play *Smash Bros.?*"

"Always."

He chuckles, and kicks the beanbag over so it's at the foot of the bed. Attached to his TV is the newest PlayStation, and the newest Nintendo console. He has a bunch of games, and I recognize most of them. I've played, and loved, most of the ones he has, and the others I've been meaning to play at some point, including *Horizon Zero Dawn*.

He has good taste, is all I'm saying.

"Have you played all of those?" I ask, pointing at them.

"Most, yeah."

"Nice."

As the game boots up, I make my way over to his bookshelf and scan his books. It's smaller than his sister's but still nearly full. He has a complete set of *Harry Potter* hardcovers, and all the A Song of Ice and Fire books. He also has a rainbow section of books, including ones by Adam Silvera, David Levithan, and Benjamin Alire Sáenz.

He's out, so he's allowed to display them like this.

That's pretty cool.

I've read a few gay books, but I hide them. If they're obviously gay in any way, I borrow them from the library and hide them in my closet as I read them. I hide them well, too, just in case Dad snoops.

"Am I passing your test?" he asks.

"Only just."

I look down and see he has all the Grishaverse books. I run my fingers along the spines. This is at least one good thing. It in no way makes up for how tragic the sports stuff is, but you know. It's a start.

Right beside them is a little plastic Arcanine figure. I pick it up. Jason closes the door behind him. It dawns on me that I'm in a gay dude's bedroom, with the door shut. It doesn't mean anything, though. Two gay dudes can be just friends. I'm sure of that.

"I love this," I say, lifting the figure.

Jason's face totally lights up, and he smiles that super-cute smile again. "Me too. She's my favorite."

"Not to brag or anything," I say. "But I can name, like, all of them. Even the new ones."

"Are you trying to impress me?"

"Maybe a little."

"Well, well done. I am impressed. Which is your favorite?"

"Oh, it's tough. I like so many. Like Goodra is cool, and I like Chandelure a lot, as well. If I had to pick, though, I'd pick Umbreon. Specifically shiny Umbreon. I just made it my phone background."

"Show me."

He moves in so close that his arm touches mine. I don't exactly hate how it feels.

I turn my phone and show him. It's a picture I found on Tumblr of shiny Umbreon looking up at the night sky. I like it more than normal Umbreon because his circles are blue instead of yellow, and blue is my favorite color.

"That's awesome," he says. "I really like it."

"Thanks."

"Take a seat anywhere you want, by the way."

I sit down onto his beanbag, breathless, and wait until he hands me my controller. As he does, he touches my fingers again.

I ignore it.

We start playing. I let him pick Pokémon Trainer, and I pick Pikachu Libre.

As we fight, I glance at him. He's totally focused on the game, his stare intense.

It's pretty hot. He lounges on his computer chair, with his legs resting on an ottoman. Weirdly, I find myself staring at the stretch of ankle showing. I know ankles were, like, scandalous in the olden days, which I've always thought was weird. But now I somewhat get it.

"Hey," I say after the match ends. He won, but it was because he used an Assist Trophy, so I'm not sure it counts. "I was wondering if you wanted to talk more about what we talked about on the roof?"

"Family stuff?"

"No, er. I meant . . ."

"Oh," he says. "Gay stuff, you mean?"

"Yeah."

"What about it?"

"Um, anything. I'm so new to it all, so I have questions."

"About sex? Well, when two guys really like each other, they play rock-paper-scissors to decide who's topping, and then—"

"Shut up! I know how sex works. I mean, like, what's being out been like for you?"

"Oh. Um, mostly good."

"Only mostly?"

"Yeah. I think I'm lucky I'm a big dude, so people don't tend to be homophobic to my face. Some girls treat me like I'm a cute play-thing, which I don't like, and sometimes I feel like guys on the team say stuff behind my back. That sucks."

"What do they say?'

"I dunno. I think they might be less cool with it than they let on publicly. Like, even though I'm on the team, I'm not really close with anyone. We're just acquaintances, really. All my actual friends are girls. Which is great, but I think maybe me being gay is part of the reason I haven't clicked with other guys. Does that make any sense?"

"For sure. But wait, do your parents know?"

He nods. "Yeah, everyone does. It's not a big deal, it's, like, the tiniest part of me. I actually hate it when people make it my main thing, you know? I feel like my being gay doesn't actually mean anything. I just like dudes in the way some guys like girls. It's not a big deal. I'd rather people think of me as a gamer or a student coun-cil rep or a baseball player."

I don't really agree that it's not a big deal. But to each their own. He's gay, he should be able to decide what it means to him.

"You're on student council?"

"Yeah."

"Nerd."

His mouth drops open. "If you want to talk smack, you're going to need to be a lot better at this game."

I laugh. "That's fair."

"Anyway, do you have any other gay questions?" he asks. "I'm always happy to give you advice, if you want it. I can be like your gay Jedi master. Teach you the ways of the gay force and all that."

"Like a rainbow Yoda?"

"Exactly. Much to learn about tongue pops, you still have, young master."

I laugh.

"Seriously, though, did anyone have any issues with it?" I ask. "Sorry I have so many questions, I've just never actually talked to a gay guy before. I've always wanted to, I just . . ."

"I bet you have, just not one who's out," he says. "And nobody had any issues. Not to my face, at least. For a while people thought I was going to go pro at baseball, and some people thought being gay would make that harder. Honestly, it just made me work more. You don't get any crap if you're the best, you know? Even if you like guys. But . . . I guess that's not really a problem anymore."

"Wait, why?"

"Well, um. I wasn't good enough."

"But you've won so much! I saw all your trophies."

"Yeah, but that's minor leagues. I tried to play at nationals and got spanked. It was bad, dude. You have no idea."

Tears fill his eyes, but he blinks them away.

"Oh man, I'm sorry. That really sucks."

He runs a hand though his hair. "You know, nobody has ever said that before? Normally people just get mad that I messed up. Like if I'd just been better, I would've won. They didn't know I gave it everything I had, and even though I did, I wasn't good enough. People seem to have a hard time wrapping their head around that. Sometimes, people just aren't good enough. I lost a few friends over it, actually. They only liked me because they thought I was going to be a big deal."

"They sound like assholes."

"I mean, I don't disagree."

He clearly is pretty torn up about it.

"And for the record, I don't care if you win or lose," I say. "If you become a big deal, I'll be happy for you. But you don't need to for me to be friends with you."

"Thanks, Matt. That means a lot; you have no idea."

Now I feel like I know Jason a little better. What I felt on the rooftop feels so distant. I can trust him. He's just a guy, and we have a lot in common. It makes sense that he'd want to be friends with me.

He doesn't have an ulterior motive. That's just my stupid paranoid brain talking.

Still, I can keep my wits about me. We can get close without me talking about my family. I already feel like I know so much about him, and I hope he feels the same way about me.

So what if I don't know his last name?

It's just a word, right?

CHAPTER ELEVEN

WE END UP PLAYING *SMASH BROS.* FOR ABOUT AN HOUR. Again, it takes me a while to get over the nerves, but now I feel like I've settled into a comfortable groove with him. I just feel like we mesh really well. I can be myself around him, and he seems to like it.

I haven't mentioned my sexuality again, but I know that he knows. This is so new. And so freaking awesome.

After Jason wins yet again, he turns to me.

"Hey, do you wanna go for a swim?"

It's pretty hot out. Even in the AC, my shirt is stuck to my back.

Plus, if we go swimming, I'd get to see him shirtless.

There's one small problem, though.

"Yeah, but I didn't bring any trunks," I say. "Sorry, I didn't think."

"Dude, I've already seen you in your underwear, it's fine. Or you could borrow some of mine, if you want?"

"I . . ."

He pushes my leg. "We don't have to if you don't want to. We can keep playing."

"No, I want to. Is it weird to borrow your clothes, though?"

"If it was weird, I wouldn't have offered."

"Okay then, sure. As long as you're cool with it."

"I'm more than cool," he says, then grins, so I know he's about to say something stupid. "I'm ice-cold."

"Ugh."

Still smiling, he stands and walks over to his dresser. He rifles through it, then pulls out a pair of trunks.

"Here," he says, and he quickly tosses them at me. I catch them with one hand. They're bright blue and have neon-pink watermelon slices on them. They're also pretty short, and feel silky and expensive.

I raise an eyebrow.

"I know," he says, smiling. He saunters over to me. Damn, he's so tall. And just . . . so big. His chest is broad, and his biceps look especially great right now. "They were a present. But they don't fit. I've never even worn them."

He's standing really close, and I can smell his cologne now.

"They're not exactly my style," I say.

He smirks. "Don't worry, I won't tell anyone you wore color."

"You better not."

He beams. "You can get changed in the bathroom; it's down the hall."

I leave his room and enter the hall. He closes his door behind me, presumably to get changed into his trunks.

The bathroom is just as well designed as the rest of the house. The decor is stone gray, and I really like it. I step out of my jeans, then switch into the trunks. Once I'm done, I pull my shirt off and check myself out in the cabinet mirror above the sink.

My chest is skinny, pale, and totally smooth. My ribs kind of jut out, and you can see the bones on the top of my shoulders and my collarbone. Also, my attempts to get a good tan haven't really worked, but at least my farmer's tan is mostly gone.

Still, the paleness kind of works with the trunks, because they're so bright. I flex and can see a faint curve of muscle on my arms and can sort of see some definition on my chest.

Actually, maybe I'm not *that* skinny anymore.

The trunks are shorter than my normal ones; they cut off at mid-thigh. I know a lot of guys wear theirs this short, but I never have. It doesn't look bad; it's just . . . different. I'm anxious about a lot of things: how hairy my legs are; a mole I have on my chest, near my heart; and how skinny my thighs are.

I don't think this much of my thighs has seen the light of day in years.

Literally years.

I tug my shirt back on, then walk back to Jason's room. His door is open, and he's standing in front of his mirror, putting sunscreen on his shoulders.

He's wearing tropical-print trunks and his tank. The trunks are pretty baggy, reaching his knees. I know that's a less cool length than mine, but he makes them work.

He looks down at my trunks. "I was right."

"About what?"

"I knew those would really suit you. You can keep 'em, if you want."

"Really?"

"Yeah, man. It's not like I'm going to get smaller. You can have 'em."

I can't help but smile. "Wait, really?"

"Yeah, it's really no problem."

"Well, thanks. It's very nice of you."

He rubs sunscreen onto the back of his neck.

"Sunscreen?" he asks.

I take it from him and rub it into my face and neck.

He glances at me, his gaze soft. A cold jolt pulses through me, like he can tell I'm thinking about how hyped I am to see him shirtless again.

Maybe this was a bad idea.

Jason showing skin off clearly does something for me. I'm not sure that's a normal thought to have about a friend.

But anyway.

"You missed a spot," he says. "On your forehead."

I touch there and feel the excess sunscreen. I rub it in silently as we both go downstairs. Sunlight is streaming in through the glass windows. On the dining table is a silver MacBook, along with a leather journal.

Dad has one just like it.

We reach the pool, and I notice there are two towels hanging on the black metal pool fence.

So this is happening. How should I act? He's about to take his shirt off, and I know how hot he is. I guess I should be totally blasé about it. I have to act like I don't care that he has a great body.

Yeah, that sounds like the best strategy. Feigning total obliviousness.

Abs? What abs?

We enter the pool area, stopping beside the water. Fuck, it's about to happen. I smell chlorine and sunscreen. Around us is white sandstone, along with a few deck chairs. There are a bunch of pool toys floating on the surface, slowly drifting in the breeze. Jason taps on his phone, and "Happier" by Marshmello and Bastille starts playing.

I lean my head back, and look up at the blue sky.

"I love this song," I say, because I do.

"Me too! I . . ."

And then, just like that, mid-conversation, Jason grabs the collar of his tank with two hands, and pulls it off. Like it's no big deal.

"They're so good, right?" he says. "I work out to Marshmello a lot."

"Oh, cool."

I try my hardest not to look. I really do.

But I can see him out of the corner of my vision. He's perfect. Even in broad daylight, with nowhere to hide, he's perfect. It's bananas. I don't even know how a body can look like that IRL. His skin has this glow about it that's weirdly captivating. I think he might shave his chest, as it's completely smooth.

He hangs his tank by the towels, then comes back and stops in front of me, resting his hands on his hips. I keep my stare up, looking at his face. *Not his abs, not his abs.* Nowhere on his body is safe, though, I like it all so much.

I wonder if this is how straight guys and some queer girls feel about boobs. If like, being in the presence of them takes over their mind.

Shirtless guys do that for me.

That's all this is.

It'd happen with any guy. It's not Jason specifically that's making me feel this.

I promise.

He's smiling a small smile, and it's still the cutest thing. Also, when he took his tank off he kinda messed up his hair, so there's now a dusty-brown spike sticking up on the crown of his head.

"Want me to hang up your shirt?" he asks. "Unless you plan on swimming in it?"

"Not yet."

"Dude, what?"

It's Jason, I figure I can be honest.

I swallow. "Sorry, just . . . you look so good, and I feel like I can't compete."

"Oh, hey." He sits down on the edge of the pool, facing me. Seriously, his skin looks so nice. "Want to talk about it?"

I cross my arms. "You're, like, perfect, man. How am I supposed to take off my shirt around you?"

He laughs. "Well, thank you. But, dude, this isn't a contest, and I'm not going to judge you. I promise."

"That sounds like something a judgy person would say."

He rolls his eyes. Okay, I deserved that.

"Besides," he says. "You're forgetting that I've already seen you, remember? I know I like how you look, so you have nothing at all to worry about. Trust me. Your beach body is whatever your body looks like right now."

It's so nice my first thought is that he's lying. I'm gay and have access to the internet. I know gay dudes seem to like only ripped jocks. I wish that wasn't the case, but the evidence is pretty overwhelming.

But why would he lie?

"You do?" I ask.

He nods. "Trust me, you have nothing to worry about."

I grin. "Okay."

He puts his hand out. I take off my shirt and hand it to him. He walks it over to the fence and hangs it up beside his. They're side by side, barely touching. I keep my focus away from him as he walks back to me.

Being shirtless feels good right now. It's warm, and it's nice to feel the breeze on my skin. I made the right call.

"You work out," he says, then he steps down onto the first step. Again, he moves dangerously close. Now that we're both shirtless, I'm even more aware of the space between us. Any contact might lead to a dangerous situation, given that I'm only in trunks.

"You didn't tell me that."

"What?"

He points at my chest. "You're pretty buff, man."

I've never been called that. Ever.

"You're buffer." I straighten up and tense as hard as I can. I stretch and catch him watching. "I just do push-ups in my room sometimes, it's nothing."

We both sit down on the first step, so our legs are in the water but our top halves are totally dry. I enjoy the sunshine.

"So what's your routine?" he asks.

I push away the urge to make a joke. "Push-ups and body-weight stuff in my room, but that's about it."

"Really?"

"Why?"

"Nothing, just stick with it. Maybe you could give me some pointers?"

"Oh, please, you so don't need that. You've got, like, abs and stuff. You're doing fine on your own."

He stretches out, so his arm is behind me. "Thanks, man. They finally came in, I'm so happy."

I stare down at the water. *Crotch, behave.*

But now he's inches away from me, and we're talking about our bodies. It's like he's trying to get a rise out of me.

"How about you?" I ask.

"Well, I play baseball, obviously, which is great cardio, and I work for my uncle as a mover. Since I've been doing that, it just sort of happened. Seriously, moving couches is one hell of a workout."

I look. His abs really are defined. They look shiny right now, because of the sunscreen.

Or maybe he's starting to sweat.

He smiles and leans a little closer. "I'm totally lying. It was a lot of work. I do this YouTube ab workout, like, every day, and I track my calories. Abs are made in the kitchen, don't let anyone tell you otherwise. And they don't show all the time; I worked out this morning because I thought we might hit the pool."

So he prepared. I guess maybe he'd wanted to be impressive. And he is. But still.

"Your shoulders are nice," he says, glancing at me. "So's your back."

"Um, thanks. So are yours."

There's a moment of silence.

"Speaking of," he says. "Can I ask you something deep?"

"Anytime."

"Are you happy with your body?"

"What makes you ask?"

"What you said before. Do you really have body-image issues? We can talk about them, if you want."

"Um. Maybe I do? For the most part I'm happy, I guess."

"Why just for the most part?"

"I know I don't look like the standard definition of hot for a gay guy." I show him my arms. "I'm so twiggy."

"You're not twiggy. Look at me, dude, you're not. You've got nice arms, and I'd kill for your frame. You're kind of a twink, actually."

"Fuck you, I'm not a twink."

I can tell from his grin he's messing with me.

"Yeah you are."

"Shut up, bear."

"Excuse me, do I look big and hairy to you?"

"Maybe."

"You're an asshole!"

"You started it."

"That's fair." His smile fades. "But seriously, Matt, I just want you to know you're hot. You're too good-looking to not know that about yourself. I feel that way about all my friends, actually."

"Thanks. So are you, in case you doubt it. You're, like, so hot. Seriously, man, it's, like, *whoa*, sometimes."

"I'm glad you think so. But hey, if you want to put on some muscle, we could work out together sometime. You could get a guest pass to my gym, and I could show you the basics."

"You'd do that?"

"'Course! It'd be fun for me, too."

"Cool."

He takes a step lower into the water so it reaches his waist. I wince, bracing myself, and follow him. He waves his fingertips through the water.

"I have another deep question," he says.

"Go for it."

"What do you want to do after school?"

"Like, for college, you mean?"

"Yeah."

I decide to be honest. I've never told anyone this, but I guess that's pretty typical when it comes to Jason. He just has this way of making me open up, like it's easy.

"Um. I like the thought of studying film."

He nods. "I should've guessed that."

"I dunno. It's a long shot."

"No way, I can totally see you doing that. You clearly have the passion for it."

I let myself fantasize for a second. "Being a movie critic would be *really* cool. It's so hard, though. It's, like, who do I think I am, you know? It's so competitive, and I'm not naturally talented. I don't have a chance."

"Don't worry about that, everything is hard these days. Promise me right now you'll at least try to make it."

"Ha, sure thing."

"Shake my hand on it." He offers his hand.

"All right, if I ever . . . ," I say.

"Not if, *when*."

"Okay, sure. When I make it, I'll call you and thank you for that time in the pool when you told me to follow my dreams."

"You better."

I like the thought of that.

Us, still friends, even as adults. I'm not even sure how that'd work, though. By that point, we'll both be full-fledged members of our respective families. We'll have all these responsibilities. Dad doesn't have any friends; he doesn't have time for it. His whole life is about his family.

We shake hands. Our grip lingers maybe a second longer than normal, so I pull my hand away.

"How about you?" I ask.

"Um, I dunno." He cracks his knuckles. "Baseball's the only thing I'm really good at, but I'm not good enough to go pro. I thought it was my ticket out, but it's not. I know that now."

He winces, and he starts blinking rapidly.

I hit a nerve. I should be careful of it.

But oh man, do I relate. I often fantasize about being so good at something I'll be able to leave my family behind. I can't ask about it, because of our deal, but still. It's nice to know he's thought about leaving as well.

"Okay, that sucks," I say. "But is that what you want? To go pro?"

"I did want that, before. Now I know I can't. I guess I'd like to be involved with it in some way, because I really do like it."

"You do?"

"Yeah."

"I didn't know that."

He grins. "Well, now you do."

He falls backward, fully into the water. So I guess that conversation is over. I step into the water. It's nice, just warm enough. I swim up to the inflatable unicorn floating by the edge and try to pull myself up onto it. As I do, a Lizzo song starts playing on the speakers.

I lose focus and tumble off the unicorn. The seam scratches me.

Damn it. I grimace, and check my forearm, to see I have a brand-spanking-new paper-thin scratch. It stings like a mother.

"Aw, buddy," says Jason. "You all right?"

"Yeah, it's nothing."

I swim back up to the unicorn and try again. This time I manage to get onto it, with one of my legs on either side.

"Huzzah!" I say, throwing my hands up in victory. I almost lose my balance, so I put my hands back down. Jason laughs.

"Nice work," he says. "That one's tricky."

He wades through the water, making his way up to me. His hair is wet and spiked now.

"Back off," I say, because I can tell from his smile what he's going to do. I splash him, trying to keep him away. He keeps advancing, so I try to swim the unicorn away, which obviously doesn't work.

Jason reaches me and flips the unicorn over. I fall off, sinking under the water. I kick up, break the surface, and get a breath in. I wipe the water from my eyes, slicking my hair to the side, so it's out of my eyes.

Jason is smiling, which makes me smile, too.

"That was rude," I say.

"You loved it."

He puts his hands on my shoulders, and before I can react, he pushes me under. And just holds me there. I struggle, but he's holding me tight.

My lungs start burning.

He lets go, and I push up and take in a huge breath.

I wipe the water from my eyes and see he's standing a few inches away from me as I cough and splutter. Then he smiles, and a weird crash of emotion hits me.

It's like an intense surge of like.

We both laugh.

"You're going to pay for that," I say, swatting at him. He raises his hands to defend himself.

"Hey, stop. Let's make it official. First to get the other in a head-lock wins?"

I take him in. He's buff, sure, but I've wrestled with Luke since I was a kid.

"What are the stakes?" I ask.

"Winner gets to decide what we do next time we hang out. Could be anything."

"Deal."

We get into position, facing each other, our hands up. I look into his eyes and am distracted for a second. They're so pretty, such a delicate shade of light green. God. He's so pretty, with his short, spiky hair and dangerous smile and that freaking body.

How did this even happen?

How did I end up here?

He takes advantage of my distraction, easily swatting my hands aside and then putting his hands on my shoulders.

He pushes me under.

I struggle, but it's useless.

When his grip slackens, I kick off the bottom of the pool and tackle into him hard. He grunts and loses his balance. We tussle. I manage to get my hands on his shoulders, so I jump up and push down as hard as I can.

He barely budges. He just plants his feet, so instead of sinking under, I'm held up.

Defeated, I fall back down.

"Is that all you got?" he asks, then he laughs.

"Not even close. Wait, I have an idea, don't move."

I swim around, so I'm behind him. Slowly, I loop my arms under his, and squeeze his back to my chest. It feels really good, but I'm not going to think about that.

Not even a little.

Nope, not at all.

"What are you doing?" he asks. "This is . . ."

I jump forward and grip him like a koala, my legs looping around him. I didn't want to hear the end of that sentence. I pull back hard, pushing my knees into him, making his spine arch. I twist to the side, trying my hardest to get him under.

He grunts and shrugs me off more roughly than before. I stand up, and he gives me an additional push on the chest for good measure. But he's smiling, so I know it's okay.

I totter back.

"Too rough?" I ask, and I grin at him. "Sorry."

"No, you're good. I just didn't know you had that in you. Nice work." He flicks my chest. "Try again. Really try and beat me, don't hold back even a little. I can take it."

"All right."

I grab his wrists and try as hard as I can to bring them together. He grits his teeth and pulls his hands apart, easily overpowering me. His biceps bulge as he does it.

"Come on, try," he says.

"I am!"

"Barely. Give me everything you've got, I want to see it."

"I am! Are you holding back?"

"Yeah," he says. "I'm sorry, but I am."

We pause.

"Then stop," I say.

He blinks. "You sure?"

"Yeah."

His eyebrows narrow, and he moves forward. I spin and try to swim away, but he grabs my wrist, stopping me in my tracks. He puts his hands on my biceps and roughly spins me around, then pulls me to him, so my back is pressing into his chest.

He picks me up, lifting me out of the water.

"Fu . . . ," I start, but then he drops me and clamps his hand down hard over my mouth.

I try my hardest to get out from his grip, but he's holding me too tight.

He grips me and falls backward, pulling us both under the water. My lungs start to burn as my hands scramble against him, but I'm stuck to him. He pushes me up out of the water, and I take in a huge breath. He takes that second to interlock his fingers on the back of my head . . .

Trapping me in a headlock.

My arms are stuck.

He won.

I had no idea he had that in him.

No freaking clue.

"See?" he says. He moves me around like I'm a rag doll. "Easy."

I'm no quitter, though, so even though I know it's dire, I keep fighting, kicking and bucking and trying with everything I have to throw him off. But no matter how much I spin and fight he holds on.

He's too strong.

I give up.

I stand motionless, my heart jackhammering.

I don't even know how I wound up here.

And I can't lie, I love this contact. It's . . . like, so good.

His chest is flush against my back, and I can feel his rapid heartbeat, and his heavy breathing right by my ear. It tickles my scalp.

At least I gave him a run for his money. We both catch our breath. His chest is heaving, becoming fully pressed against my back every few seconds.

Every second of contact makes me feel fully charged.

"Dude?" he whispers in my ear.

"Yeah?"

"Do you give up? You need to tap out."

I tap on his arm, and he lets me go.

* * *

I get home and park in my spot. I turn off the engine and just sit there for a second, thinking. My mind is stuck on that moment in the pool. It felt like I almost lost control for a second there.

And I really, really liked it.

I open the door and step outside, then jog up to the front door. Inside, Luke is playing *Fortnite*. Eddie is curled up beside him.

"Hey," he says. "Where were you?"

"A friend's place."

His eyebrows narrow. "What friend?"

"Lev, we're hanging out again."

We hung out a few years ago, but then it petered out when he found a new group of guys to be friends with. He got popular and ditched me, basically. It hurt like hell, and I've never told anyone about it. But I've decided he's the perfect cover, because Luke and Dad know him, and I figure it's not too weird that we've started hanging out again. I feel like in an alternate universe, one where I'm not a total loser, it could happen.

"That's awesome!" he says. "Lev's a cool dude. What'd you do?"

Talked about being gay.

Shirtless wrestled.

You know. Straight stuff.

"Not much. Swam for a bit."

"Nice. Wanna join? I just finished my game."

"Yeah, later," I say. "I'm going to take a nap; I'm wiped."

"'Kay."

I lock the door to my room. I should probably turn on my speaker and play some music, make some white noise, but I don't think I have time. What I'm feeling is way too intense for that sort of pre-planning. I know it might be a bad idea, seeing as I want to stay just friends with Jason, but I'm not in control right now.

I don't have a choice.

I pull off my shirt and then fall backward onto my bed.

In my mind, I go back to the pool. It's not too difficult, I still smell like chlorine and sunscreen.

I slide my hand down my pants and start.

Jason. Jason Jason Jason.

My hair is still wet, I can feel it against my pillow. I recall his body, and his smile, and exactly how it felt when he touched me. Or complimented me. Or sat right beside me. The way he laughs.

Tension builds in my shoulders, and with my free hand I yank my jeans down a couple of inches. The feelings swell, becoming unbearable, and I try as hard as I can to stop but it's too late and I . . .

It's done.

I lie back down, breathing heavy. My shoulders relax, and I smack my lips. My jeans are digging into my thighs.

Shit.

I just jerked off to Jason. And I wasn't even quiet about it. Anyone walking by might've heard.

What if they heard?

I could never look at them again. My life would be over.

I'm so majorly boned.

CHAPTER TWELVE

IT'S OFFICIAL: I LIKE JASON AS MORE THAN A FRIEND.

I tried my best to stop it, and yet, it happened. I know it in my gut; I know it with everything I have. Ever since we hung out in the pool, it's like a switch has been flipped. I always noticed he was cute, because he is, and I've always liked his company.

But now it's more than that.

It's a fully-fledged crush.

Every time I think about him, it's like my stomach fills with pissed-off butterflies. And I'm smiling so much lately that my cheeks are always kind of sore. Even though all this stuff is going on, thinking about him makes me smile *that* hard.

Fucking damn it.

* * *

I'm sitting with Dad, in his hospital room. He's finally being brought out of his coma tonight. I can't believe my timing with this crush, but it's not the sort of thing I can control.

If I could get rid of these feelings, I would. In a heartbeat.

It'd be a lot easier to stay friends with Jason. And what I need right now, more than anything, is a friend.

I can't let myself be distracted by this. Luke is here, and so is Vince, who is beside his wife, Sara, and Tony. We've been here for hours today, listening mostly to machines beeping and Dad's breathing. It's weirdly hypnotizing. All I know is the chemicals keeping Dad under are no longer being pumped into him, so he could wake up at any time, and my whole family wants to be nearby the second that happens.

It could be because they care about him.

Or they just want to make sure they stay in his good graces.

It's hard to tell.

Anyway, being here has given me a *lot* of time to think about Jason. Still I haven't figured out what to do about my feelings for him. Unrequited romantic feelings can often signal the end of a friendship. If I tell him, and he doesn't feel the same way, then things will get awkward and we'll probably stop hanging out.

My instincts tell me I need to keep these feelings a secret, until I know how to wrangle them into something controllable. Because they're totally off the chain, rampaging through my life, making me think about him nonstop.

But then there's the off chance that he's feeling something close to what I'm feeling.

In that case . . .

Across the room, Luke rushes forward to stand by Dad's bedside. He's noticed something—I guess because he's here, not miles away, like me.

Dad groggily opens his eyes.

The first thing he sees is Luke. That feels fitting. I stand up and move over to the bed. Dad sees me and smiles weakly.

"My boys," he says, reaching out and putting his hand on Luke's, then on mine.

"We're here, Dad," says Luke. "We barely left."

"I know," he says. "I could tell."

Does this mean he'll be okay? His skin looks slightly translucent, his hair is limp, and his cheeks are covered in salt-and-pepper stubble. But he's awake, that's the main thing. He doesn't look so bad for a guy who took two bullets to the gut, is all I'm saying.

"Welcome back, Mr. Miller," says the nurse.

Dad opens his mouth, but then his face twists in pain.

"Don't try to talk," she says. "Just relax."

Dad nods and then closes his eyes again.

"What's happening?' asks Luke. "Is he okay?"

"He's fine," she says as she writes something on her clipboard. "He'll drift in and out for the next few days. It might be best for you all to give him some privacy; he will need to rest for the next few hours."

I glance at Luke. He's calling the shots on this.

"Okay, you heard her," he says. "Clear out."

I turn and go to leave.

"Not you, Matt," he says.

"Oh, right."

To my surprise, my family complies. As a group, they all file out of the room, I'm guessing to head to the waiting room. The nurse follows them out. She closes the door behind her, so it's just the three of us.

"One of us should stay," he says. "You want to take first watch?"

"Sure."

"Cool. We'll swap in five hours, that sound good to you?"

"Yep."

Luke starts packing up his backpack. "Are you sure you have every-thing you need for the ball?"

To be honest, I'm surprised it's going ahead, given Dad's current situation. But it is.

"Yeah, my suit came the other day. Dad already got me everything I need."

My heart aches.

"Have you tried it on?" asks Luke.

"A bunch."

"And?"

I smile. "You might not be the only good-looking one."

"Bring it, little brother."

"Oh, I will."

He smiles, but then his attention falls to Dad, and his face drops. "We got really lucky, you know that, right?"

"What do you mean?"

He rests his hands on the metal end of the bed. "If they got their way, he'd be dead."

Technically that's true. Still, Dad isn't totally innocent. The Donovans may have started this, but he's the one who decided to turn it into an all-out war. I can't believe I'm thinking this, but I do think it's partially Dad's fault that he got shot. If he'd tried to figure out some sort of peace with them, then we wouldn't be here.

I guess I'm still hoping this is the wake-up call I've wanted him to have for ages.

"I want to kill them," says Luke. "Every single one."

"I know."

"I haven't told you, but I have all my leads tracking down the shooter."

"I thought it was Maria Donovan?"

"No, she wouldn't get her hands dirty like that. She might've called the hit, but she's not the one who did it."

That makes sense. Dad only really gets involved these days when he's showing me or Luke how things are done. Most of the time, he orders someone to do his dirty work.

"I want her dead, too," says Luke. "But nobody knows where she is right now. We're trying, but we can't find her. So my focus is on finding the man who pulled the trigger. He's just as responsible, and sure to be less protected. We can get to him."

"And what will we do if we find him?"

Luke finally looks at me.

"We'll kill him. Together."

*　*　*

My brother is being serious.

Luke wants *us* to kill someone.

That was a few days ago now, and I still can't stop thinking about it. I've spent most of that time either with Dad or at school. Dad's technically awake, but he's still pretty out of it, and we can't really talk. Every time we try, it just uses up all his energy and he drifts off again.

Right now I'm in Luke's car, being driven to somewhere I know isn't going to be good. Apparently Vince has managed to capture a Donovan and has been torturing him all day. According to Vince, he has let slip some information he thinks everyone needs to hear.

"What do you think it is?" I ask.

We're on the bridge to the port now. It's a massive structure, lit by blue lights underneath. We're over water, which makes the air pretty cold, but Luke insists on keeping the top down.

"What do you mean?" he asks.

"What do you think the Donovan gave up?"

"No idea. But it must be big for Vince to want all of us to hear it."

I want to ask him what will happen to the Donovan they caught. I'd like to think that they'll let them go, but deep down I know that's not how it works.

Someone is going to die tonight.

And I can't stop it.

Against my leg, my phone vibrates. I switched it to vibrate mode because I've been waiting for a text from Jason.

I messaged him earlier, before I knew about what was going down tonight. We were talking about our favorite TV shows, and I asked him who his favorite *Friends* character is. He said he had to go to baseball practice and he'd respond when he's done. I pull my phone out, unlock it, and read his message.

Hey. Why would you ask that? I can't choose, man. I guess Chandler is my favorite? I dunno. The only one I don't love is Ross, but I think he's necessary to the plot, even if he can be annoying. Who's your favorite?

So he's a Chandler guy?

I like that. It makes me think he likes jokes and dry humor. It just fits.

Phoebe. How was practice? And who's your favorite Brooklyn Nine-Nine *character?*

That's so cute that you like Phoebe! Practice was good, I'm wiped now, though. And so disgustingly sweaty. My favorite is Holt, obviously. You?

Same, he's the best! And how sweaty are you talking?

He sends me a selfie. His shirt has a deep V of sweat on it. Still, he manages to look really cute in the photo.

Shit, you must've worked hard.

Haha yeah. My coach doesn't mess around; he makes us do endless shuttle runs. Anyway, how about The Good Place?

That sounds like torture. And hmm. I'm going to go with Janet for this one.

It is. Believe me. I'm sure you could handle it, though. And nice! Love her. Mine's Chidi.

I really like all his choices. My phone lights up again.

What are you up to right now, btw?

"Who are you texting?" asks Luke.

I freeze.

"No one," I say.

Luke grins. "Oh my God, it's a girl, isn't it?"

"What? No, I swear!"

"Dude, you so are. How'd you meet her?"

"I already told you, it's not a girl. It's nobody."

"So you're texting no one?"

"It's a school thing. History group project. Kill me now."

"You dirty liar! Come on, tell me everything."

I chew my lip.

"I'm not lying, it's for a group project."

"Dude, nobody has ever looked like you just did while working on a group project. Not even once."

I mean, that is true. Group projects are worse than sleep paralysis. But still.

"Okay fine," I say. "You were right. I just don't want to talk about it, it's too early."

Luke grins. "Don't stress, I get it."

"You do?"

"Yeah, for sure. I'm just happy for you! For a minute there I thought you were going to end up as one of those virgins on the internet who always complain that nobody will screw them."

"You thought I was an *incel*?"

"Not yet. But I thought you might become one."

He's got to be messing with me. I give him the finger. It just makes him chuckle.

I know I should let it drop and stop messaging Jason now that Luke's aware I'm messaging someone I care about. If he found out I am acting this way because I am messaging a guy, then, well, I guess he could think I'm gay.

I don't want that.

But I want to know what Jason messaged me so badly.

I lift my phone.

Hey. So. Changing topic: There's this school dance coming up. It's probably the worst theme ever, and it's bound to be hilariously bad. Do you want to come? It's cool if you can't, but you know, if you wanted to, you could join. ☺

I stare at the message.

I think he just invited me to a dance.

This is, like . . . so amazing.

The typing bubble appears.

As friends, obviously!

Oof.

Yeah, obviously.

Sounds fun! What day is it? If I'm free, I'm there.

It's next Friday. Hope you can make it! It'd be more fun with you there.

Nobody has ever said that to me. *More fun with you there.* What a dream. I'm going. I already know it. I'm not going to miss this dance for anything. Not to be dramatic, but even if I had a chance to meet David Lynch or Spielberg, I'd pick this dance.

Cool! I'm free, so I'm in.☺

Amazing!!! I'm so glad. I'll get you a ticket. You have a suit already, right?

I sure do.

Sweet. I can't wait to see it.

I type out: *I can't wait to see you in yours.*

I delete it. It's too flirty, and I think it might give away how my feelings for him have escalated.

I look up and see that we've pulled into our destination.

It's a shipping area, filled with hundreds, if not thousands, of shipping containers. I can see the dark ocean, along with a few massive hauler boats, moored to the dock with thick chains. The space is lit by floodlights scattered around the place, but there aren't enough to properly light a space as big as this, so it has a gloomy darkness clinging to it.

I'm not going to lie, it's pretty freaky.

I wish I could stay in the car.

I know I have zero chance of that, though. I sat out last time we did something like this without getting punished. I'm not going to get lucky like that again.

Jason distracted me for a while, but this is my real life. What's happening right now, this is what my life is really about.

It's a miserable, bleak nightmare.

Even though I resist it, everyone in my family wants me to be a part of this world.

And that's kind of the appeal of being a criminal.

Whatever you want, you get.

Luke parks in a lot that's surrounded by a wire fence.

Other cars are in the lot. I recognize some of them. They're all from other family members. A few of them are out of their cars, leaning against a shipping container, smoking. *Gross.* They're all wearing dark clothes: suits for the men, long coats and dresses for the women. It's like a uniform.

I'm in my ill-fitting suit again, because I'm saving my new one. Dad probably would've called me on it, but so far, Luke hasn't. I tug at the sleeve.

"Ready?" asks Luke.

"Yep."

We get out of the car.

I spot Tony, Vince, and his wife, my aunt Sara. Her dress is white, with black flowers on it. She seems nice, but she's married to Vince, so I've always felt like it needs to be an act. No one truly nice could be married to someone who tortures people. It must require a hell of a lot of cognitive dissonance to even spend any time with him.

None of the older members of my family are here, like Grandma, although it seems like all of Dad's generation is here. The only one missing is Dad.

It's only Millers, though.

No allied families.

Meaning no Jason.

Phew.

I don't want to see him here.

He's my escape from this world. Seeing him here would make that way harder. I really like that, because of our deal, our friendship is totally separate from all this stuff.

So what if it's a little like playing make-believe?

There are definitely worse things that people can do.

I have a feeling I'm going to see that firsthand tonight.

We approach our family. Vince is staring at me like I'm one of his victims. There's this evil gleam in his eyes and in the curve of his smirk. He has his switchblade out, and keeps opening and closing it. The silver blade shines. I notice there are bloodstains on the white cuff of his shirt.

"You're late," says Vince. "I'm guessing it's Matt's fault?"

Luke scowls. "Don't be a dick, traffic was bad on Palm Ave."

"If you say so."

Vince clicks his switchblade closed. His daughters are behind him. Even though they're two years apart, they both have the same haircut, with bangs that cover their foreheads. It makes them look like twins.

I hate those two.

They seem way too into the fact that their dad tortures people.

It freaks me out.

As a family, we start walking through the shipping-container area. The containers are stacked on top of one another, so they dwarf us. It's sort of like a giant metal maze. Vince leads the pack, and he seems to know exactly where he's going. He keeps up a quick pace, still clicking his switchblade, and the crowd follows behind him.

"Hey, Matty," says Becca, the older of the two. She's fourteen.

"Hey."

"You going to keep it together tonight, or nah?"

One time, years ago, Dad yelled at me at a dinner, after I spilled my soda on the dining table. I cried. They haven't let me forget it.

"Back off," growls Luke.

The two giggle, but then fall back out of step with us.

"Thanks," I say.

"I shouldn't need to stand up for you," he says. "You don't have to take any crap from anyone."

"That would imply they bothered me. Which they didn't."

"Well, good."

They kind of did, though.

I want to go back to the car so bad.

I know whatever is waiting for me is something I'm going to hate. But I can't turn around. Everyone already thinks I'm soft, but I haven't actually given them a concrete reason to think that yet. If I went back, it'd be more than a suspicion.

It'd be a fact that'll follow me for the rest of my life.

I'll be known forever as a coward.

Plus, even if I did have the guts to ask, they wouldn't let me go.

I know that I'm a weak spot in my family. Dad is so strong, so the one way that they can all get to him is through me. Because I represent him, much to his chagrin. It's even more important now that he's been taken out of the game, at least for a while. Luke and I need to represent him while he heals.

Still.

If I don't leave, I'm going to see a guy Vince has tortured.

And I'll never be able to get it out of my head. I slow my pace. I need to do it. I need to leave.

I turn, and see that Luke is watching me. He shakes his head slowly.

Okay.

He knows.

That's okay.

I should trust him. Luke has always been so good at this stuff. If he tells me I should stay here, then I should listen to him. Seeing whatever is waiting for me might be bad, but leaving would be worse.

Probably way worse.

Vince stops walking and pockets his switchblade. His two daughters are grinning.

The shipping container in front of us is totally unremarkable. It looks pretty much the same as the thousands of others. Rusted metal, chipped paint, and a damaged door that's seen better days.

Vince lifts up a roller door, and I have to hold back a gasp.

Sitting in the middle of the container is a boy.

Or, a man. Just, a young one.

He's chained to a chair, and there's a bloody burlap sack over his head.

He's shirtless, and his body has been cut a few times. Rivers of dried blood run down from the cuts. He's still breathing, as his chest is rising and falling, but he's alarmingly pale and limp. His hands are tied behind his back and are lying slack.

How long has he been here, like this?

"I'm back," says Vince. "Did you miss me?"

The boy starts thrashing. He strains against his bonds, but his hands are tied tightly, and his ankles are bound to the legs of the chair, so he's helpless. He struggles, but he's not going anywhere.

"Now," says Vince to us, ignoring the thrashing guy. "What I'm about to show you will shock you. But I think it's in all your best interests to see this yourselves. I want you all to hear the story from the horse's mouth."

The boy starts shouting, but I think he has a gag in, as he lets out only a muffled sound.

I would honestly give anything to be somewhere else right now.

"Are you ready?" asks Vince.

Everyone nods.

Vince goes up to the boy and pulls off the burlap sack. His face is covered in dried blood, and the skin around one of his eyes is purple and puffy. I was right before: He has a balled-up cloth in his mouth.

Holy shit.

I recognize him.

He's one of Barbie Barker's rent boys.

The one who checked me out on the night I met Jason.

What's he doing here?

"Does anyone recognize this man?" asks Vince. He puts his hands on the guy's shoulders and scans the crowd.

I look into the guy's eyes. They're wide with fear.

They find mine. A flicker of recognition.

Crap.

Nobody says anything. And I'm not about to admit that I recognize him. He's a gay sex worker. If I point out that I know him, people will ask questions. More than that, though, I don't want anything to do with what's going on right now.

I can't help him.

I want to, but there's nothing I can do.

I look into his eyes, and at least try to convey that I'm sorry. I hope he gets it. I hope he knows that if I had my way, this wouldn't be happening to him. That I hate this stupid war and the way that my family can do this to someone.

"He used to work for Barbie," says Vince, then he slaps his face.

The boy growls, baring his teeth.

"But that wasn't why he came to the bar."

"Who is he?" asks Luke.

"I could tell you myself, but I think it'd be best to hear this from him."

Vince reaches down and pulls out the gag.

"HELP!" shouts the guy, but his voice is hoarse. I don't think it carries very far. "SOMEONE HELP ME!"

Silence answers him.

He changes tack.

He looks at me.

"Please, help me. One of you must have a heart. Please. I have a family. My mom, I'm her favorite. You can't let him kill me, I—"

"Quiet," says Vince. He presses the flat of his blade against the guy's throat. He falls silent.

"Good lad. Now, talk. Tell them what you told me."

He shakes his head.

"Come on now, play fair," says Vince. "We had a deal, remember? I won't hurt you . . . as long as you behave."

Vince moves the blade in front of the boy's face.

He stares Vince down. "You can't make me."

"You want to bet on that? I already know, this is just for dramatic effect. Either way, they'll know everything. You may as well save yourself the pain."

The guy looks down, clearly thinking hard.

"Too slow." Vince grins, and moves closer, raising the blade.

"Stop!" he shouts. "I'll talk, just don't!"

"Then do it, and make it good. You've wasted enough of our time."

The boy looks up. He can't be that old, midtwenties at the latest. Vince pats him on the head, smoothing down his matted hair. He looks totally beaten down, defeated. There's this desperate look in his eyes.

I think he knows he's going to die.

He must.

I guess he's just trying to decide how much pain he's going to go through before that happens.

This is monstrous.

I can't be here. I can't be a part of this.

I turn to leave, but Luke's hand ends up on my shoulder. He presses down. The message is clear: *Stay*.

"Tell them what you told me," says Vince.

"I don't work for Barbie," he says. "Not really, anyway."

"Go on."

"We were losing the war, so my aunt came up with a plan. The idea was to infiltrate your ranks, posing as your friends, your allies. We wanted to learn how you work so we could take you down from the inside. We called it the Friend Scheme."

He takes his gaze to the floor.

"This is their plan," says Vince. "This is why they've gone quiet. They're trying to break into our ranks and destroy us from the inside. They could be anyone, someone at your school, someone who cuts your hair, a passerby who has taken an interest in you. Anyone. They might seem like your friend, but all they want is to know our secrets. You must be extremely wary of anyone new who has come into your life. Anyone who has taken a new shine to you cannot be trusted."

Holy shit. There's no way this is the same, though. No. Way.

"Now," says Vince. "Why don't you tell these fine folks who you really are?"

He swallows hard, then he looks up.

"I'm Ryan Donovan."

Vince walks around him and presses his blade to Ryan's throat.

I know what's about to happen.

I look away just in time.

PART TWO

CHAPTER THIRTEEN

I'M FREAKING OUT.

It's the night of the dance that Jason invited me to.

And I think I'm going to go. Even knowing what I do now.

He's part of the Friend Scheme. A Donovan. I know it in my gut.
That means someone in his family shot my dad. *He* might've even
done it, for all I know.

He lied.

My first true friend, and it was all a lie.

All he wanted was for us to become friends, to learn about my
family, through me. It fits too perfectly to not be the case. It explains
why he wouldn't give up his last name, why he asked me about my
family, and why he even talked to me in the first place.

I know what I should do. I should tell Dad everything, starting
with meeting Jason in the bathroom of the bar.

The diner. Swimming. Hanging out at my place.

I need to tell him about all of it.

I haven't done anything wrong yet. Sure, I snuck him into our
house, but I was with him the entire time. He couldn't have done
anything. Right now, I haven't messed up at all. I fell for the scheme,
sure, but they can't get too mad at me for that. What I do now is
what really matters.

I have to tell Dad. But I know what'll happen if I do. It'll lead
Vince or someone else to Jason.

They'll kill him.

I also haven't been able to stop thinking about Ryan Donovan. I've been adjacent to death for so long, but that was the first time I saw it up close. I mean, I looked away, and didn't look at him again. As a crowd we quickly moved away, because death is necessary but ugly. Vince and Tony, along with Luke, dealt with the body (burned, to leave no evidence). I waited in Luke's car.

Someone I sort of know was murdered.

And I'm supposed to not care about it.

I do, though. So much. I haven't been able to sleep properly, and the sleep I do get is plagued with nightmares. I've pretty much given up on eating; it makes me feel too queasy. I think I've lost a few pounds, as I can now see my ribs jutting out even when I'm in a T-shirt.

I think that's part of the reason I'm not mad at Jason. He might've tried to trick me, but a man died.

It puts things into perspective.

I mean, I am angry at him, but that's not my main emotion. Mostly, I'm confused. Because our connection feels so real to me. Even knowing about this scheme, it still feels real.

Maybe he's just a really good actor.

So I want to talk to him. Because I need to be sure about this. Like, maybe this is all in my head. Maybe he *isn't* a Donovan, and it's just a coincidence it lines up so well. Because if he's been trying to betray me this whole time, he's a freaking incredible actor.

I'm going to hear him out. But there can't be any more secrets between us.

He needs to tell me who he is.

* * *

I have a plan. I'm going to talk to Jason tonight at the dance and find out who he is. If he's a Donovan, I'm going to drop him from my life. I'll ghost him if I need to.

Simple as that.

If he's not, which I so hope is the case . . . then I'm going to continue on as normal.

Although even that might be risky. What if he lies? If he truly is part of the scheme, then letting him know I'm onto him could be dangerous.

Plus, I can't let Dad or Luke know where I'm going. They know about the Friend Scheme, and are sure to be wary about anyone new in my life. Even if he says he isn't a Donovan, he's still someone new in my life, so Dad won't let me hang out with him.

I need to lie to everyone, basically. And I've never been good at that.

I'm wearing my white shirt and my black pants, along with dress shoes. In my backpack, I have my new suit and my tie. I hope they don't get too wrinkled. I'll put them on once I get to his school. It's my new one, the one I'm supposed to wear to the Miller ball. It actually fits me, and it makes a big difference. In this suit, I think I look a lot older. I finally look how I'm supposed to.

My thoughts drift back to Jason. If he truly is some undercover sleuth trying to figure out my family secrets, he must know that inviting me to his school is an epically bad idea. I could literally go up to any student in his grade and point at him and be like: *See that guy over there? What's his last name?* If I asked enough people I'm sure *someone* would know.

Then again, there's a chance that's not the case. At school, people know me as Matt Thomas. It's the name Luke and Dad go by when in the real world, too. *Thomas*. Our civilian name.

It's boring and blends into a crowd.

If Matt Miller enrolled into a school, I'm sure the cops would keep an eye on him.

Matt Thomas, though?

Nobody cares about him. Same with Luke Thomas, and the rest of my family. Other Millers have different fake names, so if they get caught, they won't be able to find everyone. This level of stealth allows us to have another life. Some of my relatives have day jobs, and their coworkers would have no idea they're near a member of a powerful crime family.

Anyway.

If Jason is a Donovan, then maybe their family uses the same trick.

But still. If he cares about keeping his last name a secret from me, then inviting me to the dance is a bad idea.

Maybe I just want to keep my *one* friend, even though I know it was probably all a lie.

It's just . . . what would I be doing tonight if it weren't for him? I'd probably just be staying at home, watching stuff on the internet. Which I like, obviously . . . but it's nice to do stuff other than that and school. He feels like my ticket to all these new things. And I don't think I'm confident enough to be one of those people who goes out and does things alone.

Like to the movies.

It'd be *so* nice to have a friend to see movies with. Going alone makes me way too anxious, like everyone is judging me. I'm also so scared of running into someone from school, and them knowing I saw a movie by myself.

I can't give up on this. I just can't.

I check myself out in the mirror. I need a haircut, as my hair is looking especially shaggy right now. I smooth down a wonky bit in the back and then preen the front bit that hangs over my forehead. I'm not going to say bangs, because that's so not what they are.

"You're dressed up," says Luke, making me jump. He leans against my doorframe and smiles at me.

My door is half open, my thoughts have been spiraling so much I didn't notice.

"Looks good, but what are you up to?"

"Nothing."

"So you're just going to hang out in your room in a suit?"

"Ugh, fine. You know that girl I was texting?"

"Yeah?"

"She asked me to a dance."

"Holy shit!" he says. "That's a definite sign."

"Of what?"

"That she's serious. For some reason she wants your sorry ass as a boyfriend. Are you okay with that, because that's where whatever this is is heading? Trust me."

I shake my head. "It's a friend thing."

This is new territory. Us, talking about my dating life. Not that I had one before. Plus, I'm not sure how much he actually knows about this stuff and how much is just bravado. For all of Luke's ways, he's never actually had a girlfriend. He's had plenty, and I mean *plenty*, of hookups, sure, but nothing serious or long-term. I've always assumed he doesn't want that.

But right now I sort of get a vibe from him. He seems jealous.

"A dance is a big deal, man," he says. "Even you must know that."

"I already said, it's just a friend thing. She doesn't . . . you know. See me like that. At least I don't think she does."

"Oh," he says. "But it's more for you?"

I mean. I guess it is. I can't stop thinking about him. I'm not sure that's a normal friend thing.

"I dunno."

"Dude, you're a Miller. Don't forget that. Just be brave and go for it."

"That's hard, though. I think I might be in the friend zone."

"I know. But trust me, it's worth it. You've got this. Anyone would be lucky to get with you. We own this city, remember? Just don't say that to her. Trust me, it doesn't go down well. And don't say *friend zone* again, it's a pathetic, sexist concept."

I mean, agreed.

"Thanks. My pep is officially rallied."

"Good. But, hey, you're being careful, right?"

"What do you mean?"

"Given the scheme and everything, are you sure it's a good idea to be hanging out with her?"

"Are you going to stop hanging out with girls?"

He chuckles. "Touché. Last thing, then I'll go. This is going to be awkward, but, do you need condoms?"

He's right.

It's so incredibly awkward.

"I have some. Thanks, though."

That's actually true. When I turned fourteen Dad bought me a box and explained that he doesn't expect me to need them, but he said I should use them if the situation ever came up. He's given me a new box every year, usually around my birthday.

It feels like the one good bit of parenting he's ever done.

"Cool," he says. "Take some just in case, and if you get lucky, you better use one. I don't care what she says, or how much you don't want to, you use one, okay? Trust me, you don't want the stress."

"Noted."

"And, hey," he says, smiling proudly, "have a good time tonight, you little Romeo."

I start blushing, and not just because of the condom talk.

Me, a Romeo? Since when?

But maybe it's not so out of place.

Plus, I love this. Normally I'm the one who stays at home when Luke goes out.

"Thanks."

For the first time, I wish I wasn't lying to him.

* * *

Jason was right when he said the theme of the dance was bad.

It's *so* bad: It's disco themed.

Seriously.

I hate it so much.

I step inside and look around the room. Oh boy.

There are psychedelic floral prints everywhere, and the teachers are all dressed up accordingly. They're so into it I'm slightly embarrassed for them. Even the young ones, who should know better, are dressed up. There's a young male teacher standing by an archway of golden balloons. I'm guessing he's a PE teacher, as he's ripped. He's wearing a massive curly wig, pink circular sunglasses, and a fake mustache.

He's still hot, but *yeesh*.

A huge banner hangs on the far wall. It reads: PANIC!

I guess it's a reference to the band. I don't need the sign to tell me what to do, because the gym is packed.

There are so. Many. People.

And Jason is here.

I walk farther into the gym, looking for him. There's very little room to move, and the air is already warm in a gross, stuffy way. A guy bumps into me, then glares at me, like it was my fault.

"Sorry," I say, then I shut my mouth.

I have no idea why I apologized, it was totally his fault.

Stupid brain.

My plan of attack is to talk to Jason and get out of here ASAP. I mean, it's a dance, filled with strangers. So, a horror show. It doesn't matter that the golden lights around the place look kind of magical, or that everyone is dressed up so nice, and I think I look the best I ever have.

I don't belong here.

There's a stall by the door, where you can buy cans of soda or bags of chips for a dollar. I walk over to the stall and buy a Coke, mostly so I'll look busy, or like I'm someone who knows what to do at these things.

I crack it open and walk over to a section of wooden bleachers and sit down on the first row. Up the back, a straight couple is making out. Already?

I sip my Coke.

Seriously, what am I doing?

I shouldn't be here. I should've told Dad my suspicions about Jason and let him deal with it. If Jason finds out that I know about his plan, then he might react badly. If he really is a Donovan, and he finds out that I know, then I might be in the line of fire.

But I can't see that happening.

I really can't.

If he meant to hurt me, I'd know. Right?

I rub my temples. I really don't know what I'm doing. I look up. And holy shit.

He's here. And he looks *amazing*.

He's wearing a maroon suit over a white shirt and a skinny black tie. It's perfectly tailored to his body, and the color does wonders for his hair, making it look a richer brown than usual. I'm *so* here for it. He'd look right at home on a red carpet.

I walk over to him. My shoes click on the floor. Everything else blurs away.

I might be walking up to Jason Donovan.

My enemy.

Here it goes, I guess.

"Matt!" he says, smiling a gorgeous smile. His eyes light up. "Thanks so much for coming. Dude, you should never take this off, you look so handsome."

If this is an act, he could win an Oscar.

The song changes to that one that repeats *I feel love I feel love I feel love* over and over again.

Good one, universe.

"No worries, I wasn't doing anything," I say. "And thanks, um. You look handsome, too, like, I'm sure you know that, but yeah. You do. Sorry. I'm bad at giving compliments. And receiving them, actually."

He laughs. "You're doing better than you think."

Now's the time. I need to ask him to talk.

"Er," I say. "Listen, I . . ."

"What?"

I can't get the words out. I don't even know why.

"You okay, man?" he asks.

"Yeah, I'm fine."

He eyes me warily. "Well, good. So, do you want to meet my friends?"

Not really. I want to talk to him about the scheme. No matter how hard I try, though, I can't get myself to.

"Sure."

He leads me through the party to a spot on the dance floor. There are two girls there.

One has short black hair, shorter than mine. She's wearing a floral dress that's freaking cute. The other is in this über-cool green dress that contrasts really well with her warm-brown skin.

They both look amazing.

So this is them, Jason's friends.

And they're clearly cool.

Whelp.

Jason puts his hand on my back.

"Hey, friends," says Jason. "This is Matt. Matt, meet Naomi and Bri."

Naomi, the girl in the floral dress, blinks. "Is this *the* Matt?"

"The one and only," says Jason, and he squeezes my shoulder. "He's a cutie, isn't he?"

Wait, he talked about me?

And he just called me cute? On top of calling me handsome earlier?

I don't know how to process all this.

"I hope I don't disappoint," I say.

"Omigosh," says Naomi. "Sweetie, no, you don't at all. Look at you in your suit! You look like James Bond!"

"Shucks. You look great, too. That dress is . . . something else."

She frowns, then her eyebrows narrow.

"Shit, dude," says Bri, laughing. "You've got a way with words."

Oh fuck.

"I mean that in a good way! Um. I just mean, like, it's next-level good. Sorry. You seem really cool, so I'm nervous. Ugh. Ignore me."

"Hey, it's cool." She beams. "I'm used to making boys nervous. Okay, Jase, I like him already. You can keep this one."

He squeezes my shoulder again. "I was planning on it."

And my heart threatens to burst out of my chest like a Xenomorph. How can a feeling like this not be real? How can he fake it?

I really wish I knew what was going on.

More than that, though. Despite everything, I want him to do what he said.

I want him to keep me.

"You boys wanna dance?" asks Bri.

Um.

No.

My answer to that question is always no.

No no no, a million times no.

But Jason nods, and suddenly I'm walking with him to the dance floor. Soon, we're surrounded by other students, who are all dancing. Lights flash around us, and it's just dark enough for me to feel a little anonymous.

I must say, it's a little infectious.

Seriously, he called me cute?

Plus, Jason introduced me to his friends like I was his date.

Like he was showing me off.

Even though I know about the scheme, I want to feel nothing but this.

Seeing as I have no other option, I awkwardly join their dance. I have one dance move, which is just jumping along to the beat. Sometimes I move my arms a little. But that makes me feel weird. I'm just not good at this. A few more songs play, mainly vintage disco, and I grow increasingly uncomfortable with each one.

It's more than the fact that I'm uncoordinated, though. And even a night like this can't make me like disco music.

I'm dancing with Jason and his friends.

I'm acting like nothing's changed.

But it has.

I can't do this.

The Friend Scheme is the real reason I'm here. I'm not here to have a good time. I'm here to find out if Jason is really a Donovan.

I can't forget that.

I need some space to think this through. Because once I bring it up, there's no taking it back, and I will probably lose all of this. Even if it's fake, a part of me thinks it's better than nothing. I want to ignore it and string him along for a little while, just to keep it going.

That's a terrible idea, though. I know it.

"Hey," I say, sliding in close to him so he can hear me. "I need some air. I'll be back in a minute."

Jason frowns. "Are you okay?"

"Yeah, it's nothing," I say as I start walking away. "It's just hot in here; I'm feeling a little light-headed."

"Do you want me to come with?"

"No, you're good. I'll be back in a sec."

With that, I turn and walk away. It's not exactly a graceful exit.

I leave the gym and walk down a hall and then take a left.

I should've expected this to happen. That I'd see Jason and he'd make me feel like I'm someone else. Someone cool and handsome. And I'd do anything to keep that feeling . . . even pretend I don't know who he really is, and why we're friends.

Because I know what's going to happen.

As soon as Jason knows that I know his secret, we'll never talk again.

I shouldn't have given myself the chance to feel how great it could've been if we were different people. If I was Matt Thomas, and he was whoever he's pretending to be.

Because I don't even need to ask him to know, I know it in my gut.

He's a Donovan.

We're enemies.

I need to be strong and end it.

I find an empty stairwell and sit down, leaning my back against the wall. I'm sweaty all over and feel like throwing up.

All because of my stupid family.

I breathe in deeply a few times.

I clench my palm, then release it. Clench, release.

This is so unfair. Why can't I just have it easy, like everyone else does?

My family is to blame. I make one friend, my first ever, and it's considered a bad thing. This is so messed up.

I push the thoughts away and focus on breathing deeply.

When I no longer feel like the walls are closing in as much, I open Instagram on my phone, hoping it'll be a good distraction. I mostly follow celebrities and movie fan accounts, as well as Luke. He's posted a bathroom selfie, and in it he's lifting his black tank up, to show off his abs.

I roll my eyes and go past it.

I scroll for a while, liking everything. It feels so hollow, though.

It's not as fun as hanging out with Jason is. With him . . . I was even starting to like dancing. If that doesn't show how much I like being friends with him, I don't know what will.

I look up. The hallway in front of me is totally empty.

I think for five minutes.

Then ten.

Then fifteen.

And I decide.

I'm just going to leave.

I'm not going to tell him that I know. That's too risky.

I'm also not going to tell Dad about him.

I'm going to drop him from my life. I know he's a Donovan. At this point, I'd be shocked if he wasn't. So this is it for us. This party was a last hurrah. And I've been too freaked out the whole time to actually enjoy it.

I round a corner and walk straight into someone's chest.

I spring back. They do as well.

"Hey!" says Jason. "Watch where you're going, shark bait."

It's like an instant sugar rush. He came looking for me. Nobody has ever done that before.

It's not real, I think.

I can't forget that.

"Sorry," I say. "What are you doing here?"

The only sound is the faint throbbing of disco music in the distance.

He puts his hands in his pockets and looks up at me.

Are those puppy dog eyes? Aimed at me?

"I was looking for you," he says. "Are you okay? You kind of ran away."

"Yeah, I was just taking a breather. Loud spaces and people and stuff, they mess with me sometimes. I know it's weird. I was on my way back."

"It's not weird, I totally get it. It's an anxiety thing, right?"

I nod.

"Want to talk about it?" he asks. "We could find somewhere quiet, if you want."

"Um, not right now. Actually, I was thinking I might go home."

His eyebrows raise. "What?"

"Yeah, I just feel like . . . I dunno. I think I should go."

I turn and jog toward the exit. I don't like being dramatic, but I

153

know myself. If I keep talking to him, I'll bail on my plan. Because as much as I hate to admit it, I can't stop noticing how good he looks in his suit.

He follows after me. "Hey, Matt, wait. What's going on?"

I ignore him. It's so hard, but I do it.

"Do you want me to beg, to get you to say here?" he says. "Is that it? Please, talk to me, tell me what's going on. You're freaking me out."

It sounds so real.

I stop and turn around.

I look into his eyes. He's looking at me in such a kind, hurt way, like me doing this is really bothering him. I'm freaking him out.

"What do you want me to do?" he asks.

"I really don't know," I say. "I'm sorry I'm such a mess. I'm really trying to be cool, I just . . ."

"Just what?"

"I can't tell you."

I turn and walk away again, but he grabs my arm and pulls me back.

"Seriously, let me go!" I say. "It's better for everyone."

"First, tell me what's going on," he says. "I'm getting all these mixed signals from you right now."

"You're one to talk about mixed signals."

"What does *that* mean?"

"I . . ."

I need to say it. I need to tell him that I know.

He watches me, and then his eyes widen a fraction. In that second, I think it hits him. He knows I've figured it out. He knows I'm onto him.

"Let's find somewhere quiet," he says.

"Okay."

We walk down the hall. He tries the door of a classroom, but it's locked. The next room is a men's bathroom.

He pushes on the door. And success.

We go inside. The tiles are this really hideous shade of green. All the stalls are open, so we have privacy. I feel breathless, like my lungs are working overtime but can't take in enough air.

He steps closer.

If it weren't for the scheme, I'd think he's about to kiss me.

"Talk to me, Matt."

"I know, all right?" I say. "I know about everything. So you can cut the act and stop looking at me like that. You don't need to anymore."

"Know what?"

His voice is low. Dangerous.

"I know who you are," I say. "I know you're a Donovan. I know you know who I am, and I know you've been pretending to be my friend this whole time, just so I'll tell you secrets about my family."

He's watching me, his features still.

"It's true," he finally says. "Nice work."

I'm stumped for a second. He shrugs.

"I knew you'd figure it out; you're too smart not to."

"What?"

Of all the ways I pictured this confrontation going down, I never imagined this.

"I dunno, man. I mean, I figured me being so cagey about my last name would make it obvious. But, like, for the record, I gave up on that plan, like, the moment I had dinner with you. I might've met you because of the scheme, but after that, our friendship has been real."

"What?"

"Yeah, I liked you too much to hurt you like that. I decided pretty early on I wasn't going to go through with it."

"What about your family?" I ask. "Even if you gave up on it, they'd still want you to do it, right?"

"They think you're just really good at dodging the questions I've asked you. But that's not what I'm doing, I promise. Anything I've asked you is because I genuinely want to get to know you."

"What are you saying?" I ask.

"I'm saying that this is more than that. It's real."

"I . . ."

"Come on," he says. "Don't you feel it? We have a connection. I've never felt anything like it before. I think you might be my best friend."

"I feel it, too. Of course I do. But . . . it's like, if you are who I think you are, we shouldn't be friends, right?"

"Says who?"

"Our families. They hate each other."

"They do," he says.

"And you only wanted to get to know me just so you could tell them my secrets."

He rubs the nape of his neck.

"Yeah, but only for, like, five minutes. I'm telling you, I bailed on that plan as soon as I realized how much I could like you. Which happened pretty fast. I just . . . I feel so connected to you. It's true what I said before. It's unlike anything I've ever felt. We just click, you know?"

That's sweet and all, but . . .

"How can I trust you?" I ask.

"You probably shouldn't. But I'd like it if you did."

"You're . . . you're a lot, you know that?"

He grins. "That's the nicest thing I've heard all week."

Infuriatingly, him saying that drives me pretty wild.

"So you aren't going to drop me?" he asks. "Seriously, you have nothing to worry about."

"I don't know. I honestly didn't know what to expect after telling you, but it wasn't this."

"I'm glad. I'm not a threat to you, I promise. You are to me, though. Have you told anyone else about me?"

"Not a soul. I wouldn't do that."

"Good."

I take him in. This is so not how I thought this would go down. But I buy what he's telling me. I just don't feel like he'd be able to fake it that well.

"So you're really not just pretending to be my friend?" I ask.

"I swear, I'm not. I truly do like you. Do you still like me?"

Isn't that a loaded question?

"I do," I say. "And I don't. I can't believe you lied to me, but there's this other part of me that . . ."

"What? What does this other part of you want?"

"It wants to kiss you so bad."

He grins. "Then do it."

"Really?"

"Yeah. Show me what you got, Miller."

Hearing him say my name sends me into overdrive.

"Sure thing," I say, and then I step closer to him.

A smart person wouldn't do this.

But that smart person wouldn't get kissed.

So how smart are they, really?

I put my hand on the side of his face and hold it there. He closes his eyes at my touch. Then I lean forward and gently press my lips to his. He smiles, tilts his head, then kisses me. My eyes widen, and I'm so shocked I only just remember to kiss back at the last second. Because I'm so aware that my first kiss is happening RIGHT NOW.

And the kiss itself? It's incredible. It's just, different from what I thought it'd be. I can feel it everywhere. His lips are so soft, backed with just enough pressure to be worth my time.

He pulls back. "Want to keep going?"

"Yeah."

The word is filled with want. I didn't even know I could sound like that.

He pushes me up against the wall and starts kissing harder.

I lose myself.

He starts unbuttoning my shirt. I do the same, with his. It's sort of a scramble. We're still in suits and ties, but I want to see as much of his body as I can. I run my hand down his bare chest, to his stomach. I've wanted to do this the whole time, and now I finally can.

But then I come back to myself.

What am I doing?

"Hey," I say, pushing him back.

His shirt is hanging open now, and every part of me wants to touch him even more. His chest is all smooth, hard planes.

"What?"

"I want to hear it from you. Who are you?"

"I'm Jason. You know me."

"But what's your last name?"

He lowers his hands and looks into my eyes. My whole body sort of aches.

"Donovan," he says. "Should I stop?" he asks.

I shake my head.

He grabs me by the shirt, pulls me to him, and kisses me again.

CHAPTER FOURTEEN

I kissed Jason Donovan.

I'd be totally lying if I said I regret it. Because I straight-up don't.

But it might be the stupidest thing I've ever done. It might be the stupidest thing anyone has *ever* done.

He's a Donovan, and I'm a Miller. We're supposed to be mortal enemies. We shouldn't even be friends. And yet, I keep finding myself thinking about how it felt.

Right now I'm standing at the back of a ballroom. It's the Miller ball, so everyone around me is either from our family or one who's allied with us. It's a totally over-the-top spectacle, complete with waiters in white suits serving canapés. There's also this massive swan ice sculpture in the middle of the room. A band in tuxedos is at the back, playing slow classical music.

The room we're in is pretty over-the-top, too. The walls are this pretty soft gold color, and a crystal chandelier hangs from the ceiling. I wonder how much it's worth . . . and how many people were hurt so our family can afford all of this.

It's cool, but also probably not worth however much it cost.

But who cares.

I kissed a Donovan.

I keep finding myself thinking about how it felt to be kissed by him. Because seriously: He's a *great* kisser. He acted like he knew exactly what he was doing, like he's done it a bunch before. I get all the hype about kissing now, because there's nothing else like it.

I don't know how people do anything other than make out all the time.

It was my first kiss, but I know it was a good one. That was the kind of kiss people write songs about. It was magical and perfect, and I want almost desperately to do it again.

I can't, though.

I went to the dance to find out if my theory is correct. To find out his last name.

Now that I know what it is, I can't ever see him again.

Donovans and Millers have hated each other for so long. Dad has told me countless stories about what treacherous, bad people they are. Like Victoria Donovan, who is the reason hard drugs are so popular with many of the youth of the city. She targeted them and made the drugs readily available. And then there's Christopher Donovan, who killed five people over a debt of five grand. He wiped out a whole family because the poor sucker who loaned from him couldn't pay him back on time.

This is the story I've heard, over and over.

Donovans are the most selfish, awful people around. They can never be trusted. The only good thing to do with them is kill them.

Because as much as we're criminals, at least Millers care about the people of the city. We make ourselves rich at the same time, too, sure. But we're forgiving. And considerate. And we never put ourselves above the general well-being of the city. People like illegal stuff, and we're happy to provide it.

Jason acts a lot more like us than any Donovan I've ever heard of.

I turn my attention back to the ball. I'm surprised it's even going on, given everyone knows about the Donovans' scheme now.

As long as I never talk to him about my family, he can't ruin my life. Right?

No.

This is just me being stupid.

I had no idea how much I needed a friend until I got a taste of it. To use an expression Dad uses a lot: I've swirled the drink. It can't hurt me.

But if I were to see him again . . .

Ugh.

I wish he was an ordinary guy.

"Hello, earth to Matthew."

I look up and see Cassidy standing in front of me. She's holding two glasses of champagne. She looks amazing right now, in a sleek, floor-length black dress.

She offers me a glass.

"Thanks," I say, and I take a sip, even though I don't like drinking. It's very crisp, and probably superexpensive. It's still gross, though. Who even likes this stuff? "Sorry, I was just thinking."

"No worries," she says, leaning against the golden wall beside me. "Having a good night?"

"Clearly."

She laughs and tilts her glass toward me. We cheers.

"Yeah, me too," she says. "My mom drags me to these things; it's the worst."

"Oh, really? What would you rather be doing?"

She pauses, thinking. "Pretty much anything. You?"

"Yeah, same."

"Figures. Why do they make us come here?"

I shrug. "I guess they want us to learn how stuff works. We're going to be like them, one day."

"That's a scary thought."

"Right?"

Silence falls over us. We both watch the crowd. It is actually a pretty great spectacle. Everyone has gone all out with their outfits. Luke has taken off his suit jacket, revealing a white shirt and suspenders. He's slow dancing with a girl in a red gown. Her hair is straightened, and she reminds me a little of a femme fatale. He dips her, then snaps her back up, so she's fully pressed against him. She looks breathless. So does he.

I wonder if Cassidy is jealous.

She smiles. "I know you're gay, by the way. I know it's not just a rumor."

"What?"

"Oh, dude, listen. I'm not going to out you. It's our secret. But if you want people to stop talking, you should probably be a *little* more careful. I watched you for like five minutes and saw you check out every single even remotely hunky waiter in here. Plus, I'm in *this* dress, and you don't seem nervous to talk to me. Nor have you looked at my décolletage."

I've known Cassidy for ages. I've never considered her a threat. But I don't trust how I feel anymore.

"I . . . um. Listen, I . . ."

"Hey, it's okay. I just want you to know I think it's a good thing, if it is true. Maybe it's even a great thing. This world has enough straight dudes. I think it's time for the queers and the women to take over."

I nod. I feel like I can't say anything.

She smiles. "You know, we should hang out more."

It kind of surprises me. I've always thought Cassidy was way too cool for me.

"Really?" I say.

"Yeah!"

What if she's trying out the Friend Scheme?

But there's no way. She's Cassidy Strickland; I've known her since she was five.

There's no way this is a Friend Scheme thing.

She wants to be friends with me. For real.

"Why?" I ask.

"I feel like you're really coming into your own lately. I don't know. It's like everyone has been underestimating you. Luke gets so much attention, and don't get me wrong, he's a cool guy, and he's *so* fun to hook up with. But you have potential I don't think many people see."

I laugh. "Potential for what?"

"To change things! God, haven't you noticed how old-fashioned this world is? Look at the women in this crowd and tell me you think they look happy. They don't. And it's because men like your dad and Luke have been running things for so long. But if a Miller like you was in charge . . . things could get better."

"Believe me, I'm not going to be in charge."

"If you want to be, you could. You're a Miller, man! This whole world is yours. And if you want a friend who can show you how to take it, I'm here. Together, we could change this world, so people like us are happy here. We could use your last name to do some good. For us, anyway."

It's kind of a cool idea.

"I'll think about it," I say.

"You better," she says.

She lifts off the wall and walks away.

Huh.

Maybe being friends with Cassidy would be a good thing.

Maybe if I wasn't so lonely, I'd be better able to resist the temptation that is Jason.

Because I know that's what I should do. I should resist.

The band stops playing, and Vince steps up onto the stage to go up to the microphone. He's wearing a white suit jacket, so he sort of matches the waiters. I'm sure he hates that.

"Can I have your attention, please?" he says.

I push up off the wall and walk closer.

The curtains at the back of the room open, and oh my God.

It's Dad.

He's in a wheelchair and is being pushed by Sara. He's dressed in a white shirt and slacks. I'm not sure he should be here. He looks really pale, and he still hasn't shaved. He looks so ill. Sara pushes the wheelchair up to the microphone, and Vince hands Dad the mic.

"I wanted to thank you all for coming," says Dad. "I hope you're all enjoying yourselves."

Vince claps Dad on the shoulder. "We have, buddy."

"I'm glad, but there's another reason I'm here," says Dad. "I want you all to know that I have heard about the Friend Scheme, and I am currently working my hardest to root out any Donovan moles within our ranks."

Holy. Shit.

Dad's talking about the scheme. It makes my skin crawl.

"To that end, I have a request. If any of you have any suspicions about someone in your life, I ask that you come to me immediately and tell me all that you know. I understand that it will be hard, if you have formed a bond with them. But it's what must be done. We must find every single Donovan in our ranks and put them down."

I finish my champagne in one go.

"If you refrain, you are my enemy," says Dad. "And you all know what I do to our enemies. Never forget that. Now, enjoy the rest of the party."

Dad is wheeled backstage.

What he just said rings in my ears. *If you refrain, you are my enemy.*

I'm not willing to give Jason up.

It means I'm my dad's enemy.

CHAPTER FIFTEEN

JASON HASN'T TEXTED ME BACK.

I'm in my room, lying on my bed, staring at my phone.

My room is a wreck. There are discarded clothes all over the floor, the carpet needs a vacuum, and dirty dishes are scattered around my desk and on my bookshelf. I've been distracted, and Dad isn't around to tell me to clean up, so I haven't.

It's been over a week since the dance. Eleven days, to be exact.

We kissed, and he hasn't messaged me.

I can't stop thinking about it. Maybe it's because the Friend Scheme is out in the open between us.

Or maybe it's because I'm a bad kisser.

Oh my God, what if I'm a bad kisser?

This is making me feel things I've never felt before. I want him to message me *so* badly. It's, like, the only thing I actually want to do. Then again, a part of me thinks our ending things is the best idea. It's definitely safer than continuing to hang out, given who he is and how we met.

Maybe he's realized that, too.

But on the other hand . . . He said he gave up on the scheme, and I believe him.

I'm in my room, lying on my bed, staring at my phone. I consider inviting him to the fair. I can picture it now. Me and him, strolling down the main strip. We'd play some games, eat some junk food, and have a good time.

We could talk, too.

The fair would be a perfect place to hang out, as it's a public place. We'd both be safe. Plus, I think if we hung out at either my house or his, I have a feeling we'd make out the whole time. He must want to do it again as much as I do. Which would be so hot. But bad.

There's a knock on my door.

"It's open," I say.

Luke appears. He's clearly on his way to the gym. His earbuds are hanging down the front of his tank.

"Hey," he says. "Are you free?"

I sit up in bed. "Do I look busy?"

"Don't be a shithead."

"Sorry."

He enters my room and sits down on my bed. Eddie follows behind him and curls up at his feet. Today must be one of his needy days. Luke scratches the top of his head, and Eddie's tail thumps against my bed.

"Just give it to me straight: Are you and Cass a thing now?" he asks.

Oh boy. I don't know how Luke can be so aware sometimes and so damn wrong at other times.

"What do you mean?" I ask.

"I saw you two talking at the ball, and I know you've been hanging out. So I was just wondering if she's the girl you've been dating."

"Oh, no. This is new. Cass and I are just friends."

"Really?"

"Yeah."

"I wouldn't be so sure, man," he says. "Cassidy doesn't give

anyone the time of day she doesn't think is worth it. If you're hanging out with her, she must see *something* in you."

"She doesn't like me like that," I say. "There's no way."

"Dude, why are you always so down on yourself?"

I shrug. "I'm not. She likes me as a friend. That's not a bad thing."

I actually do think that. I think there's way more power in friendship than people realize. Anyone who's never had friends would
agree with that.

He eyes me warily.

"Seriously!" I say. "Besides, you two have history. It'd be weird if
we hooked up, right?"

"She's not used goods, Matt."

"That's not what I mean! I mean emotionally." I stare up at the
ceiling for a second. I need to be careful. His thinking I'm secretly
dating Cass is definitely better than his figuring out the truth.

"Nothing's going on, I promise," I say. "And I'll tell you if that
changes. I mean, it's not going to. But if it does, you'll be the first
to know."

He nods. "I better be."

He leaves my room, closing my door behind me. He knows me
well enough to know that I always want it closed.

I open my messages to Jason. I know I shouldn't, but . . .

I finally cave.

*Hey. It's cool if you don't want to, but I was just wondering if you'd
like to go to a fair? It's in the city. Again, it's totally cool if you can't. I
know I shouldn't, but I miss you.*

And send.

The typing bubble appears right away.

Oh my God.

Please don't disappear, please don't disappear. A message comes in.

You don't think it's a bad idea?

No, I do. But I still want to risk it.

Me too. Let's just do it. Whenever and wherever you want me, I'm there.

* * *

Jason is waiting for me by the entrance of the fair. He's standing in the middle of the walkway, with his hands in his pockets. He's wearing a gray T-shirt, and chinos.

Very cute.

"Hey," he says, as we hug. There are so many people around, but it feels a little like we're the only two here. That this whole place belongs to us. He rocks me back and forth, and it makes me feel unstoppable.

I look out at the ocean. The sun is starting to set.

"Wanna check this place out?" he asks.

I nod, so we start walking down the main strip. We walk fairly close to each other, so it's obvious we're together. Not together-together. Just a pair. I don't know how I'll be able to explain this if anyone I know sees us.

Now that I'm here, this feels like a catastrophic mistake.

But whatever.

"What do you want to do?" he asks. "Maybe we could go on the Ferris wheel? Or are you hungry?"

I shake my head. "Honestly, I just want to talk. Can we find somewhere quiet?"

That might be hard. It's crowded. Maybe I didn't think this through enough.

We walk to the very end of the fairground and don't spot anywhere quiet. Seriously. It's like almost everyone in the city has shown up tonight.

"Sorry," I say. "I should've thought more. I think we should talk. If we're going to stay friends, we should make some ground rules."

"Agreed."

We eventually find an empty bench at the far left of the fairground. It gives us a great view of the whole place. I love how the lights look against the pink sky. I can hear the rattling of the Wild Mouse coaster and carousel music, and can smell cotton candy. I look across, out at the ocean, in the distance. The sun is just setting.

It's magic hour.

Perfect.

"So," I say.

Where should I start? The scheme, the friendship, or the kiss? There's so much I want to ask about, but I can't decide what to begin with.

Jason's posture is slightly hunched, and he's staring at his hands. They're shaking. I want to take them in mine and tell him that it's okay, that I get it. I'm scared, too. And I'm still not sure if we're friends, or something else, now that we've kissed.

This feels a little ridiculous.

I'm sitting next to a Donovan, and we're both tongue-tied. Not because he's my enemy, but because I care so much about saying the right thing.

"I should apologize," he says. "For, you know, keeping the secret."

I nod. "You don't have to; I get it. I'm guessing your family made you do it?"

"Yeah, they did. How'd you know?"

"My dad makes me do stuff I don't want to all the time. So I totally get it. If my dad asked me to, I would've done the exact same thing to you."

"Still," he says. "I'm sorry. They did make me, but I don't want to deflect the blame. I'm still the one mostly responsible." He taps his fingers on his legs. "I got into a huge fight with my parents over it, actually, I didn't want to do it that much."

"Really?"

"Yeah. It was terrifying. I never stand up to them."

"I get that. I've been a little salty with Dad sometimes, but I've never gotten into a big fight with him."

That's way too scary a prospect.

But oh shit, I just talked to Jason about Dad. I can't do that again.

"Fuck," I say.

"What?"

"I just said something about my dad. I really shouldn't do that."

"I mean, you can, if you want to. The jig is up, I'm not trying to learn your secrets anymore, I promise."

But what if he is?

"I don't think I should," I say. "I do trust you. Mostly. But, dude, what if this is all part of your plot?"

"That'd make me the worst mole ever."

"Or the best."

"If you don't trust me, I can go. It was your decision to hang out again, remember?"

"Oh, right."

We both fall silent. I watch the Ferris wheel spin.

"I'm really glad you did message me, though," he says. "I really liked getting to know you."

"What'd you like about it?" I ask.

He leans back. He puts his arm out, so it's on the backrest behind me. "Just being able to be, you know? I'm Jason *Donovan*. A lot of the time that's all anyone cares about. As if that tells them everything that's important about me. It was nice to meet someone and just be myself, because I couldn't tell you who I am. Does that make any sense?"

"It makes *so* much sense. It was nice to be someone other than *Little Matty*."

"Wait, Little Matty?"

"Yeah, that's what my family calls me. I used to be short."

"Assholes."

It makes me laugh, out of sheer shock. "It's just a nickname."

"Yeah, but a mean one. Not that there's anything wrong with being short, but you know, it sounds like they weren't saying it affectionately."

"They weren't."

"Then I stand by what I said. Assholes. All of them."

I get another rush of affection for him. I'm weirdly relieved I can still feel that, even though I know who he is now.

"So you don't like being a Donovan?" I ask.

My voice shakes as I ask that.

He stares forward, thinking. He blinks a few times, like he's never thought about it, and now it's hitting him hard.

"I guess I don't. That sucks, right?"

"Yep, it really does."

"Can I ask if you like being a Miller? Or is that too close to asking about your family?"

I mean. It *is* asking about my family. And I'm scared about this being a slippery slope. I know Jason is that, for me. The fact that I'm even here shows how much he can sway me. Not that long ago, I was thinking that I shouldn't hang out with him.

And here I am. Figuring out a way to keep this going.

I trust him. Which might be stupid.

But I do.

"I'm the black sheep of my family," I say. "So yeah. I'm like you. I don't like it. From now on, though, I don't want to talk about my family with you, okay? That's my rule. If you ever ask me about them, I'll ghost you."

"Deal."

He stares at me for a moment, with a small smile on his face.

"What?" I say.

"I thought I was the only one," he says. "It's nice to know I'm not. And I just really like you, man. Thank you so much for not dropping me over this."

Tears fill my eyes. I don't even know why.

It's such a perfect thing to hear.

"Are you okay?" he asks.

I blink rapidly. "Yeah, sorry. I've just never really had a good friend before. I'm not sure if you know that. So this is all messy now, but it's more than I've ever had. I'm just really glad we're staying friends. Sorry, I'm being a sap."

He laughs. "You're being yourself, which is the best thing you can be around me. So please, be a sap, if you want. Doesn't bother me."

"Careful," I say. "I can get really mushy sometimes, so you might start to regret that."

"Trust me, I won't," he says. "Whatever you want to be, I'm here for it. Well, I think the rules have been firmly established. Now, want to go on some rides?"

"Yeah, I do."

* * *

Jason and I ended up spending about an hour and a half at the fair.

We went on a few rides, played a few games, and won some candy, and then we had corn dogs and two giant cups of Coke.

It's been so much fucking fun.

And now I have a fairly epic sugar high.

At least I think that's what it is.

We weren't done with the night yet, so now we're going for a walk. After escaping the crowds of the fair, we headed for the palm-tree-lined tourist strip, right by the beach where we first went swimming all those weeks ago. In the distance, there's a neon-drenched strip of bars, and past that, towering skyscrapers.

"Do you like Florida?" he asks.

"What makes you ask?"

He shrugs. "Just curious."

I look around. I mean, it is pretty picturesque at the moment. This spot is, at least.

"I mean, yeah? I hate the humidity, but it's still home, you know?"

"Yeah, for sure."

"Do you?" I ask.

"I'm the same. It's home."

He stops walking in front of a pathway to the beach.

"Want to go for a swim?" he asks.

"I'm guessing you do?"

He nods.

"You know it's weird that you do this, right?" I say.

"What's weird?"

"That you like swimming at night."

"Oh. Yeah, I'm aware."

"Then why do you do it?"

He looks out at the water, and shrugs. He sort of shrinks into himself a little. I'm surprised. I didn't think he was self-conscious about anything.

"I don't know. I know why I want to go swimming with you, though."

"Why?"

"I want to see you take your shirt off."

I suppress a laugh.

"I'm serious!" he says. "What's funny about that?"

"Nothing, I guess. I just . . ."

"What?"

"This is just so new for me. You're a guy, and I'm scared of saying the wrong thing, I guess. I know I'm not good at flirting. You're so good at it, and I'm . . ."

"Just be yourself, man. You have no idea of how much of a killer you could be if you were confident. You've got everything you need."

Huh. I do like the thought of that.

"Okay, let me give this a shot," I say.

"Flirt away," he says.

"Um. I really like your . . . ears."

I wanted to say something other than his chest or his biceps. I felt like that'd be too obvious.

He laughs. "What?"

"Yeah. I like your ears. They're cute. Is that weird?"

"No, it's not. You're so cute, you don't even know."

We reach the sand and take off our shoes. We leave them to the side, and then start walking toward the water.

"For real, though, it's weird, right?" he says. "That I do this? I've actually never told anyone that I do this before. I was too worried about what they'd think, I guess."

"No," I say. "I like it."

We reach a spot on the edge. He stretches.

"You coming in?" he asks as he takes off his shirt.

"For sure."

"Sweet."

We both undress to our underwear, and then walk up to the water. I step in, and it's pretty freaking cold. Jason goes behind me, and puts his hands on my arms, holding me in place.

"What are you doing?" I ask.

He whispers in my ear: "I heard something on the news the other day."

"Oh really? What?"

He rubs my arms, and he's standing so close that I can feel his body warmth on my back.

"That shark attacks are on the rise."

He leans in close, and lightly presses his teeth on the back of my neck. Laughing, I push him away.

"Seriously, though, are you actually scared of sharks?" he asks. "I just like messing with you. You get so flustered; it's so fun."

I look out at the water. "It's fine."

"Okay, then. In that case, I dare you to go in by yourself."

"What?"

"Come on, be brave. Go in without me. You can do it."

I guess he has a point.

Going in alone is way scarier.

"Fine," I say, and I trudge forward.

I want to impress him. And myself, I guess.

I go even deeper than we did last time, and start treading water. Okay, this is *way* freakier by myself.

"How long are you going to make me wait?" I call.

He smiles and wades in. He dives into the water and swims up to me.

He reaches me and slicks his hair back. His chest is heaving, and his mouth is hanging open. He's breathless. I stand up.

"You're so brave," he says.

"It takes more than this to scare me."

"I bet," he says, stepping closer. "Now, dare me to do something. Anything you want, I'll do it."

I look into his eyes.

And I have the guts to say it.

"I want you to kiss me so much I can't breathe anymore."

He pulls me to him.

CHAPTER SIXTEEN

FOR THE FIRST TIME EVER, I HAVE TWO SEPARATE INVITES for tomorrow.

The first is from Cassidy.

She's asked me to go to a dumpling place in the city she's heard is amazing. After that, Jason has asked me to come and watch him play baseball. I feel so lucky. I'm not sure what I did to have my life change like this . . . but I'm really enjoying it.

All that stuff is happening tomorrow, though.

First, tonight, Dad is coming home.

It means today is weirdly hectic.

I'm really relieved he's coming home. He's still going to need a lot of rest, but his being home will make me feel less anxious. To me, it means he's out of the woods. Luke's gone to get him now, and they'll be home at any minute. I thought they'd be here by the time I got back from school, but they're still out. I hope it doesn't mean anything has gone wrong.

Ever since I got home I've been cooking pasta for Dad, because it's his favorite. There's a bubbling pot of sauce on the stove, and the whole house smells like tomatoes and garlic. I've been cleaning as I go, because I know any mess will undo any goodwill I've built by cooking for him. I know I don't make it as well as he or Luke do, but I thought I'd at least try. It still tastes good if you drown it in Parmesan anyway.

I stir the pot, then lean against the island and check my phone.

Cassidy's invite was for six thirty, and Jason's game starts at seven. Which means I don't have time to go to both, unless I alter one of the plans slightly. That makes me kind of nervous, though. Like I'll piss them off by asking.

It's not a big deal to move the plans by an hour. If I keep telling myself that, hopefully I'll start believing it.

I open up my messages to Cassidy. My hand is shaking.

Hey, I was just wondering if we could we make it five thirty? I have plans at seven.

I'm so nervous. I know I shouldn't be stressed over something so minor, but I can't help it.

On top of that, I'm anxious to tell her that I have plans. Because then she's sure to ask me what those plans are, which means I'm going to have to lie to her. I can't tell her I'm hanging out with Jason Donovan, after all.

I hate lying.

It's messy, and I'm really not good at it. Keeping a secret by omission, like what I normally do with my sexuality, and how I feel about my family, is one thing. Actual lying is way harder. I feel like I need to create this whole elaborate story in my head about what I'm doing if she asks. I need to make sure it all fits, like it's something I could actually be doing.

My phone buzzes.

Look at you, busy man! 5:30 actually works great for me. See you then, rock star ☺

I find myself smiling.

I think I might be making another legit friend.

I hear a car pull into the driveway. Eddie stands up and runs over to the door. That'll be Luke and Dad. Still, I peer out through the glass to make sure. I was right, it's Luke in his car. Dad is sitting beside him.

I go outside. It's cloudy today, and the sky is gray.

Dad makes his way up to me. He's walking on his own, but every step is clearly labored. Sweat has broken out on his brow, and his teeth are clenched.

"Hey," I say.

"Grab my bags," he says. "They're in the trunk."

I don't think he's being mean, I think every word hurts, so he doesn't want to waste the energy on manners.

"Sure."

I jog down and grab his suitcase. I heave it out and bring it inside. It's really heavy, but I'm not about to complain. No way, no sir. I wheel the suitcase to Dad's room. His room is the biggest in the house and is really nice. The walls are cream colored, and the furniture is all designer.

Dad lowers himself down onto the bed, wincing in pain. Through his shirt, I can see a white pad over his stomach. Luke moves the covers aside and then puts them over his legs. They look really thin. I'm surprised Dad is letting Luke take care of him like this. I'm sure if I tried it, he'd lose his shit at me.

"Did you make dinner?" he asks.

"I did," I say. "It should be ready soon, if you want some."

"I'm not up for it tonight, but we'll eat as a family tomorrow. I need to rest. Thank you, though."

"No problem," I say, trying to ignore how my chest is aching. I can't help but feel like it's just because I made it. "Take all the time you need."

* * *

Whoever recommended this place to Cassidy was right. The dumplings are amazing.

The restaurant is getting hyped up online, so it's crowded. We even needed to wait for ten minutes, which Cassidy assured me is the sign that a place is worth our time. She said she tries to not eat anywhere she can just walk into.

I lift one of the pork-and-chives dumplings, dip it in soy sauce, and take a bite. It's so damn good. I could live off these.

"It's official: I love this place," says Cassidy.

"Me too," I say, my mouth full. I swallow, and wish I'd taken the two seconds to do that before I spoke. That would've been way cooler.

She takes another. "So what are you doing after? I have no plans. Pathetic, I know."

"Story of my life."

She laughs, which makes me smile. I'm glad she thinks that I was joking.

"Um," I say. "I'm going to my friend Lev's place. We're just going to be huge nerds and play games all night."

She scoffs. "And here I was, thinking you were cool."

"I'm surprised you thought that for even a second."

She laughs. "I'm just messing with you. I like games, too." She sighs. "But okay, I guess I'll let you two have your nerdy guys' night." Her eyes light up. "Wait, are you and Lev, like . . ." She makes a pretty obscene gesture with her fingers.

I laugh.

"God no," I say. "We're just friends. He's straight."

"You're friends with a straight guy? In *this* economy?"

"I know, right?" I guess I'm out to her. I actually love this.

"Do you have pictures of him?" she asks.

"Yeah, I do," I say. I take out my phone, and show her Lev's Facebook. At least we actually are Facebook friends. I don't know what I would've done if I'd said I was hanging out with someone else.

She swipes through his photos.

"Oh wow, he's cute. Nerds with muscles are such a weak spot of mine." She narrows her eyes. "Are you sure this is a just-friends thing for you? Straight guys are off-limits, in case nobody has told you that. I've seen too many of my gay friends get crushed by them. I don't want to see that happen to you, too."

"Yeah, I know. He's not my type, anyway."

That's not true. He totally is, at least physically, but I want to change the subject.

"And what is?" she asks.

I've never talked about this. With anyone.

I glance across at a waiter. He's got black hair, cut neatly, and has scruff on his cheeks. I noticed him, like, the second I walked in here. There's also a tattoo poking out from under his shirt, running down his beefy forearm. I tilt my head toward him.

She grins. "Oh, honey. You, me, and the rest of the male-loving world like that. Trust me, they're a bad idea. Fun, for sure, but definitely a bad idea."

"Noted."

We have a few more dumplings.

"Hey," I say. "Can I ask you something?"

She nods. The restaurant is so loud, I figure we can talk, as long as I keep my voice down.

"What do you think of the Friend Scheme?"

"The plan of the Donovans', you mean?"

I nod.

"I guess . . . I dunno. A part of me thinks it's risky, but also it's kind of genius? Even now that it's been found out. Like, I have this theory that the whole point of it might've been to freak us out."

"What do you mean?"

"Well, ever since we found out about it, everyone has been super paranoid. And your dad has closed ranks, Mom told me. Some of the big meetings have changed to be Millers only, and Mom's been left out of some stuff. She says she gets it, but I can tell she's pretty upset. If you look at it that way, it's genius."

Ever since he was shot, meetings have been taking place in Dad's hospital room instead of at Jimmy's. It's not ideal, but Dad paid the hospital a lot of money in order to ensure privacy. I haven't been invited to these meetings, but Luke's been to a few.

"Right."

That actually does make sense.

If we're fractured, not as strong as we used to be. Maybe that was a big part of their plan, and we played right into it?

I should talk to Dad about this as soon as possible.

But after I've watched Jason play baseball. I'm not going to miss that for anything.

"What are you thinking?" she asks.

"Just that you might be sort of brilliant."

"Sort of? I'm offended, Matt."

"Okay, you're *totally* brilliant."

"Thanks," she says, and she grabs another dumpling with her chopsticks. "I know."

CHAPTER SEVENTEEN

MY PHONE LIGHTS UP.

It's a text from Jason.

You're still coming to the game, right?

Sure am.

I'm in my car, in the lot of the restaurant where I had dinner with Cassidy. In front of me is a huge tropical mural, with a few red birds and butterflies on it. I rest my head against the headrest and smile. Hanging out with her has made me feel so damn good. I wonder if she knows how great it is for me to talk about being attracted to guys around her, and for her to not even care.

It's new for me. I love it. Plus, she's cool and smart and funny. Being friends with her would be a good thing.

My phone buzzes again.

Sweet! See you then.

I should enjoy this for a second. I know things aren't perfect, but this a big deal for me. I'm making friends. I'm maybe even becoming more than friends with Jason, which I never would've expected even only a few weeks ago. I picture the way his eyes light up when he smiles, and his laugh, which is sort of goofy. It's like he lets slip who he really is for a second, because he can't control it.

I lock my phone and turn on the engine. A pop song starts playing on the radio, and I don't even change it.

What can I say? Things are good.

After a short drive I reach the baseball field, which is behind

Jason's school. The bleachers are already crowded. There are so many people here.

When I get to the bleachers, I see Naomi and Bri sitting in the back row. Naomi waves at me with both arms. I jog up the metal steps. When I get there, I sit down beside her. The bleachers are crammed, so everyone has to touch (eek), and a bunch of them are holding up signs in Jason's school colors, which are yellow and blue. A Nicki Minaj song is playing over the speakers.

"So," says Bri. "You and Jase. What's happening there?"

"Wow," says Naomi. "You couldn't even give him two seconds to sit down? Jesus."

"I mean, why not just cut to the chase? So, Matt. Tell us *everything*."

"Um, we're friends."

"*Just* friends?"

"Yeah."

"Oh. That's disappointing."

"Why?" I ask.

"I thought you might be dating, or at least hooking up. I've got to say, you and him together would be, like, *the* cutest. I would just die."

I swallow hard. "Sorry to disappoint."

So what if we've kissed a few times? They don't need to know that.

Plus, even though we did that, we *are* still just friends. I actually hate that saying, though. *Just friends*. Like it's a consolation prize. If he wanted to stop making out and stay friends, I'd do it. At least that way we'd avoid total disaster, given our families.

"Don't be," she says. "I'm not gonna lie, I'm a little bummed, but it's fine. At least he's finally made a good guy friend. He needed one."

"Agreed," says Naomi. "He's always sort of been the odd one out of the guys. We love him so much, but he's never really clicked with them. He says he's fine, but he's the only out dude on the team. That must be hard."

"Yeah," says Bri. "Wallace says he avoids most of the team when they're not playing. Like he thinks he's too good for them. Wallace, you don't know him, but he's the captain of the team. Anyway, he's actually worried Jason thinks he's homophobic, even though he's not. Has he talked to you about that?"

I shake my head.

She rolls her eyes. "Typical boys. You should talk to him about how he feels, because he has a lot going on. He's under *so* much pressure, you have no idea."

"Because he's gay?"

"Nah, I think he's fine with that. His issue is his parents. My moms are so on board with me being whatever I want to be, but his mom and dad, well, let's just put it this way: He needs to be the best at everything in order for them to be happy."

"For real?"

"It's bad, dude. His mom especially, she's sort of a nightmare. He gets perfect grades and is so polite and nice and stuff to everyone, but she acts like he's still not enough. I know it hurts him."

Bri swats her leg.

"What?" says Naomi.

"I bet Jase doesn't want you spilling all his family drama to a new friend."

"Oh, right. Forget I said anything, Matt."

"Done. It's not a total surprise, though. He's talked about it a little, but I didn't know it was *that* bad."

"Yeah, it really is. So I think having a new friend is good for him. It might make him chill out a little, finally. He's definitely changed since you started hanging out. How'd you meet, by the way?"

Luckily, I have a lie prepared.

"He's friends with a mutual friend of mine, and we just clicked. We both like the same games." It's another lie I have prepared. "But wait. What do you mean about him changing?"

"He seems happier, I guess? And a lot less high-strung. He's always been our anxious little stress ball, and now he's way less stress-y about everything. I think that's because of you. Something has definitely changed in him. It's got to be you."

"Wow, um . . . That's awesome."

The thought of making Jason happy makes me freaking giddy.

One team runs out onto the field, getting into their positions. I scan the field and spot Jason. He's pitching. I find myself smiling. Look at that guy! He's so cute. I must say, he looks great in his uniform. It's blue and white, and the pants are really tight. It'd be pretty fun to make out with him while he's wearing it. I wonder if he'd be down for that.

The crowd goes silent, and the game begins.

Jason pitches . . .

It's a strike!

Jason pitches again and gets another strike.

Then another. He pumps his fist.

The batter walks away, his shoulders hunched.

I won't lie, baseball isn't my favorite thing to watch. And it goes on forever. But I don't mind watching Jason play.

I have to keep reminding myself: We're just friends. I have the situation under control.

"Hey," I say to Naomi, who is beside me.

"Yeah?"

"Does Jason have Instagram?"

I already have my phone out. I'm so ready for this.

"Wait, you don't follow him?"

I shake my head.

"Weird. I mean, of course he does."

"Can you show me?"

She pulls out her phone, and loads Instagram. I do the same.

"It's Jason_todd11," she says.

Jason Todd.

That's his alias?

That's also the name of a superhero: Red Hood. He used to be Robin, until he went down a dark path.

I search for it.

And there it is.

Jason's Instagram. The name might be fake, but it's still his.

This is a treasure. I want to add him, but I'm a little nervous. Even though both our profiles use fake names, who I follow is public. Not that I seriously think anyone is looking at me that closely.

"Are you going to add him?" asks Bri.

"Yeah," I say, and then I lock my phone and slide it back into my pocket. "Maybe later, though."

"Oh, I know this game," she says. "You want him to add you first, don't you?"

"Yeah."

"Power move. I respect that."

I laugh, and then we bump knuckles.

After the first inning, the teams both file off the field.

Bri stands up and waves. "Wallace! Over here!"

Wallace jogs up the bleachers. Jason follows behind him, along with another dude. When they reach us, Jason runs a hand through his hair, pushing it back up.

It's wet with sweat, and messy, in a way that makes him look a little more rugged than normal.

He's also breathing heavy, and there's this energized look in his eyes.

I can't stop looking at him.

"What are you doing here?" asks Naomi. "You're not supposed to leave the dugout."

"I know," says Wallace. "But I had to see my girl."

Wallace kisses Bri on the lips, which makes Naomi cringe, then make a sign of the cross. Then she turns to the remaining two.

"What's your excuse?" she asks. "You could get detention for this, you know?"

They both shrug, but Jason looks at me. The other dude raises a hand at Naomi, and I swear she blushes so hard I can feel the heat radiating from her face. It's all sorts of adorable. I kind of want to push the two of them together and be like, "Now kiss."

Maybe I'm just in a romantic mood at the moment. Who knows?

"Hey, man," says Wallace, offering his hand. "I'm Wallace."

"Matt," I say as we shake.

"He's Jason's friend," says Bri. "The new one."

She gives him a very pointed look. Wallace glances at Jason, his mouth hanging open slightly. I wonder if he's thinking that we're together.

I don't hate that thought.

Oh wow.

That's terrifying. I can't date Jason, I know that. But still, now I'm picturing it. Us, in sweats, cuddling as we watch TV and eat junk food. Showering together. Kissing, like, all the time. Him calling me his boyfriend when we meet someone new.

The truth is, I love all of it.

"I'm Scott, by the way," says the third dude.

"Hi. Matt, obviously."

I shake his hand and start blushing. It dawns on me that I love feeling like one of the group. I smile and notice Jason is looking at me in, like, the softest way. I'm blushing, and he doesn't seem to care.

"Hey," he says, tilting his head up. "Having fun?"

"Yeah! Like, so much! Dude, you're amazing at this."

"Shucks. I'm glad you think so. I feel like I've been playing better than normal today. I think it might be because of you."

He looks at me, then glances away, hiding his expression.

"Guys, we better go before Coach notices," says Scott. "And thanks for coming, Naomi. Um. I'm glad you could make it, I know you're really busy and stuff."

Seriously.

They're both such awkward cinnamon rolls.

I already ship them so hard.

"Sure thing!" says Naomi. "I love watching people prove their masculinity via hitting tiny balls."

"Me too!" says Bri.

"You guys are the worst," says Scott with a smile. "Even you, new guy."

With that, the three turn and jog down the steps.

Jason turns back and waves, just at me.

My stomach plummets.

CHAPTER EIGHTEEN

It's time.

I need to talk to Dad.

I've been trying to muster up the courage ever since I got home from the game. I need to tell him what Cassidy told me. Now that the moment is here I'm reconsidering. I've always been low-key afraid of him, and avoid him as much as possible, but lately it's gotten a lot worse.

I guess I have more to lose now.

Plus, this is the first time I've ever gone brazenly against his wishes. I've always done what he wanted, with a sort of reserved acknowledgment that it's just the way things need to be.

I did "forget" my mask that one time.

But that's nothing compared to being friends with a Donovan.

I've seen him mad before, but if he found out, I'm sure it'd be next-level.

I'm lying on my bed, stalking Jason's social media on my phone. His Facebook was easy to find, once I had his Instagram. He uses Jason Todd as a name there, too. His likes include *Attack on Titan*, *Avatar: The Last Airbender*, and *She-Ra*. I love that they're there, I'm obsessed with all three.

Obviously.

I'm not even surprised when we like the same thing anymore.

I load his Instagram for what feels like the millionth time and scroll down. He's posted a bunch of cute selfies of him just going about his life, mixed in with staged-looking ones of him hanging out with his friends, often at the beach, or at this cute coffee shop he seems to go to a lot. It has a wall of dog photos. My favorite of his photos is one of him at Harry Potter world, freaking out over Butterbeer. Impossibly cute.

Still, it feels very staged to me. I prefer Instagram to feel a little more real.

But, hey, what do I know? He gets a lot more likes than I do.

There are two shirtless photos of him. One is at a pool party, but he's holding an inflatable duck in front of him, so I can't see much. It's still really cute, though, because his smile looks so genuine . . . like he's giddy levels of happy.

He's the cutest boy ever.

The other is on a gorgeous beach in Thailand. He's emerging from the water, dripping wet, staring at something off camera. No smile. Dead serious. It's *totally* a thirst trap, and I'm here for it. His followers are, too, it seems like everyone he knows commented on how hot he is. I read a few of the comments.

GET IT BUDDY!

fire emoji fire emoji fire emoji

THOSE ABS THO! MURDER ME.

I tap, scroll up, and see the follow button.

My heart racing, I jab it.

I leave my room to go to Dad's. I reach it and knock on the door.

"Hey," I say. "Can I come in?"

Dad mutters something, which I take as a yes.

I step inside. He's got his reading glasses on, and his computer is on his lap.

"Why are you up so late?" he asks.

I mean, I do stay up late a lot. But most of the time I just hide in my room. Being out here, trying to get his attention, is weird and he knows it.

"I wanted to talk to you, if you have a sec?"

"Go on."

I know he's recovering, so I shouldn't be too harsh, but he looks *old*. There are big bags under his eyes, and his hair isn't as perfectly kept as it normally is. I wouldn't go so far as to say it's messy, because it's not, but you know . . .

It's not as perfect as I'm used to.

"How are you feeling?" I ask.

"Fine. What did you want to tell me? I'm working, so make it quick."

"Well, I was hanging out with Cassidy earlier, and she . . ."

"Cassidy Strickland?"

"Yeah."

"When did this start?"

"Um . . . at the ball."

"Did you not listen to what Vince said? The only people we can trust right now are our family. Everyone else is a threat."

That's not true, though. Vince said we should be worried about *new* friends. Not old ones. But I can't challenge my father. That's not how our relationship works. He knows best, always. Surely if Luke said exactly the same thing he wouldn't be mad at him. He's mad because I'm the one who said it, and I can never do anything right. I forgot that for a second.

"But that's the thing, this is *about* the Friend Scheme! She had this theory, and I think it's a really good one. Like—"

"Matthew!" he shouts. "Be quiet!"

I shrink back.

I could cry. Obviously I'm not going to. But I could.

"I'm sorry," he says as he rubs his temples. "I didn't mean to yell, I've had a long day. And you just frustrate me sometimes. Why is it so hard for you to do what I tell you? We can't trust anyone right now, so you should just know you shouldn't be spending time with her, at least until we've gotten to the bottom of this."

I frustrate him sometimes. He's never said that to me, even though I've assumed it for a while. Hearing it is a totally different thing.

It makes me feel broken.

"Don't worry about it," I say. "You're right; it's dumb."

I turn to walk back to my room.

"No, Matt, wait."

I ignore him, because I know he doesn't really mean that. He doesn't want me to wait.

He wants me to be like Luke. To be good at this stuff.

He wants me to not be me.

I go back into my room and close my door.

It's just so dumb. He's wrong, anyway. Vince said we can't trust anyone new. Why would he be mad about me being friends with Cassidy? There's nothing wrong with me doing that, so I have no idea why he got upset.

Whatever.

My phone is resting on my bed. I lift it and see I have a new notification. It's from Instagram.

Jason has followed me back.

He's also liked a bunch of my pictures. He's even sent me a DM.

Who knew you were such a good photographer! Just when I think you couldn't get any cooler. ☺

In spite of everything, I smile. I start typing a response.

You're the cool one!! But hey, are you free? I really want to see you.

I hit send.

Hey! Yeah, I am actually, my parents are out for the night, they took my sister to a movie. So I have the place to myself, for the next hour at least . . .

It feels risky. An hour isn't much time. But I can't be here right now.

I just can't.

Can I come over?

YES PLEASE!!! I would love that!

Haha, okay. I'll head over now, then?

See you soon, Mr. ☺

CHAPTER NINETEEN

I DRIVE TO JASON'S PLACE, AND I'M *FREAKING* PISSED.

At Dad. And my stupid life. And the fact that it's so unfair that my first real friend is completely off-limits. It's making me want to speed, or hit my steering wheel, or just pull over and scream until I've gotten everything in my chest out.

But that isn't what I really want.

What I want is to not even have to think about this.

I wish Jason and I were ordinary guys.

If that were the case, we could just hang out at each other's places, and it wouldn't be weird. It'd maybe be awkward to transition into something more romantic, but it'd be cute awkward. Rom-com awkward. Our parents might even be nosy, and get too involved, and it'd be a little embarrassing, but I'd secretly love it.

I want a *Love, Simon* life, basically. Not this. Not a dad who I frustrate. And a boy I can never truly have because of our last names.

I reach Jason's place and park out front.

This is the Donovans' house.

I shouldn't be here.

I step out of the car and walk up to the front door. The air is still, and I can hear chirping crickets. I love this sound. I reach his porch and pause. Time to do this. For some reason knocking makes me anxious, so I message him that I'm here.

A few moments later, the door opens.

"Hey there," he says, tilting his head up. "You look great."

So does he. He's wearing a black T-shirt with a Poké Ball on it and gym shorts. His feet are covered in black ankle socks, and his hair is a little limp, not pushed up like it normally is.

I realize this is Jason when he hasn't put any work in.

He's gorgeous.

I feel lucky that I get to see this. Him, with his walls down. He beckons me inside and closes the door behind me.

Then we hug. I sink into it.

I can't tell him about what happened with Dad, so I just try to get as much out of the hug as I can.

"What's going on?" he asks.

"Huh?"

"I'm just picking up a vibe that something's happened. Want to talk about it?"

I chew my lip.

And decide to test him.

"Um, my dad's been kind of shitty lately."

His eyes widen. "Oh. Right. Well, I mean, you don't have to tell me about it if you don't want to." He rubs my arm. "Whatever he did, I'm sorry."

And he passes with flying colors.

I sigh. "No, I can talk about it. He told me I frustrate him sometimes. I know that's not much, but like . . . I don't want to frustrate him. He's my dad, you know?"

"I completely get it. I'm sorry. But I'd bet he'd be really upset if he found out he'd hurt your feelings. I know my dad says hurtful stuff all the time, and I don't think he has any idea he's doing it. I think it's just a dad thing, you shouldn't take it personally."

I like the thought of that.

"That was the perfect thing to make me feel better," I say. "And you just, like, knew it."

He grins. "I'm glad. It gets better, too. I actually have something in mind for right now. I've always had this idea of what I'd do if I got you in my bedroom."

UM.

"Oh God, not that!" he says. "I mean, that could be fun, too. But that's not what I'm talking about. Just, come with me."

He leads me to his bedroom and closes the door behind him. Then he locks it.

"So what's the plan?" I ask.

He turns his TV on.

"I was thinking we could watch *Mulholland Drive*? I've been meaning to ever since you recommended it, but I haven't gotten around to it yet."

Oh my God.

My favorite movie.

He needs to be less cute. I can't handle this.

"You remembered," I say.

"Of course," he says, shrugging. "Like I remember you love *Donnie Darko*, and how you had a crush on Jake Gyllenhaal when you were a kid, and how you can name every single Pokémon."

"And here I was thinking guys were supposed to be bad listeners."

"Normally I am. Just not with you."

I'm floored.

"I remember everything you've told me, by the way," I say. "Like how your favorite Pokémon is Arcanine, and how you love the Bartimaeus trilogy, and your big crush as a kid was on Sam Winchester. It's easy with you, for some reason."

"I feel the same about you."

"Cool. Anyway. Um, should we watch the movie?"

"Yeah, I guess."

He sits down on his bed, propped up against the headrest. I think he'd be cool with me joining him on the bed, but I don't want to assume anything, so I wheel his desk chair over to the side of the bed.

I don't know exactly what we're doing.

I sit down on the chair.

He watches me. I think he's going to say something, but then he turns away, and scrolls through the apps on the TV. He loads Netflix, then searches for *Mulholland Drive* and finds it.

"Do you like horror, by the way?" I ask.

"Yeah. They freak me out, though. I think it's because, like, I sort of believe in that stuff. Like, I totally think ghosts and stuff could be real. That might be dumb."

It's not. It's really cute.

"It's not dumb. I sort of believe in it, too. I'm, like, paranormal agnostic."

"Dude, that's the perfect description! I'm exactly the same! Like, I'm not totally convinced that they're real, but like, I think there's a chance. Enough to get scared by a horror movie, anyway."

I love it when he gets like this. All hyper and excited.

It's so. Damn. Precious.

We smile at each other.

Again, I feel overwhelmed by how cool I think he is. I fall back to that mental image, of us, in sweats, just hanging out together. I don't know why I like that picture so much, but I do. Us, as boy-friends.

Naomi was right.

It would be really cute.

"Is this going to scare me?" he asks.

"Probably."

He lifts the remote, and then lowers it. He tilts his head toward me.

"Hey," he says.

"Yeah?"

"Is there a reason you aren't on the bed?"

"Oh, I just thought . . ."

"Thought what?"

"I didn't want to assume."

"Well, you're totally welcome to join me. Sitting there is cool, too, if you want to. No pressure."

I move to the bed.

"Much better," he says.

He scoots across as I start unlacing my shoes. I kick them off, and then put my legs onto the bed. He's watching me, smiling.

"What?" I ask.

"Nothing."

I think he wants me to lean forward and kiss him. The twinkle in his eyes makes me think that's what he wants. I take him in. Per-fect hair, broad shoulders, and soft-looking lips. Military boy par excellence. He hasn't shaved today, so there's a slight shadow on his cheeks.

Kissing him would be unbeatable.

But what if I'm wrong?

What if I make a move, and he doesn't want me to, and then things between us become so awkward that we never talk to each other again?

Plus, he's a Donovan. I really shouldn't kiss him.

Instead, I just lean against the headrest, keeping a comfortable distance between us.

"Do you want more pillows or something?" he asks.

I adjust the pillow behind me so it's a proper backrest.

"I'm good. Thanks, though."

"Cool."

He starts the movie.

And here I am.

Sitting in a bed. With a Donovan.

I wonder if we're going to have sex.

I can't even believe I'm actually thinking that. I mean, it wasn't that long ago that I hadn't even been kissed, and now I'm thinking about sex? If it were any other guy, I think I'd be nervous. But with Jason, I think I could handle it. I wonder what position he'd prefer. I've always felt like I'd like both, although I get a vibe that Jason is more of a . . .

Okay.

I need to stop thinking about this.

I focus on the movie. Luckily, it's a pretty fantastic distraction, because it's so weird and dark and I love it so much.

I'm still thinking about *it*, though. I've never done it before, but I don't think I have any hang-ups about it. It's never seemed like that big of a deal to me. So I'd probably try it if he suggested it, as long as we were safe. Either position, I don't care. Or something else; I know that kind of sex takes prep work. But I have condoms in my bag, so like, we could totally do it.

I wonder if he's a virgin, too.

I have no idea. I don't like to assume this sort of thing.

Anyway, it doesn't matter. This is just a fantasy.

I start to feel a little brave. I tilt my foot across and touch his foot.

"Finally," he says, and he leans across to kiss me.

I pull back.

"What?" he says.

I'm thinking about Dad. About how I frustrate him. And I think my doing stuff like this is part of the reason why. Maybe I'd be less miserable if I at least tried to do the stuff he wants me to.

Being friends with a Donovan is one thing. Going further is different.

"I dunno, just, maybe we shouldn't . . . ," I say.

"Oh. Why not?"

"Because we're us, you know? I want to, but I also want to be smart. I think this is going to be really embarrassing to admit, but . . ."

"But what?"

He says it so softly, like he already knows, and it's okay.

"I think if I'm not careful, I could start to like you," I say. "As more than a friend, I mean. Obviously I like you. But it could be more for me, if we keep doing stuff like this. Which would be bad, right?"

I hang my head. I can't bring myself to look at him.

"Why would it be bad?" he asks.

He raises his hand to touch me. I pull away.

"Because you're a Donovan," I say. "We're on opposite sides. I gave myself a rule, and I need to stick to it. We can be friends, but that's all. Look at me. Please. Let's just be friends. That's as far as I can go."

"Why'd you touch my foot, then?" He doesn't ask in a harsh way, it seems he genuinely wants to know.

"I didn't mean to."

He stares at me blankly.

"Okay, sorry," I say. I bring my knees up to my chest. "Maybe I wanted to see what would happen. Because I do like you, I just . . . I wish I could show you what's going on in my head right now."

"Use your words. What were you hoping would happen?"

"Truly, I don't know."

"Just tell me: What do you want?"

I know what I want. But I'm not allowed.

Then again, maybe I should just say screw it and go all in.

I get very hyped up at the thought.

Ryan Donovan flashes in my mind. Then he shifts to Jason sitting on the chair, with slashes on his chest. Vince slices down, killing him.

"What are you thinking?" he asks. "Talk to me."

"I think it all boils down to the fact that I'm scared of how much I could like you."

"I'm scared of how much I could like you, too."

That sinks in. I can't think of anything to say to that. I guess he can't, either, as we both turn our attention back to the movie.

I can't focus on it, though. It's hopeless. I like him too much.

Even though I know I shouldn't, I brush my arm against his. It's only a tiny amount of contact, but it sends a crackling static feeling through me. He keeps watching. I stop paying attention to the movie, to focus instead on how close I am to him. It feels as if time has slowed down.

Our arms are almost touching, and we're nearly skin to skin.

I keep watching.

I brush my arm against his again. He doesn't move.

I do it again, and then he moves his arm out, so it's resting against mine. I glance at him, and he's focused on the movie.

"Hey," I say.

He swallows. "Hey. Did you decide, is this okay?"

"Yeah, I like it," I say.

"Cool, I like it, too. How about this? Tell me if I go too far."

His foot moves across and touches mine. I tilt my foot and touch his. And all of a sudden it's on, we're bumping and touching each other.

I like it so much.

I can't do this.

"Sorry," I say, my voice coming out a little raspy. "Stop. We can't."

He goes still. "Dude, talk to me. What do you want?"

"I just . . . I keep going from wanting to be friends to not wanting to see you at all, then wanting to be, like, more than friends with you. And I can't figure out what the smart thing to do is."

He moves away, and his foot goes still. "Okay. I'm really confused. Do you want me to stop?"

"I don't know. I like this. It's just, I think kissing is too far, but urgh. I want to; I *really* want to. But I feel like it's a mistake. I'm sorry if I'm being frustrating. I just don't want to do the wrong thing. I still don't know how much I trust you."

"You can trust me. I swear, I'm not here as a Donovan. I'm here as your friend."

"Okay, I get that."

"Then what makes you feel like kissing is the wrong thing?"

I push my thumb into my palm. "It's just what my instincts are telling me. Even if you don't have some scheme, it can't end well, right?"

"Okay. I'm getting the impression that you like me, and you like fooling around, but you don't want to get into a relationship, because of who we are."

"Yes, exactly! That's, like, totally it!"

"Right. Well, what if we just say that we're friends who sometimes do stuff? We're not dating or anything. We're just two guys . . . trying stuff out. No pressure, and we can stop at any time. Would that be okay with you?"

"Like, friends with benefits?" I ask.

"I mean, yeah?"

Would that be okay? It doesn't mean I'm being any more disloyal to Dad and my family than I would be if we were just friends. Nor am I putting my family in danger. Jason already knows I like guys, so even if he did tell his family about this, it wouldn't matter.

"I think so," I say.

He shakes his head. "I need more than that. I don't want to do anything with you unless you're fully sure. The last thing I want to do is make you uncomfortable."

"Okay," I say. "Then I'm in. Friends with benefits it is."

"In that case, screw the movie."

"Yeah, screw you!" I say to the TV. "I can't believe I just said that.

You know that's my favorite movie, right? That'd be like you saying screw you to *Skyrim*."

"Trust me, I know, and I appreciate it."

He laughs, and puts his hand flat on my chest, and just holds it there.

I chew my lip. "What are you doing?"

"Touching you," he says.

"Okay."

He slides his hand under my shirt, until his hand is in the same spot as it was before, but under, so his palm is on my bare skin. I let myself stop thinking so much and just enjoy how it feels to be touched.

I get really into it.

"You like this?" he asks, his voice low.

"Uh-uh."

"God you're cute."

He slides his hand out from under, and brings it up to my face. Then he leans down and kisses me. I open my mouth, and tease my tongue against his. He's moving his mouth slowly, and I try to mirror him. It feels really good.

He pulls back.

"Good?" I ask.

"So good."

"Should we take our shirts off? We don't have to go further than that, but, do you want to?"

"Definitely." He tears off his shirt, and then he frantically takes mine off me.

We take a second to look at each other, both shirtless. He's so perfect. I run my hands down his chest, to his stomach. I touch his abs, feeling the individual ridges of muscle. They feel different from what I was expecting. More solid. I didn't even know a stomach could feel like this.

He knots his hand through my hair, and for a second I think I should stop.

I'm not sure if I can be just friends with benefits with him.

I think I like him too much for that.

When he leans down, I let him kiss me.

CHAPTER TWENTY

I'M AT JIMMY'S, SITTING AT A BOOTH NEAR THE BACK, by myself. I'm thinking about Jason, trying to figure out what I'm going to do about the epic shitstorm I've found myself in.

Being friends with benefits with him is never going to work.

I know that.

I like him way too much, and I'm *way* too attracted to him.

In fact, I'm genuinely worried about us getting so close and going so far that when it all falls to pieces, I'll be ruined. I really can see us getting *that* close. Or at least my liking him that much.

Let's be real, though.

Even with the risk, deep down I know I'm not going to stop seeing him.

I don't know if I *could* stop, even if I wanted to.

The bar is dim, like always. Sara is drinking a Scotch alone at the bar, and Grandma is talking to Barbie. Dad's upstairs. It's his first night back.

Ending things with Jason now would be a really good call. I know that.

And I want to be smart. I really do.

But hanging out with him . . . it's everything to me. I like it way more than anything else in my life. I can't give it up.

I swirl my drink and take a sip.

It's just Coke, but I'm hoping people think it's got bourbon or something in it. I feel like drinking just Coke is too childish, and for some reason I care about that right now. Not that anyone is giving me much attention. Cassidy isn't here tonight, so I'm back to sitting by myself, waiting for the night to be over.

The bar looks quieter than normal. It seems like a lot of allied families have sat this night out. Maybe Cassidy's theory was right. That this exodus is because of the Friend Scheme. Like the Mackenzies, who we're allied with because they are the best at supplying weaponry. Or the Davidsons, who help run the illegal gambling rings we have set up around the city. They're not here, and we need them.

I guess that's paranoia for you, though.

It's not rational by definition.

I just wish Dad would listen to me. He can't see this because he's so sure he knows everything. But us losing allies is *really* bad. We need them, even if he thinks we don't. I know in my gut that he should listen to me, but I don't think he's ever going to.

It makes me wonder if I'd like being a part of this world a little more if I were at least somewhat respected.

I'm not, though, and I don't think I ever will be.

I'll always be Little Matty. The black sheep. The only person who listens to me is Jason.

I . . .

I pause, because Dad appears on the steps that lead up to the top level of the bar. He winces, then presses his lips together. He's wearing a suit now, so the gauze on his stomach is no longer obvious. The bartender turns the music down, and the bar falls silent.

"Family meeting," says Dad, his voice filling the room. "Millers only, upstairs, five minutes."

He turns and slowly walks back up, having to use the handrail for support.

There's a lull, and then chatter breaks up among the bar patrons. The music turns back on. Most of the people from allied families look seriously pissed. I get that. Nobody likes being left out. They're probably wondering why they even showed up.

I finish my drink, then stand up. Luke is at the bar, talking to a girl with strawberry-blond hair. I've seen her around a few times, but I don't know her name. I probably should, because I'm expected to know everyone here.

I guess Dad would be fine with his talking to her because he trusts Luke more than he trusts me.

As I walk over, she crosses her arms.

"I'm sorry," Luke says to her. "I know it sucks."

"You have no idea," she says. "And hey, Matt."

I wave. "Hey."

"This is Dad's idea, not mine," says Luke. "If it were up to me, you'd be in there, too, I promise. He's just been paranoid lately, because of the scheme."

She turns away.

Luke touches her arm. "I'll make it up to you, okay?"

She finally turns back. "You better."

He grins, which makes me think he's going to enjoy making it up to her.

The girl turns around and waves down the bartender.

What *is* her name? I think it's S-something. Stacey?

Luke and I cross the bar. Once we're out of earshot, he huffs.

"That seems to be going well," I say.

He nods.

"Nice work," I whisper. "She's really cute."

He chuckles. "You're the only guy I know who'd call her cute."

"But she is cute."

"Yeah, but . . . she's hot, too. There's a big difference. Most guys know it."

I mean, I feel like one of these days Luke is going to stumble face-first right into the truth.

"It's sweet," he says. "Sometimes I wonder if there's a romantic bone in my body. The only bone I have is in my—"

"Stop!" I say. "I so don't want to hear the end of that."

He chuckles. "That's fair."

Together, we go upstairs.

It's a long hallway, lined with windows. The wooden floorboards beneath me creaks. If I look out, I can see the parking lot, lit by neon. I think back to when I first got in Jason's car, and how scared and excited I was.

He still makes me feel that way.

My blood chills. It would've been so easy for anyone standing where I am now to see me get in his car. So maybe we were watched. But surely if someone saw, I would've gotten in trouble by now.

Luke and I go inside a room to the right. It's a conference room, with a long table in the middle, surrounded by high-backed chairs. About ten family members are already seated. There's an unlit fireplace at the head of the room, although I think that's more for decoration than anything, as I've never seen it lit. On the table are glasses of Scotch, a few bottles of red wine, and a bowl filled with fresh fruit, mostly red apples and grapes.

I think I've been here maybe three times in total.

I've hated it every single time.

Hanging on the wall opposite the fireplace is a portrait of my grandfather. He's wearing a black suit, and I swear the artist did a great job of capturing his disapproving sneer. I catch Grandma looking at it, her eyes glassy.

I wish I could say I miss him.

But I blame him for the Miller legacy. The darkness and our lies.

Luke and I sit near the head of the table, where Dad is sitting. He has a half-empty glass of Scotch beside him. In the dim light, he looks gaunt. He lost weight while in the hospital and hasn't put it back on yet, which is even more obvious now that he's shaved. He's clearly mad about something. His hands are resting on the dark wood of the table, and one of them is clenched into a fist.

Soon, everyone is seated. Silence falls over the room.

"Now," says Dad. "Given recent events, I need all of you to promise that what we talk about tonight will not, under any circumstances, leave this room. Not a word, to anyone, do you all understand?"

He glances at me.

Okay, ouch.

But message received.

Everyone nods.

"Good," he says. He sips his Scotch. "I've called this meeting because I've come up with a plan to end the war."

The energy in the room changes. Everyone is now listening intently.

Dad smirks. "I propose that we call a truce."

There's an uproar. Almost everyone is shouting, trying to get their opinion in.

I might be the only one not doing that.

Can this really be happening?

Is he going to finally ask for peace?

If a truce happens, there will be nothing keeping Jason and me from being friends, or maybe even escalating.

This would solve everything.

"Quiet," says Grandma.

And everyone listens. The room stills.

It still feels charged, though.

"Now," says Dad. "I want you all to know that I have no intention of actually honoring this truce. It's too late for that. They took my father from me, and they tried to kill me. They need to pay."

The crowd seems to like this, as the energy changes. They're on board, I can feel it.

Everyone is but me. For a second I let myself fantasize about a world where Jason and I are allowed to be together.

That was obviously a mistake. Now I just feel down.

"So, what?" asks Luke. "You want to call a truce but lie about it?"

Dad nods. "Let me finish. I propose we call a truce. They will agree. They know we have larger numbers, more funding, and more allies."

For now.

"If this war continues as it has been going, then it's only a matter of time before they lose, and they know it. I do believe they will start lashing out soon, though, in their desperate attempts to rebalance the scales. We need to end this war now, in order to ensure our side doesn't take heavy losses."

Vince has his switchblade out. He opens it. "Just tell us, what's the plan?"

"I say we ask them for an unarmed meeting to discuss ending the war peacefully. We tell them we are willing to give them the north side, as long as we keep control over the south and the beach. They can take back control of narcotics, and we will take back full control of gambling. We'll go back to how things used to be."

I know that a meeting like this is a sacred agreement, a safe space. On the streets, we can fight like animals . . . but if a meeting is called, violence is strictly prohibited.

And I think I understand what Dad is suggesting . . . It's so dark. Surely he can't be serious.

"And when they come to the meeting," he says, "we have snipers ready. We can capture a few, and Vince can get them to give up the identities of the rest. We will wipe them all out in one swift strike."

Nobody says anything.

The tension is so thick.

To break tradition like this . . . it's a stink our family will never be able to get off us.

"We can't," says Grandma. "It's not the way things are done."

"They killed your husband," says Dad. "They tried to kill me. Enough time has passed, and now we need retribution."

"Did you learn nothing from him?" asks Grandma. "To suggest this spits on his memory."

"To do nothing spits on his memory. We need to stop them."

"I agree, but our allies won't stand for this," says my aunt Sara. "We could lose all of them. You would take out the Donovans but ruin our family."

"I DON'T CARE!" roars Dad. "I want them dead! All of them! They need to pay!"

Grandma is fuming now.

"And they will!" says Sara. "But in the right way. Joe, we can't do this. If you stop and think for a second, you'll realize you aren't thinking clearly. There *has* to be another way."

Dad nods. "Enough. I propose a vote. Everyone in favor of my plan . . ."

Dad raises his hand.

Luke does, too.

As does Vince.

Luckily for me, everyone else keeps their hand down. Dad sees that I've kept my hand down, though. I don't think I'll ever be able to get the look he gives me out of my head.

"And now," says Dad, "everyone who thinks we shouldn't . . ."

Everyone else raises their hands. Once again, I keep my hands on the table. He already knows my vote. There's no point rubbing it in.

"All right," says Dad. "It's decided. The plan will not go ahead."

I feel like I just dodged a bullet. But the damage is done.

CHAPTER TWENTY-ONE

Jason wants me to meet him at the baseball stadium at the back of his school.

I know I'm going down a dark road . . . one that might just lead to him chained to a chair and tortured, then killed.

Or me. Or both of us.

But as long as I'm careful, we're safe.

I think.

I'm ready to go. I'm wearing a gray tank, black skinny jeans with rips in the knees, and my boots. I leave my room and walk down the hall as quietly as I can. Nobody is around, and the house is dark. Eddie is asleep in his spot. Good.

I hear a noise, the fridge opening.

It's the worst timing in all of freaking history.

That *might* be a slight overreaction. But it's up there.

I pause. But as I take a step backward, my shoe squeaks.

Shit.

I really regret deciding to wear boots right now.

"Who's there?" says a voice.

I'm so relieved. It's just Luke. I step out from the darkness.

Luke's features soften, and he smiles. He's wearing a white tank, and his hair is mussed. I haven't seen it this messy in ages and hadn't actually realized how long it's gotten. When it's slicked down, it looks way shorter. This is a good look for him, though. It brings out the delicate parts of his features. I wonder if he got those from Mom.

"What are you up to?" he asks.

"I got invited to this house party, and I was thinking of going. Don't tell Dad. Seriously, you can't."

"Whoa, calm down, I won't." He leans against the open door of the fridge. "It's about time you started sneaking out; I've been doing it for years. Dad's a heavy sleeper, he won't hear the car. You want some beers?"

"Huh?"

"For the party? I could be convinced to give you a six-pack. You'll need to pay me back, though."

"Er, yeah, sure. That'd be amazing, actually."

Drinking was already part of the plan. Jason said he was bringing some beers, and he asked me to Uber to the stadium instead of driving, so I could drink. Luke opens the fridge and hands me a six-pack.

"Thanks," I say.

"No sweat. Just remember, condoms if you hook up. Every time, you hear me?"

"Yeah, I got it."

"And don't you dare drink and drive. If you get wasted, call an Uber, or me, and I'll come pick you up. Anytime, okay?"

"Okay. Thanks. Well, see ya."

"Have fun."

I carry the beer outside, where the car I ordered is already waiting. The window slides down.

"Matt, right?" asks the driver.

I nod and get in the car.

* * *

Jason is waiting for me in the parking lot of the stadium.

He's leaning against a fence. Beside him is a six-pack of beer, a baseball bat, a black mesh bag filled with baseballs, and a tee.

I want to take a snapshot of him. American boy, in his element. I know there's a lot more than that going on with him, but that's what he looks like right now. A corn-fed golden boy.

I thank the driver, then grab the beers and climb out.

"Hey," he says. "You brought refreshments?"

I kick the door shut. "Luke gave 'em to me."

"Nice."

I point at the stuff. "We're going to play baseball?"

"Not exactly. We're just going to hit a few balls. It'll be fun, trust me."

"Those sound like famous last words."

He laughs. "They sure do."

We talk up to the front gate. The entire area is surrounded by a chain-link fence. It probably wouldn't be that hard to climb over, so I wonder if that's what he's got in mind. But he pulls a key from his pocket and opens up the padlock. He pushes on the gate, and it swings open, the metal screeching.

"You have a key?" I ask.

"Yeah, man."

"How?"

"Coach gave it to me. He wanted me to practice here whenever I have free time."

"You come here?"

"I do, yeah."

"By yourself?"

"Uh-huh."

"Isn't that lonely?"

He shrugs. "Tonight it's not."

We reach the diamond, and he puts the tee down. It's nearly a full moon, so the stadium is pretty bright, even though the spotlights are dark. The stars glow. It feels kind of epic for the two of us to be alone in such a massive space.

I hand Jason a beer, and then I take one. We crack them open.

I watch as Jason drinks his, finishing it quickly, his Adam's apple bobbing up and down as he drinks. He lowers the can and wipes his mouth on his sleeve, then he throws away the empty can. It skitters across the ground.

"Don't worry," he says. "I'll pick them up after."

I finish mine, and throw it away, too. I've never drunk beer that fast before. He takes a ball from the mesh bag and puts it on the tee. Then he picks up the bat, twirls it around a couple of times, and offers it to me. I take it.

"Have you ever done this?" he asks.

"Not since middle school."

"Just do what your instincts tell you. I'll correct from there."

"All right."

I move up to the position and do a practice swing. It feels good, so I pull back, and hit the ball as hard as I can.

It flies a couple of yards, and then drops down onto the dirt.

"Good, right?" I say.

"You're very cute, but dude, no. First things first, you're holding the bat wrong. Two hands on the handle, like this."

He stands behind me, looping his arms around me, so his hands are also on the bat.

"Like this."

He corrects my grip on the bat. Next, he puts his hand on my chest, straightening me up. Then he nudges my front foot forward. God, these little touches are enough to overwhelm me.

"You want to stride out a little and keep your hands back. That's steps one and two."

"Sure."

He moves his hand down to my hip. I stand very still. "Now, when you go to hit, you explode this out, toward the ball. When you do it, your hands should follow."

"*I* don't follow."

"Sorry, all right. Like, this."

He gets into position in front of me, and then swings his hip forward. He does it so fast I know there's no way I'm going to be able to do it.

"What's next?"

"Step four is throwing your hands toward the ball. Like this."

Again, it's deceptively complicated for such a small movement, but maybe that's because I'm so freaking untalented at sports. Still, I want to at least try.

"Then swing. That's five. And six is extension through the ball. That's how you get lift."

"Okay."

"And step seven is follow through." He finishes his swing, then pokes me in the chest with the end of the bat. "And that, my friend, is how you hit a baseball."

"Got it. I think."

He puts a ball on the tee.

"You ready for this?" I ask.

"So ready."

I get into position, moving my foot forward. And then I swing. The baseball makes a really nice sound, and it lifts off. It doesn't go much farther than last time, but it *felt* a lot better.

"You're a natural," he says.

"Don't be condescending."

"I'm not."

I give him my best death stare.

"Okay," he says. "Maybe I was, just a little."

I laugh. "Why don't you show me how it's done, if you're such a pro?"

"I can do that. Prepare to eat your words, Miller."

I hand him the bat, and he walks up to the tee. I put down a ball and then stand behind him. His stare fixes, and he goes through the motions once. Then he gets into position, and swings.

Thwack.

The ball goes flying, up and into the darkness. If it were a real game it'd have to be a home run. He's so good, it's hot as hell.

I whistle. "How do you do that?"

"Practice." He strides up to me. "Lots and lots of practice. You impressed?"

"I am, actually."

We take turns hitting for a while, breaking the hits up by drinking beer. It honestly feels like another perfect night. I'm starting to like the taste. Soon, I'm pretty drunk, and am barely focused on hitting the ball. I'm concentrating on Jason, and how cute and hot he is. He loves baseball so much, it's infectious. And his shirt fits snuggly against him. His muscles . . . I must say, they're so great. He's sweaty now, making his shirt slightly transparent, and it's stuck to his back. I find myself staring at his lower back, at the muscles around his spine.

So hot.

Once we've hit all the balls in the bag, I go to retrieve them. I collect them all and then make my way up to him.

He smiles. "I'm just going to go grab something, give me a second?"

"Okay?"

He goes back to his car. I sit down on the first row of the bleachers and pull out my phone. Cassidy has sent me a link to a cat-fails video she thinks I should watch. I know I'll like it, but later.

Jason returns, and he's holding a picnic rug.

"Is this weird?" he asks. "I was thinking we might lie down on it or something? I thought it could be fun, but we don't have to."

"I love it," I say. "I mean, it's not weird at all. Same wavelengths, remember?"

"Right."

He throws the rug down in the middle of the diamond. And then we both just stand there.

It's not very big.

"I guess we should just lie down?" he says.

"Yeah, I guess."

So we do.

We're both on our backs, looking up at the night sky. Our bodies are sort of angled, so we're leaning in toward each other. Our hands are inches apart.

"Want another beer?" I ask.

"Obviously, yeah."

I hand one to him, then crack mine open and take a sip. I focus on the sky. There aren't many stars visible, but still, it's pretty cool. It's so massive. We drink our beers and finish them at about the same time.

Then we both lie down.

I put my hands behind my head and get really comfortable.

I'm hoping for a shooting star.

"I really like this," says Jason.

"Me too."

He reaches out to touch my side. It feels like crackling electricity. His hand runs up my side, then across to my chest. Static, all over. He shifts, until he's propped upright, with his hand resting on me, looking into my eyes.

"What are you doing?" I ask.

His lips look so soft and pink. He's bound to taste like beer right now. His hair is as messy as his can get, and there's this sort of dazed look in his eyes. He's drunk.

"I don't know," he says. "I've just always had this fantasy of kissing a guy here. Of doing exactly this. I . . ."

I stop listening.

I shouldn't, I know I shouldn't, but . . . .

Fuck it.

I sit up and kiss him.

I don't even care about anything. He repositions so we can properly kiss. Our mouths open at the same time, and my tongue goes into his mouth. It feels so wet but weirdly so nice. I sit properly up, and we try out this sort of kissing. I feel like I know his rhythm now. I know how to respond when he moves, and I know what to do with my tongue. It all just works.

We break apart, and I open my eyes.

"Like this?" I ask.

"Exactly like this."

He pushes my chest, and I fall back down. Then he moves across . . .

He sits on top of me.

And I'm really hard. I'm sure he can feel it. I just wasn't expecting him to do this.

"Sorry," I say. "I . . ."

"Don't be," he says, and he cups my face with both hands, and kisses me. "You're fine, dude."

He does taste a little like beer, but it's definitely not bad. It's actually great. He takes my bottom lip between his teeth, which tells me going for it is okay.

We crash together, frantically kissing. I scratch down his back, and his eyelids flutter. His shoulders are so bulky, and I love how they feel. But mostly I just like how he kisses me. He does it so intently, like this is the only thing on earth he wants to be doing.

"I have a serious question for you," he says.

"Anything."

He touches my tank, lifting it up a little.

"Why is this still on?"

"Because you haven't taken it off me."

I'm not sure it's the safest decision, because we are out in the open. But I still pull off his shirt, and then he takes mine off me. I explore his chest and arms with my fingertips. Then he leans down again, and kisses me deeply.

It very quickly becomes apparent that I need to stop, like, right now.

I break away and press my head against the blanket. It smells earthy, like grass.

"Fuck," I say. "Don't move."

He laughs a throaty laugh. It's so hot. He doesn't move, though, and the feelings pass.

"Hey," he says. "I need to tell you something." His voice is thick.

"What? You want me to take my pants off?"

"I mean, yes. But before that, you need to know something."

I sit up. "Oh, okay. What?"

He looks nervous. I don't think I've ever seen him nervous. It's painfully endearing.

"This, um, it's more than a friends-with-benefits thing for me. I think it always has been."

Oh. Wow.

I mean, it is for me, too. But there's a big difference between feeling it and saying it.

"But . . . ," I start.

"You don't need to say if you like me back," he says. "It's okay if you don't."

"Dude," I say, and then I gesture at my current predicament. I'm shirtless in the middle of a baseball field, and he's sitting on top of me. How can he doubt how I feel about him? "I obviously like you as more than a normal friend."

"But we're on opposite sides," he says. "You said that, remember?"

I want to tell him everything I'm feeling.

But I can't.

He's a Donovan.

Things between us have to end at some point. There's no future where we'll be allowed to be together. We're always going to be who we are, and our families are always going to be our families.

But I'm not strong enough to turn down this wonderful boy.

And I owe him the truth. That's always been our thing.

"I know what I said before. But it's more than a friends-with-benefits thing for me, too."

He smiles. "Sweet."

It makes me so happy I think maybe it's too late. I don't know how it works. But I might already kind of love him.

Oh boy.

This is bad.

So freaking bad.

"How about we go on a date, then?" he asks. "I have something in mind, actually."

"Do you, now?"

He nods and then kisses me in the middle of my forehead. "Next time we hang out, it'll be a date, if that's okay with you?"

"It's more than okay," I say. "It's, like . . . so exciting."

"I'm glad you think that."

He puts his hand on my face, and rubs my cheek with his thumb. I need to shave, because it feels a little prickly.

"What made you decide?" he asks.

"I guess . . . I can't help myself around you."

"I can't help myself around you, either."

It feels so perfect. Maybe too perfect.

What about the Friend Scheme? And why we met in the first place?

What if he's still manipulating me?

It's as if he knows what I'm thinking, because he leans down and kisses me hard.

My doubts fade away.

CHAPTER TWENTY-TWO

I'M IN A SHIPPING CONTAINER, SHIRTLESS, CUFFED TO A metal chair.

It's cold. My arms and legs are bound to it with thick leather straps, so I can't really move. I pull against my bonds, but they're too tight.

I can't move. I'm helpless. Utterly at the mercy of . . .

Vince.

He's standing in front of me, with a too-big grin on his face. He's holding his switchblade, and he keeps opening and closing it. The container is dark, so the paleness of his skin really stands out.

He's my uncle.

And he's about to torture me.

I doubt he's going to show me any mercy. Actually, he might even be more vicious with me, because I betrayed my family.

His family.

I need to outsmart him. What he wants is for me to give up Jason. To tell him his identity, and for me to tell him everything we've been doing. I can't do that, though. I know what'll happen if I do.

He'll kill me, and then Jason.

"I won't talk," I say, trying to sound as stoic as I can. I splay my hands, as they're starting to cramp.

"You will," he says as he circles me. "Everyone knows how weak you are, Little Matty."

"That's just a rumor. You'll see."

"I almost hope that's true." He leans in close, so he's whispering in my ear. "You might be a traitor, but I hope you aren't a coward as well."

I straighten up and stare him down.

"Just get on with it, then."

I don't know where this bravery is coming from.

I guess it's because Jason's life is on the line. I can't let anyone hurt him.

"Okay, then," he says. "Let's start. Tell me who you've been spending time with."

Vince runs the blade along my skin, walking in a circle around me. There's not enough pressure on it to cut, but I know that's coming very soon.

I start hyperventilating.

As much as I want to be brave and not give him any satisfaction, I know he's about to badly hurt me. Right now he's just playing with me. But soon, I'll feel the real thing.

"Just a friend," I say. "That's all we are, I swear."

I only just manage to say it, because I'm shaking so much.

"You're lying," he says.

"I'm not, I promise I'm not. Please don't hurt me. Dad will kill you if you do."

"Who do you think asked me to do this?"

He slowly moves the blade down, closer and closer, until it's touching me. I struggle, but I can't move, and then I feel the cold of metal on my skin, and I go totally still. My heart is pounding, and I want to scream, but it's trapped in my throat.

"Last chance," he says. "Tell me everything."

I shake my head.

He tilts the blade slightly so the edge is touching me . . .

And then he presses down.

A thumping on my door pulls me from my dream.

I sit bolt upright and touch my chest.

I can still feel his knife cutting into me. I pull my blankets away and see that my skin is fine. I'm wearing a white tank and my boxers.

It was just a dream. I'm okay.

The knock sounds again, a fist pounding against my door.

I slide out of bed and walk over to my door. Moonlight streams in through my window, and my curtains flutter gently. I unlock my door and swing it open. Luke is standing outside, wearing a black suit.

He's holding his mask.

"Good news," he says. "They found him."

I rub my eyes. "Found who?"

"The man who shot Dad. How fast can you get ready?"

"Huh?" I say.

"How fast do you think you can get into your suit?"

"Pretty fast, why?"

"Do it. Tony and Vince are already in the car. He's vulnerable, but we need to act fast."

Vince.

"Do you need me? I have school tomorrow, and . . ."

"Dude," says Luke. "Do you really think Dad will be okay with you sitting this out? He's the guy responsible. We need to make him pay. Key word: *we*."

He's right.

Dad would never let me sit this out.

I close my door and lightly slap my face a few times to try to totally wake up.

Come on, dude, get back here.

As quickly as I can, I get dressed in my suit. I haven't done my tie up yet, but I figure I can do that in the car. I push my feet into my dress shoes. Last, I retrieve my mask. I look at it for a second, then I shove it in my pocket and step outside.

Luke is still out in the hallway, leaning against the wall.

"Have you got your mask?"

I nod and show him.

He stares at me for a second, and I think he's going to say something. But then he just turns, and we go through the house. Dad is waiting for us. He's leaning against the kitchen island.

"Make him pay," he says. "I would, if I was strong enough."

"We will," says Luke.

I just nod.

Then we go out the front door to a burner car that's waiting for us in our driveway.

Inside, classical music is playing. Tony is in the driver's seat, and Vince is beside him.

"Are you sure you're up for this?" asks Tony.

I nod and put my seat belt on.

Tony starts the engine and pulls away from the curb.

* * *

I feel queasy for the entire drive.

This is so wrong.

Someone is going to die tonight, and there's nothing I can do to stop it.

They tried to kill my dad. I should want this. I should need this, like everyone else in the car needs it.

I don't, though.

I stare out the window. It's pitch-black outside, and the road is empty.

I'm too scared to even cry. Mostly I feel like I'm going to throw up.

I hate this.

I hate it so much.

All I want is to be someone else. Someone who doesn't have to do stuff like this.

We end up driving for about half an hour. I only just manage to keep myself from freaking out and telling Luke that I want to leave.

Tony parks in front of a single-story, slate-gray house.

There's a flower garden out the front. It's nice.

Vince hands each of us a pair of black earmuffs. Military-grade.

"Masks on," he says. He sounds just like Dad.

I pull mine on.

It feels tight and scratchy against my face. Then, copying Vince, I put my earmuffs on, and the world falls into fuzzy silence. Luke is wearing a mask now, and with his new, bulky frame, and dressed in a black suit, he looks like a true criminal, just like Vince and Tony.

Tony glances at me, and then at Luke.

We both nod.

We open the car doors at the same time.

I get out of the car on the side that isn't facing the house and duck down so I'm shielded. Just in case they're expecting us.

Vince and Tony open the trunk of the car.

There are four black guns. One for each of us.

Vince grabs one. Then Tony does, followed by Luke.

I grab the last of the guns. It's cold and heavy in my hands. We walk out to the middle of the road and stand in a line.

I can't do this. I can't be this person. I can't shoot at someone.

Vince raises his gun. Luke and Tony do the same thing.

I do as well.

And then Luke pulls the trigger.

The gunfire is so loud. Deafening, even. The glass front window of the house shatters as bullets shred the house. Bits of plaster explode off the walls. The peppering of bullets is relentless.

I join in, aiming low. I know how to shoot; Dad made me take lessons when I was younger. I started with a handgun and then moved up until I learned how to shoot one of these. I hated it even then, I guess because I knew I wouldn't be aiming at paper targets forever.

I aim at the garden out the front. I hope our shots will all blend together so nobody will notice what I'm doing.

There's a gunshot, higher pitched than the others, and then I see a spark on the ground to my left.

They returned fire.

I crouch and run back to the car. There are more sparks on the ground.

My heart pounds so hard. Luke, Tony, and Vince join me behind the car.

Bullets speak against the front of the car. Luke is staring at the ground. I think he's concentrating. Counting, maybe.

There's a lull. Luke stands up, and aims his gun over the roof of the car.

He fires. I hear a single shout.

I know I'm never going to get that sound out of my head. For the rest of my life, it'll be etched in.

The night stills.

I think he hit him. Luke has finally done it.

He's killed someone.

"It's done," says Luke. "Let's go."

We all climb into the car, and I catch a glimpse of the house. It's totally shredded. Through the shattered windows, I can see a body on the ground. He's barefoot. We might've woken him.

I look down.

The once pretty flower garden has now been totally eviscerated. I was a part of this. A man is dead, and I was a part of it.

That's undeniable.

I stare out the window again.

Tony plants his foot on the gas, and we speed away, into the night.

CHAPTER TWENTY-THREE

JASON IS LEANING AGAINST THE PINK WALL OF THE SUNSHINE Diner.

It was his idea for our first date.

It's the same chain as the one we went to on the night we met, but it's not the same location. That one is too close to the bar where my family hangs out, which meant I wouldn't be able to relax. If it's even possible to relax on my first-ever date. Or at all, given everything.

I can't stop thinking about Ryan. And about the unknown man Luke killed a few nights ago.

Yet we keep pretending we're just ordinary guys, not involved in the underworld at all. I know we both want that so badly. But still. How long can we keep pretending?

Jason has his earbuds in. He's nodding his head along to whatever he's listening to. He's so damn cute. Even with everything going on, I can't help but notice that. He's wearing a casual green button-down, skinny jeans, and sneakers.

I love that he's wearing a button-down. It nails home that this is a date.

The lot is dimly lit, with most of the light coming from the neon sign on the front of the diner. I weirdly love the mix of neon and nighttime. Something about it is kind of cinematic.

Jason notices me and raises a hand.

Everything feels so surreal.

I'm on a date. Not only with a boy, but with *Jason*. The sweet, gay gamer, who gets me in a way nobody ever has. A freaking star baseball player, who is smart and funny and *so* damn hot.

But he's Jason *Donovan*.

How can I keep ignoring that part of him?

But I needed to see him. Even though he's a Donovan, he's the one person who gets it. Nobody else I know understands how I feel about this world. Everyone else expects me to be fine with the fact that Luke killed someone a few nights ago. I'm supposed to be happy about it, even.

Not Jason, though.

I feel like he gets it. Gets *me*.

It's hypnotic.

I climb out of the car.

"You're early," I say as I close my car door.

I'm also early, as it's ten to seven, when we planned on meeting at seven. It's only just dark out.

"What can I say," he says, shrugging. "I was excited."

I get that.

"Me too."

He walks over and hugs me, which sends a buzz straight to my head. We step away from each other, and through my daze I realize he's had a haircut since I last saw him. The sides are buzzed to his scalp, and the top is perfectly sculpted, swept over to the side and pressed down with product.

It's very militaristic.

It makes me think of him as a soldier. That's what he is, I guess.

"What?" he asks.

"You got a haircut."

He chuckles, and touches it. "Yeah. Do you like it?"

"It looks so good, dude."

"Aw, shucks. You're too kind."

Inside is similar to the other Sunshine Diner. Complete with the palm tree painting on the wall.

There's an old jukebox at the far right. It's playing some old-ass song.

We both sit down at a booth near the back.

"I've got to confess something," he says.

Oh God.

"What?"

He raises a shaking hand. "I'm so nervous. So if I say something weird, let me off the hook, 'kay?"

I laugh. "What are you nervous about?"

"It's a date, you know? And I want it to be good."

"Oh, right. I'm nervous about that, too, by the way. So don't stress."

I glance around. The place is almost empty. Our company is just the fry cook and the server, plus two customers. One is a balding man who is slouched over a newspaper, drinking a coffee, and the other is a blond girl. She has a half-drunk vanilla milkshake in front of her, and her cheeks are wet with tears. I guess she's been stood up, given how nice her clothes and makeup are.

She catches me looking and gives me a pretty killer death stare.

Rightfully so, I was totally being a snoop.

I have a reason to be, though.

I just want to make sure nobody at the diner knows me. Through the window beside us, I can see the main road, and beyond that, the city skyline. Palm trees line the road, their fronds swaying in the breeze.

"I like this place," he says. "It's cooler than the other one."

"Right? I was thinking the same thing."

The server refills the guy at the bar's coffee, and the cook slaps a burger down onto the grill. It starts sizzling.

So here we are.

On a date.

Earlier today I read a few guides online to find out good questions to ask.

"So," I say. "I have a question."

"Go ahead."

"If you could live anywhere in the world, where would you pick?" I ask.

He narrows his eyes and smiles. "Did you study for this?"

The way his eyes have lit up tells me that I can tell him the truth.

"Er, yeah. How'd you know?"

"That's adorable. I don't know if I should tell you this, but I think I read that same guide. Third one down if you google 'good first date questions,' right? My next question for you is 'What band or musician do you never get tired of?' which is from that article."

I laugh. "Well, apparently first dates are about finding common ground, so I'm going to mark this as a win."

"For sure."

"But just answer my question, I actually want to know."

"All right," he says. "Hmm. I think it'd be fun to live in London. I've never been, but I feel like it'd be really cool."

"I can totally see you in London!" I sigh wistfully. "Just think of the coats."

"Dude, yes! The coats are a huge part of the reason I want to go there. I'd get a really preppy one and basically live in it. Plus, I've always wanted to do all the Harry Potter stuff you can do over there. But anyway, I'm super curious now. Same question, back at you."

"LA, hands down. But I want to be there for more than a year. I want to live there. I don't know if I ever will, but I want to. I've never told anyone that, but yeah, it's gotta be LA."

"Because you like movies, right?"

I nod. "There might be more to it, though. I feel like there's something really special about it as a city. I've wanted to move there since the first time I saw *Mulholland Drive*. I'm not sure if that's weird."

"No, that's awesome. See, now I know something new about you. Thank you, internet."

"Ha, yeah."

"But, dude . . ."

"Yeah?"

"LA is about as far away from here as you can go without leaving the country. Should I read anything into that?"

I shrug. I guess I can answer.

"Maybe, I dunno. Like I said, it's just a pipe dream, it's never going to happen. I'm going to be here forever, with my family."

"Do you want to talk more about that?"

"Dude, no."

"What?"

"I told you, I don't want to talk about my family."

"This is a date, though, yeah? How come it's off-limits?"

I chew my lip.

"Oh," he says, his face falling. "You don't fully trust me, do you?"

I try to decide how to answer. "Do you want me to be honest?"

"Always."

"Okay. It's like . . . I really like you. And I always have so much fun hanging out with you. But there's always this part of me that thinks the scheme might still be in place. So if I talk to you about my family . . ."

"I'll tell it to my family."

"Exactly."

"Well, that's going to make dating pretty hard if I can't even ask you about real stuff."

"Yeah. I guess it will. I just don't feel comfortable."

He stares at the table. I think I might've hurt his feelings.

Which I get. I'm basically telling him I don't trust him. Which I don't, at least not completely. But still. I do really care about him. And maybe I'm just being a coward. He hurt me once, by being a part of the scheme in the first place. He came clean, though. How long do I need to be distrustful of him?

A middle-aged waitress in a white shirt under red suspenders appears by our table. There are huge dark circles under her eyes, like she's been working nonstop for hours. She lifts her tablet and stares at us blankly.

"You ready?" she asks.

"Yeah, um, I'm going to go for a double cheeseburger with bacon, and a chocolate shake," says Jason. "I'm bulking. And a plate of waffle fries for both of us. Thanks."

"I'll have what he's having," I say. "I'm not bulking; it just sounds good."

"Great."

She takes our menus, then walks off to the register. Jason rests his hands on the table.

"So, my turn," he says. "Here's my question: Which musician do you never get sick of? Like who's your favorite?"

I guess we're just going to ignore what I said before. That suits me really well.

"The Killers. I like *Sam's Town* best."

"Oh, right, you told me that. Sorry."

"Oh, no worries. Anyway, um, do you like them?"

"To be honest, I only really know 'Mr. Brightside,' and that one about being human or a dancer or something. What do you like about them so much?"

"I dunno. I love them, they just click with me, they have ever since I first listened to them. I think maybe it's because I have this weird love of small-town Americana, and *Sam's Town* kind of sounds like that."

"Oh, nice."

Silence falls. I shift in my seat.

"Have you decided what your favorite band is yet?" I ask.

"Maybe? I've been thinking about it, and I really like Marshmello. I saw him at a festival Bri dragged me to, and that was fun, and I do work out to him. I listen to him the most, so he's probably my number one right now."

I open the notes app on my phone.

"What are you doing?" he asks.

"Writing a note about him, so I don't forget. I only know his big songs."

"Nice. I can message you his best songs, if you want. And you can do the same for me with the Killers."

"Yes, please!"

"Cool." He runs his fingers along the edge of his menu.

The silence gets awkward.

Is this going badly? It feels a little like it is. I get the impression he's still pretty put out that I don't trust him. It makes talking about music and things seem silly and pointless.

I never thought I'd think that.

We chat for a while, keeping it light, and soon, the server returns and places two delicious-looking cheeseburgers, along with a plate of waffle fries, down in front of us. I lift my burger and take a bite. It's *so* good.

We eat in silence for a few minutes.

"Okay," says Jason. "What's going on?"

I lower my burger. "What do you mean?"

"You seem like you're in your head, even more than normal. Are you not happy this is a date?"

"What? No, not at all. I mean, I'm very happy this is a date. Are you happy this is a date?"

"Yeah, I guess. It's just not what I thought it'd be."

I wipe my mouth. "What do you mean?"

"Well, you don't trust me; I didn't realize that. I'll be honest, that hurts."

I could lie. But it's Jason. He's the one guy I'm supposed to be totally honest with.

"I get that. And I'm really sorry. I just really don't want to be stupid. My whole family looks down on me. They think I'm stupid and weak. I really don't want to prove them right by giving up my secrets to a Donovan."

"Is that all I am now?"

I glance around, and see that nobody is within earshot.

We have privacy.

We can talk.

"No," I say. "Of course not."

"I just . . . I want to get to know you, you know? Like, who you really are."

He stares at me for a second.

"Is that okay?" he asks.

"I dunno."

"Oh."

He won't look me in the eyes.

"I like you, Jason. And I like this. Our friendship means so much to me. But I don't feel comfortable talking about my family to you. It doesn't mean I don't care about you; I really mean that."

"That's the thing," he says, leaning forward. "I think talking about our families will make this better. Seriously."

"You can't know that."

"No, but I'm about as sure as it's possible for me to be."

I pause, watching him, keeping solid eye contact. Then I glance down. It's just . . . it's not like he's been open at all about his family. I don't know anything about them because of our deal. It feels unfair almost that he wants me to go first, to take all the risk. "Can you just let me think about it?"

"Yeah, definitely."

"But would you be okay with us keeping our rule going, if I decide

I want that? Like, would it be okay with you if we *never* talk about our families?"

"I . . . I don't know. I always thought . . ."

"What?"

"I assumed we would talk about everything, at some point. I didn't realize you might never want that."

"Yeah," I say. "Right now, I think that's what I want. Anyway. This is a problem we can deal with later, right?"

He smiles weakly. "Yeah, sure."

After we've finished eating, Jason pays the bill, then returns to the table.

"No way," I say. "Let's split it."

He smirks. "It's already done."

I stand and throw a twenty-dollar bill at him. It flutters down to the table.

He picks it up, then steps closer, so he towers over me. I freeze, and my breath hitches. His expression is so serious, and I have no idea what he's doing. He rolls the cash up tightly, and sticks it into my front pocket. I go totally still and chew my lip. He taps it down, until only the top part is sticking out.

"Keep it," he says.

"You sure?"

He nods once.

I clear my throat. "Thanks."

We go outside. It's started sprinkling rain. I still feel shitty. And Jason seems really clammed up, too.

He and I stand in the lot, facing each other, lit by the neon, in front of our cars. We're getting gently rained on.

"Hey," he says. "I'm sorry. I shouldn't have asked you. We can pretend I didn't, if you want."

"No, don't be sorry. I want to know what you're thinking. But I already know. I'm never going to want to talk to you about my family. I just don't think it's a good idea."

"Oh."

"Is that okay?"

"Yeah, sure. It's like, whatever. Seriously, it's fine."

"It doesn't sound fine. Dude, talk to me."

"What can I say, Matt?" he says. "I just found out this guy I really like doesn't trust me. Why do you even hang out me with me if you think I'm capable of betraying you?"

"I don't think that."

"You do, though. You wouldn't keep secrets from me if you did."

"It's not about keeping secrets."

He hunches his shoulders, and the fight leaves him.

"Sure it is. Just tell me: What can I do to get you to trust me? Because anything you want, I'll do it. I know I made a mistake with the scheme, and I'm really sorry. But I promise you, I'm not trying to get your secrets anymore. I'm seriously not. All I want is to get to know you."

"I don't know if there's anything you can do. Just give me time, maybe?"

He smiles. "Sure. Well, thanks for a really nice night. I always have such a good time with you."

"No, thank you."

He rubs my arm. "Are you sure you're good?"

"Yeah. I'm fine. Are you good?"

"Yeah, totally. I'm going to head out, then, okay?"

"Okay."

He hugs me, but it feels nowhere near as good as the hug at the start of the date.

Oh boy. I really messed this up.

I want to cry.

He lets me go and then climbs into his car. I do the same with mine. I watch as he drives away.

And the moment he's gone, and I know he can't see me . . .

I break down.

CHAPTER TWENTY-FOUR

So my first date was a disaster.

It's totally mortifying. I can't stop thinking about it and cringing. But maybe I should've expected this. I am, you know, myself. And maybe it's possible my expectations were too high.

This isn't a movie. In real life first dates don't have to be perfect.

It's just . . . I thought my first date with Jason would be. And it wasn't. At all. That means something. I think it means something to him, too, as it's been nearly a week, and I haven't heard from him.

Maybe he's just giving me space, though. I know I wasn't the coolest. The hard part is I can see where he's coming from. Still, I don't think trusting him with info about my family is the best idea.

I truly don't know what to do.

Ugh.

Boys, man. They'll be the death of me.

I pull my pillow out from under me and quietly scream into it.

My phone chimes. I freak out. Every time in the past week that I've gotten a notification, I've had this feeling that something world-changing is about to happen. That it's going to be Jason on the other end.

But so far, the messages have been from other people. Luke, Cassidy. I stare up at the ceiling. It's not going to be him who messaged me.

The anticipation becomes too much, so I lift my phone.

And holy shit.

It's from Jason. Finally.

Hey, want to see a movie later?

I swear I can hear harps playing. Or something.

I don't even care what the movie is. I'd go see *Transformers* or some shit. I'd see anything with him.

I'm beaming as I type out my response:

Obviously, yes.

* * *

When we get to the movie theater, he opens the door for me. It's nearly empty inside, and we join the small line in front of the ticket booth. This cinema is decorated in this cool art deco style. I glance around, making sure I don't recognize anyone. Jason doesn't seem to care, which strikes me as odd.

He walks up to the ticket booth and buys two tickets before I can protest. He makes his way back and hands one to me.

"Do you want snacks?" he asks.

"I mean, always."

"Good answer."

He reaches into his pocket to pull out his wallet, but I stop him. "I can get them, you've paid for a bunch. What do you want?"

"You should be able to guess."

He grins.

"Come on, you know this, Mr. Movie Buff," he says. "They're the only acceptable movie snacks."

"Popcorn and a Coke?"

"Bingo."

"Um, you're forgetting about Junior Mints," I say.

"Wait, you actually like them? I thought they were just for grandpas?"

"That's Werther's. Junior Mints are the best. When was the last time you tried them?"

"I can't even remember."

"Want to?"

"Hell yeah."

He grins.

I buy two medium combos, and a pack of Junior Mints, and we walk upstairs. A girl takes our tickets and rips them in half. As we walk down the hall, I see a poster for the movie we're seeing: *The Tower*.

The poster shows two buff guys in front of a steel-blue background. Maybe fittingly, they're both are totally blue steel–ing it. It sinks in that this is a gay movie, so people could assume that Jason and I are on a date. I think we pass as friends normally, but here, maybe not.

We enter the theater, and see that the trailers have already started. It's playing one starring a straight white dude in his midforties who's a secret agent or something. I dunno, it's one of the dozens they make that are basically the same each year. One of the ones that might as well be called *TESTOSTERONE*. We make our way up the steps and sit in the very back row, a little to the side. The theater is maybe three-quarters full. The roof has this cool golden pattern on it, and the walls are red and black. There's a reason I suggested this cinema; it's by far the coolest in the city.

I open the Junior Mints and offer them to him, rattling them. He takes the box and tries a handful, then smiles.

"What do you think?" I ask.

"You're right," he says. "These are, like, way too good. Totally not just for grandpas."

Success!

"Right?"

He pulls them away, so I have to reach over and grab the box to take them back. We wrestle for a second, then we remember we're in public and settle, both smiling.

The movie is about this guy who interns at a new tech company, only to discover that the people he's working for are incredibly evil.

The main actor is really cute, an ex-Disney star I think, and there's a weird number of shots of him stressing about his life in a futuristic shower. The camera lingers on his newly crafted abs multiple times, which I appreciate. But I'm sitting next to Jason, and I've got a massive sugar high from the Junior Mints, so it's hard to focus on the movie.

I turn and look at him. His profile is lit up by the screen. He looks like the lead from an old classic, like the ones who had to keep who they liked a secret to be leading men.

Jason catches me looking, then his hand brushes the back of my palm.

He moves a little, close enough that his leg is as close to mine as it can be without actually touching. Still staring forward, he offers his hand to me.

I take it.

* * *

The movie was great.

Under different circumstances, it might've even become a new favorite. But I straight-up don't have the space to obsess over something new right now. We're out of the theater now, on the street. It's humid as hell, and the air is thick. Around us, people hurry by, trying to get back to air-conditioning as fast as possible.

I watch as a sleek black Mercedes drives past us.

Its windows are so dark I can't see inside.

"Are you hungry?" asks Jason, pulling me back to earth.

"I mean, always."

He smiles. "Me too. What do you feel like?"

I can't help but think about that car. What if I know them? What if, right now, word about who I'm with is getting back to Dad?

"Waffle fries?" I suggest.

"Yes! Oh my God, we're so doing this."

His smile is infectious and makes my spiraling brain shut up. It'll be fine.

He pulls out his phone and starts looking up restaurants.

"There's one a five-minute walk away."

"Perfect."

He sets off down the street. I follow after him.

He turns his hand, and offers it to me.

I know we held hands during the whole movie. But this is different. This is out in public.

"Sorry," I say. "I'm not ready."

He clenches his hand into a fist. "Hey, no worries. I get it."

"I liked it during the movie, though!"

He smiles, but it's obviously fake. We reach the restaurant. His eyes are still downcast.

"Hey," I say. "What's up?"

"Nothing."

That's so obviously not the case.

"Is this about the holding-hands thing? Because I—"

"It's not just that," he says. "Sorry, I'm being really moody."

"That's fine. What's on your mind?"

"I shouldn't say."

"No, you can. Tell me."

"Okay. Have you thought more about the family thing?"

"I mean, a little."

"And? I can't stop thinking about it. It's been a while, I was hoping maybe you'd changed your mind."

Wait, is *this* why he didn't message me for a week? So I'd change my mind?

"Oh, um," I say. "I don't think I'm going to change my mind. I'm pretty sure not talking to you about my family is the right call."

"But for how long?"

"I don't know. I'm really sorry, and I'm trying, I just . . ."

"Don't trust me."

I press a knuckle to my forehead. "It's not that. I get how this must make you feel, and I'm really sorry. Can't we just ignore this, like we used to?"

He shakes his head. "I don't think I can anymore."

"What does that mean?"

I think he just gave me an ultimatum.

"I'm trying my best," he says. "But it's really hard to date a guy who has this big section of his life totally off-limits to me. How are we supposed to get close if you're never going to talk about real stuff?"

"I don't know."

"I don't know, either. That's the problem."

That lingers between us.

"I really like you," I say. "You know that, right?"

"I do. But I also feel like I don't really know you."

"What? How can you think that?"

"I just do. You always say we're such good friends, but you never tell me anything real about you. And anytime I try, you shut me down really hard."

"I know, and I'm sorry. I just . . ."

He looks really upset, and I want to do anything I can to stop it.

"I just feel like you don't care about me," he says. "It's not a good feeling, man."

I feel tears prickle. "I do care about you! So much!"

"Then talk to me! Open up. I know it's hard, but I think this is worth it. Show me you trust me."

"I can't."

His features harden.

"I'm not really hungry anymore," he says. "I think I might head out."

"Wait, really?"

"I'll message you, okay?"

"Um, sure."

He squeezes my arm, then ducks away. He's walking, but I feel like he's running away.

CHAPTER TWENTY-FIVE

HEY THERE. I HAVE SOMETHING TO ASK YOU.

I'm lying diagonally across my bed, with my legs dangling over the edge, listening to a new playlist I made.

It's the first time in days that Jason has messaged me.

I feel like he was waiting for me to message him.

And I wanted to. Obviously. But another part of me felt like he was being pretty unfair. He tried to trick me once. I think it's fair for me to not completely trust him. I still get how he feels, but I can't just make myself trust someone. Especially someone who has tried to trick me once before.

Then again, I do see his point. He doesn't really know me, and I don't really know him. Until we're open with each other, we aren't even that close. I know we have a lot in common, but it's all more superficial things.

It's enough to be friends, but if we want to go further than that, which I guess is the whole point of dating, then we need to go further.

It's Monday night, and I've been avoiding all the homework I should be doing by listening to music. Mostly I'm listening to slightly sad songs, because I'm pretty sure Jason and I are going down in flames. And I don't know how to stop it. I just can't see myself being comfortable telling him about my family, and until I can, we can't progress.

Still, every time I hear a song I really like, I want to message him about it. Like, I want him to know about the song "For Reasons

Unknown," which makes me think of the drive Luke took me on when he first got his car, where we drove by the beach and he played it way too loud. We sung along, and it was, like, a perfect night. That was before Luke got so into the family stuff.

Would it be so bad to tell him?

I want Jason to know these things about me.

I just don't want to be stupid.

I type out a response:

What's up?

Not much. I've just been thinking . . .

Oh yeah? About what?

The family thing. You're right, I've been too intense. I'm really sorry, and I'm going to take a step back. I was out of line.

You're totally fine, man. I get it. I'm sorry I'm so closed off.

No, don't be! I know I need to prove to you I'm trustworthy. So I have this idea. How would you feel about getting out of the city for a weekend?

What do you mean?

I think you and I should go on a trip, just for a weekend. Thoughts?

I mean, I would love that.

I can't, though. Dad would never let me.

What do you mean?

I was hoping you'd be a little more enthusiastic. I've already booked tickets. There was this deal I found, and I impulse bought them. My mom booked the hotel room for me, she thinks I'm going with Bri and Naomi.

You what???

Yeah man. You, me, and LA. This weekend. You in?

My mouth is hanging open.

I can't let myself entertain this idea, though.

That's really nice, but I'd never be allowed to go. Thanks though. You have no idea how fun that sounds to me.

Then find a way, man! I booked us this hotel:

He sends through a bunch of photos. It's the Four Seasons.

So really nice.

Just think about it. We could see the actual Mulholland Drive! Plus, you, me, and this room. With total privacy. Think about it.

Is he implying what I think he is?

I read his message again and decide that, yeah, he totally is. I feel like any hotel room would do for that. I don't know why we'd need to go to LA for that, other than it's my favorite city. And it'd put a bunch of actual distance between us and our families.

That sounds so nice.

And think about it I do. I imagine Jason kissing me like he did at the baseball stadium, just, in a room.

We wouldn't need to stop.

We could do whatever we wanted.

Where'd you get the money for this?

I work for my uncle as a mover, remember? I have cash to burn, and seriously, the flights were really cheap.

This is so much.

It's, like, incredibly nice.

And I can't stop thinking about what we'd do in a room together.

And you promise not to ask about my family when we're away?

I promise. If you ever decide you want to open up to me, then I would love that. But I'd get it if you don't ever want to. I just want to go back to having fun with you. That's what this is about.

This is maybe the nicest thing anyone has ever done for me. A vacation. To my favorite city.

And just thinking about it is enough to make my heart swell.

A weekend away. From the city, from the war.

I don't think Dad will let me go, though.

But I think it's worth a shot.

* * *

It's been a day, and I've decided Luke is my best shot at getting Dad to let me go on the LA trip with Jason.

I knock on his door. I knock hard, because I know a lot of the time he has headphones in.

"What?" he calls.

"Can I come in?"

"Yeah, sure."

I open the door. Luke's been playing his guitar. He's still holding it, but he's taken his headphones off. He's wearing his college T-shirt. *Go Gators!* I go inside and close the door behind me. Eddie's dozing on the end of his bed. I give him a head scratch.

"What's up?" asks Luke.

"I need a favor."

"It'll cost you."

"I know."

He strums on his guitar. "What do you want?"

"You know the girl I'm seeing?"

"The one who totally isn't Cass, you mean?"

"Yeah, her. Well, we sort of have this weekend away planned."

"Oh shit," he says. "You guys really are serious now?"

"Yeah, I guess."

He smiles. "Nice, man. When are you going to let me meet her?"

"Soon, maybe. But I need your help. I want to go on the trip, but I don't think Dad will let me go."

"Oh, he definitely won't."

"I know. So I was wondering if you have any idea of how I could get him to let me go."

"Hmm." His eyebrows furrow. "I guess I could say you and I are going on a trip?"

"What do you mean?"

"I could say you and I are going camping or something for a weekend. We could say we've had it planned for ages. Dad never listens, anyway, so if we're casual about it, he'd buy it."

"You think so?"

"I know so."

For the first time, I allow myself to really entertain the idea that Jason and I might be able to go on the trip.

It makes me giddy.

He nods. "You'd majorly owe me, though."

"What do you want?"

"Anytime Eddie needs a bath for the next year, you're doing it."
Oh no.

Eddie's cute, but he hates baths with a burning passion. He always tries to run away and always makes a huge mess. It's an ordeal.

"Okay."

"And I want your old Xbox."

"Why do you want that?"

"Nostalgia, I guess."

It does sting to part with it, but it has been sitting in my closet for a few years.

"Fine, it's yours."

He taps his chin. What else could he possibly want from me?

"I also want to be able to use you as an excuse sometime in the future. No questions asked, all right?"

"Sure."

"Then we have a deal."

Holy shit.

That means I'm going.

CHAPTER TWENTY-SIX

JASON BOOKED THE FLIGHTS FOR PRETTY EARLY IN THE morning, so we'll have nearly two full days in LA before we need to get back for school. We've checked in, and now we're sitting in the airport lounge, waiting to board.

Luke was right, Dad totally bought the lie. I guess it's because he trusts Luke so much.

Anyway.

I'm not thinking about my family this weekend.

While we wait for our flight, I've been reading and Jason's been gaming.

A part of me can't believe this is happening.

That I'm doing this.

A really hot guy wants to go on a weekend getaway with me.

We'll share a hotel room.

I'm like 90 percent sure I'm going to lose my virginity on this trip.

I think I'm ready. I've done a lot of research on the internet about how to have a safe—and enjoyable—time. I think I've covered all the bases. After a slightly embarrassing trip to the convenience store, I have everything I'll need.

Or *we'll* need.

I'm pretty nervous. I mean, I care about Jason a lot, and I really want to have a good time. I think I will. I know I'm so attracted to him. But I just know how awkward I can be physically. My body isn't something I have complete control over.

I think Jason will get all of this, though.

I don't think he'll be nervous about it. I just get the impression he's a fairly sexual person, and he will just know what he's doing.

"Hey," he says. "Whatcha thinking about?"

"Oh, um, not much."

"You just look a little worried. Are you a nervous flier?"

I feel like saying that is better than admitting I was thinking about us having sex.

"Yeah, a little."

He smiles. "That's so cute. You'll be fine. This is a lot safer than swimming at night, and you did that just fine."

"Good point."

I feel like I finally have the old Jason back. He got weirdly pushy for a while there. Now I feel like there's no pressure on me. He's just my friend. I think we're still dating, but I'm not sure how to label us yet, as we're definitely not boyfriends. I don't think we could ever get there until I trust him enough to tell him about my family.

A voice over the intercom tells us that the flight is boarding.

"Ready?" he asks.

"Ready."

* * *

The flight passed pretty quickly.

Jason and I set up a little gaming hub, using our tray tables. We played a lot of *Smash Bros*. I even won a few matches, but I suspect he was going easy on those ones. He even had a small nap on the plane.

As he did, he rested his head on my shoulder. I let him. I didn't even care that people could see us.

It was the cutest thing.

He looks so delicate when he sleeps. So vulnerable. It did funny things to my chest.

It's kind of weird, but I feel lighter than I have in months. I'm away from my family. I have as close to total freedom as I will ever get.

This was such a good idea.

Jason moves away from me to adjust the handle on his bag. Maybe I'm taking him for granted. He's been so great. He told me about the scheme. He told me about who he really is. Why can't I trust him? What's wrong with me?

He was right, before. It really is hard to date while I keep a big part of who I am totally sectioned off from him. I am totally half-assing my relationship with him. And that will never last. Sometime soon, I'll need to decide. I should either fully commit and tell him everything.

Or I need to let him go.

The thought of that generates such a strong reaction in me. I can't do that.

"You want a coffee? I feel like we should be basic LA gays and get iced coffees."

"Yes!"

We wheel our bags through the airport and find a Starbucks. Soon we're both holding jumbo iced coffees. Basic, but delicious. Together, we head outside. And hello, there's the sunshine. It feels way different from Florida. It's missing a lot of the humidity. There's just something about this city that makes me feel good.

"Have you ever been here?" I ask.

He shakes his head. "No, never. Have you?"

"Yeah, once."

"And you liked it?"

"I loved it."

"Cool."

We find the Four Seasons hotel shuttle and board it, sitting in the back row. Like we're rebels or cool kids. For the first time, I think people seeing us might consider us as a couple, not friends. Because we're miles away from home, I actually freaking love the thought. Jason keeps bumping into me, or touching me. I have no reason to stop him.

So I don't.

I love the drive to the hotel. I spend it listening to music and looking out the window, at everything. LA isn't the prettiest of cities—it's so flat and hazy with pollution. But who cares? I love it.

For one thing, there are movie billboards everywhere.

This is where they're made.

Well, a lot of them. I know because of tax breaks they film in a lot of weird places now. Like Georgia. Or Canada. But, still, LA will always be the heart of the industry.

We reach the hotel and whoa.

It's stunning.

It's a tall white building with gleaming windows. I feel like such an adult, doing this. We get our bags, tip the driver, and then go through the automatic doors into the lobby. It's so grand, with this cool artwork hanging from the ceiling. It's like a modern chandelier.

"Happy?" asks Jason.

"So happy. This is amazing. Are you?"

"Honestly, I don't think I've ever felt better. They have no control over us now—how cool is that?"

"It's so cool."

He checks in, and then we take the elevator up to our room. We're really high up.

We reach our room, and he opens the door.

Oh my God.

There's a massive window curving around the whole space, giving a great view of the city and the blue sky. It's so vivid. I've never stayed in a room as nice as this.

Also.

There's only one bed.

"Oh," says Jason. "I asked for two beds. Let's go back . . ."

I grab hold of his shirt, and pull him to me. "Don't."

He grins. "Really?"

I nod. I guide him across the room, to the window. Behind us, the city stretches out. I hope these windows are darkened, so nobody can see him.

I push him against the wall and kiss him.

I'm just so grateful. For everything. It's been so long since we've touched like this. Far too long. My body craves it. It ramps up quickly, becoming hard and fast. Just when it starts getting really good, he pulls back an inch. I growl, then lean forward to kiss him, but he pulls back again. The part of me that craves him claws at my chest.

"What's wrong?" I ask.

"We only have two days here, we should make it count." He taps my chest. "Which for me means doing whatever you'd like. We could do anything, as long as you're happy."

I roll my eyes. "Come on."

Being here makes me feel bold.

"We could . . . ," I say.

He smiles. "You want to?"

I nod.

"Can I, then?" he asks.

"Go ahead."

He pulls my shirt off and throws it away. He turns back and kisses me. I stop him, and he gets the idea and quickly unbuttons his shirt. As soon as it's undone, we crash together. We spin. He kisses me so hard my entire back touches the cold glass.

I move away, and we shuffle toward the bed, still kissing. We reach the edge of the bed and kick off our shoes. I take my socks off as quickly as possible and toss them away.

He does the same, then slowly takes off his shirt.

So here we are.

Both shirtless, our chests heaving.

He moves toward me.

"Hey, you," he says.

"Hi."

We kiss. As we do, his hands go down, his knuckles brushing my stomach, and he undoes my belt.

Or, he tries to. It gets stuck, bunched up in one of the loops.

I laugh and press myself against him. He's really warm.

"Oh man," he says, then he rests his forehead against my shoulder. "Did I just ruin this?"

"It's just a dumb belt."

I stand still as he figures it out, and he pulls off my belt. Then he kisses me, all while his hands are busy with my pants. He gets them undone, then yanks down, exposing the top half of my underwear.

He pauses.

"Is this okay?" he asks.

"Yeah. Are you good?"

"Yeah, definitely. This happened a lot faster than I thought it would."

"Really?"

"I mean, no, not really."

He smiles. It's so cute I just have to kiss him.

I watch as he undoes his belt, then pulls his pants down. I do the same with mine. He's wearing red-and-black-striped boxer briefs. I'm in plain gray. I readjust them.

Now we're both in our underwear, but that's it.

I glance at the bed, then back at him.

This might be a bad idea.

But since when have I cared about that?

"Do you want to?" he asks. His voice is kind of froggy. "Maybe we shouldn't."

"Why not?"

"I just want this to be special. Is it, for you?"

"Hey, dude, look at me. This is *so* special. This is, like, perfect."

"You promise you're telling the truth?"

"I promise."

"Good. Because this is a big deal for me, too."

From the way he sounds, I guess he's a virgin, too. How has he not done it? Surely he's had the chance.

"So you've never . . . ?" I ask.

"No, I've hooked up a few times, but nothing like this. Have you?"

"Nope. Is that a problem?"

"Not at all."

"Good. Um, sorry to bring this up, but I want to use protection, just in case. Is that okay?"

"Yeah, me too."

He moves closer.

"Are we really going to do this?" I ask. "Right now?"

"I think so."

He smiles at me, and I smile back.

Then he pushes me onto the bed.

CHAPTER TWENTY-SEVEN

I WAKE UP AND AM HIT WITH AN INTENSE FEELING.

I might not be sure about much at the moment. But I know this.

I love Jason.

I turn my head slowly so I don't wake him. Dawn light streams in through the window that curves around the hotel room. It's really pretty. I glance down. Jason's beside me, fast asleep. He's curled and facing away from me, his lower half covered by a white sheet.

Yep.

I love him.

Yesterday was perfect. After we hooked up, we showered and then just spent the day being tourists. We checked out the Hollywood Walk of Fame, the TCL Chinese Theatre, then took an Uber to Mulholland Drive. We ended the day with room service, and then we hung out in the hotel hot tub until the security guard kicked us out.

It was perfect.

The sight of him, in bed next to me, makes me feel overwhelmed.

I love him. A Donovan.

And I could lose him.

If I'm not honest with him, I will lose him. I need to trust him. He's not going to betray me. There's no way.

It's settled.

When he wakes up, I'm going to tell him everything about me and my family.

I'm going to give him the power to destroy me.

I guess that's what love is. That's how it always seems in movies. If it's not world-shattering, something is wrong.

He shifts. I think he might be awake, just dozing. I need to tell him. I need to do it right now, before I chicken out.

But then I bail.

What if I'm making a huge mistake?

He opens his eyes. He truly is so handsome. He grabs my arm, and pulls me across, so I'm spooning him.

Oh.

This is nice.

Maybe I don't need to do anything so drastic just yet. I close my eyes, and let myself relax.

By the time I wake up, the sun is out, and Jason is no longer beside me. I sit up. He's brushing his teeth. He's gotten dressed, in a gray T-shirt and swimming trunks. His hair's already perfectly done.

"Morning," he says.

"Hey."

He spits. "Sleep well?"

I stretch. "So well. You?"

"Same. Best in ages."

I get that. Even though I know telling Jason about my family is a big decision, I am feeling very relaxed right now. More relaxed than I have in recent memory, actually. I think it might have something to do with finally getting out of the city.

"So," I say. "What did you want to do today?"

"I was thinking we could go to the beach? As long as we get to the airport by five, we'll be fine."

"Cool."

That's where I'll do it.

The beach.

He walks over to me and falls down onto the bed. He kisses me. He tastes like toothpaste.

I pull back.

"What?" he asks.

"I think I've decided."

He props himself up. "Decided what?"

"I think I want to tell you about my family. You're right, this will never be real until I tell you everything."

"You sure? You don't have to, if you don't want to."

"I'm sure."

His smile is dazzling. "Cool."

"Don't think you're getting off the hook, though. You'll have to tell me stuff, too."

"Of course."

"So should I just, like, tell you now?"

He chews his lip. "Why don't you wait awhile? This is clearly a big deal for you, and the last thing I want is for you to regret it. So why don't you think about it for a few hours, and then, if you're still sure, you can tell me."

"Okay," I say. "Sounds like a plan."

* * *

I'm sure.

I totally respect that Jason wants to give me some time, to be completely and utterly sure about this.

I don't need it, though.

I'm sure.

I'm going to tell him about my family. I've been thinking about it the whole journey to the beach, and even though I've analyzed the crap out of it, I'm still totally confident this is the right move. Telling him everything there is to know about me will make this even better than it already is.

He asked me to really think this through, so I'm going to. I'm going to try to have a good time and not obsess over it. But I think this is one of those things I won't be able to stop thinking about until I've gotten it off my chest.

We both step out of the Uber.

The beach stretches out in front of us. It's crowded. Up ahead, there's a pink ice cream truck by a path to the beach. It looks a little hipster-y.

"Want one?" he asks.

"Yeah, for sure. Do you?"

He nods, so we join the line.

I don't think I've ever felt this good.

We reach the front of the line.

"Can I get a sundae, and then whatever this one wants?" He puts his hand on my shoulder.

"Can I get a choc-dipped cone?"

"You sure can," says the server. She's dressed in a pink-and-white-striped shirt. "You two are the cutest, by the way."

"Thanks."

"He's the cute one," says Jason.

I blush.

She hands us our ice creams, and Jason pays.

Then we start walking toward the beach. We both take off our flip-flops and walk. The sand is so warm. A pair of girls in bikini tops and denim shorts totally check Jason out as they pass us. One even lowers her sunglasses to ogle. It's right out of a CW show.

He stomps onward, oblivious.

He glances my way.

"What are you thinking about?" he asks.

"Just that the beach looks really nice today."

He tousles my hair with his free hand.

I smile.

We find an empty spot, and he tosses his towel down hard onto the ground. We sit down, and eat our ice cream.

"Now?" I ask.

He shakes his head. "Not yet. You really need to be sure."

"I am!"

"Just give it a little longer, okay?"

"Fine."

We finish our ice cream. My hands are all sticky now.

"Want to go for a swim?" he asks.

"Yeah."

We both stand. Then he grabs the hem of his shirt and pulls it off. I do the same with my shirt and throw it down onto his. He stretches, then adjusts his trunks, pulling them up a little higher.

I'm not over seeing him like this. Not even close.

I grab the sunscreen from my bag and start slathering it onto my chest. I feel like the palest person on this beach, so this will save my life. Without it I'd be beet red in half an hour. I put some on in the hotel room, but I really want to be sure I'm covered. The last thing I need right now is a sunburn.

He turns to me. "Want some help with that?"

"I've got it."

He frowns. "Oh."

"Unless you want to help?"

He nods and grins. "Turn around."

I hand him the sunscreen. He puts it onto my back. I close my eyes for a second as he rubs. The skin-to-skin contact, it's blissful. Once he's done, he turns around and I put sunscreen on his back.

He's so broad, and I love how he feels with the sunscreen on him. He's so slick.

"Am I good?" he asks.

"Yep. All safe."

"Awesome." He takes a step away. "Race you to the water?"

"You're on."

We both tear off, sprinting toward the ocean.

* * *

Jason and I are sitting on a bench in front of the path to the beach. There isn't a cloud in sight.

It's been another perfect day.

I don't want to leave.

I don't want to go back to Florida.

I'd stay here forever if I could.

We're listening to his playlist, with one earbud each, and he has his arm around me. His songs are all fast-paced and electronic. So, not my usual thing, but I'm into it, because he likes it.

He smells like salt, and he's so warm. I can feel it even through his shirt. His stare is fixed on the horizon. This close, I can see his jawline is just starting to show signs of honey-brown stubble. It's lighter than the hair on his head. I'm jealous, because it looks even, and my facial hair is still so patchy.

He rubs my arm. I nestle against him.

It's time.

Or, it's close enough for me. The song we were listening to ends.

I notice he's shaking.

"Hey," I say. "What's up?"

"I think I'm going to be sick."

I move a little away from him. "Like, actually, or . . ."

He leans forward, and starts breathing deeply. He's hunched over, and his shoulders are raised.

I don't know what to do.

He turns to face me. He's gone so pale. "Listen, Matt."

"Yeah?"

"I know you said you were going to talk about your family."

Oh fuck.

Something is clearly very wrong.

"Yeah?"

"You can't. Look at me, you can't tell me anything about them."

His eyes are wide.

"What? Why?"

He looks like he's in pain.

"What's going on?" I ask.

He pulls his shirt down a little.

In the middle of his chest, nearly invisible, is something that looks like a plastic circle. He obviously wasn't wearing it before; I would've noticed it. I think back, and he left for a little while before to go to the public bathroom. He took his backpack. He must've put it on then, before we came here.

Oh no.

I think I know what it is.

And why he wouldn't let me tell him about my family until we got here.

"What's that?" I ask. I need to know for sure.

There's horror in my voice.

He peels it off his skin, wincing as he does. It looked like it was stuck tight. There's now a red circle on his chest where it had been.

"It's a wire," he says. "It's new tech."

He tries scrunching it up in his hands, but that doesn't work, it's too flexible. So he pinches it, and rips it in half. Inside, I can see tiny wires, glinting in the sunlight.

I don't know what to say.

"So I was right?" I ask. "You are still trying to learn my family secrets."

"Yeah, I am. But it's not what you think."

I feel like I could be sick.

"I'm not who you think I am," he says.

I scoff. "You're right about that."

I'm only just managing to keep it together. I always had this fear, and it's because it was founded. Jason was pretending. He was still trying to learn the secrets about my family so he could tell his. The scariest part is I was about to tell him everything. I was seconds away from doing it.

But he stopped me.

Why?

"Matt, my last name . . . it isn't Donovan."

"What?"

"It was just a cover. If we got caught, we were told to tell you we're Donovans, to throw you off the scent. My mom thought your hatred of them would blind you to the truth."

"What truth?"

"About who we are. About who I really work for."

He reaches into his pocket and pulls out his phone. He swipes through and then turns it to show it to me.

It's a photo of Jason standing with a female cop. She's wearing the full uniform. The badge gleams against her chest. I look closer, and see the similarities. They have the same face shape, the same hair color, and even the same nose.

This can't be happening.

"I'm not a Donovan," he says. "My last name is Kendricks."

I look at the woman again.

His mom.

Jason isn't who he said he is.

He's the son of a cop.

PART THREE

CHAPTER TWENTY-EIGHT

"So let me get this straight," I say. "You're the son of a cop?"

"I am."

"And this whole time, you've just been trying to get to know me so you can tell your mom about my family."

"More or less, yes."

That all sinks in.

"Shit," I say.

"But, Matt, listen to me. I couldn't do it."

"Couldn't do what?"

"The scheme. I couldn't finish it. It's why I told you, before you told me anything they could use."

"If you think I'm going to believe anything you say *now* . . ."

"What else could I be hiding? What else could there possibly be?"

"I don't know," I say. "But I do recall thinking something similar the last time you did a big reveal about who you are. I thought: *He wouldn't have another secret.* There's no way. And yet, here we are."

"I know. And you never fully trusted me, did you? You always picked up that something was off."

I feel tears prickle. "Actually, I did. In the end, I did."

"Oh."

"So you know, good job. You're very good. Have you ever thought about going into acting?"

Tears fill his eyes, too.

"Why are *you* crying?" I ask.

"Because I don't want to be this person."

I do hate seeing him so put out.

Then I remember he deserves it.

"I wouldn't want to be you, either. You might be the worst person I've ever met. You *slept* with me."

He just nods.

"You made me think I'd made a friend. Do you even know how big of a deal that was for me?"

"No, I know. You told me, remember. At the hospital."

I'm sort of surprised he remembered that.

It was all fake.

Yet he remembered.

I take him in. I sort of can't believe I didn't see it before, but he looks like a rookie cop. With his crew cut and fit body, he fits in a lot more with that side of the law. I guess that's part of the reason I was so drawn to him. He's never belonged to my side of the world.

I get why that was appealing to me.

"This trip . . . was it just to get me away from my family?" I ask.

"Yeah. It was pretty obvious you wouldn't tell me anything. I was getting nervous, because I thought the longer I was with you, the more in danger I was in. So I needed to push you. Coming to LA was Mom's idea. The whole scheme was, actually."

"What about your friends? Couldn't they have given it away?"

He shakes his head. "They were in on it. You never went to my real school or met my real baseball team. The dance was another school's that we joined. We hired a few actors to pretend to be close to me, so that you'd trust me more. This was a huge project, man, led by my mom. She was constantly thinking of ways to get you to like me."

"She sounds like a real winner."

"You have no idea. She controls everything about my life. I didn't even want to be a part of the scheme. But she made me. She said I would do it, or I would find somewhere else to live. She said if I didn't, she'd get rid of my college fund and my trust."

"You expect me to feel sorry for you?"

"No. I just want you to know why I did it."

"Why doesn't really matter to me. You still did it."

He bows his head. "I know."

"You could've said no."

"Have you ever said no to anything your family has asked you to do?"

Huh.

I guess he does have me there.

"Don't turn this back on me. You're the liar here."

"And you're the one heading straight for a life of crime."

"I . . ."

I can't even disagree, because I know it's true.

"But that isn't you, Matt. I know it. I've known it the whole time. You were nothing like I was expecting. When I was told I had to befriend the son of a criminal, I thought I'd have to deal with a monster. But then I met you."

"I know," I say. "I'm such a disappointment, right?"

"Dude, no! That's not what I mean at all. You're this sweet, thoughtful guy. I know you, and I know you'd never hurt anyone.

You . . . you're a wonderful person. You're a good guy, just from a bad family. That was obvious to me straightaway."

I stare up. A few gulls are circling overhead. It's late afternoon now, so the sun is going down.

"Why are you even telling me this?" I say. "And why didn't you finish it? I was about to tell you everything. You know that, right?"

"Yeah, I do."

"So you had everything you wanted. But then you do this. Why? I mean, the sex was good, but it wasn't *this* good."

"I couldn't do it to you." He smiles. "And hey, don't talk down, you've got skills."

"If you expect me to believe that, and that you care about me, I—"

"But I do," he says. "Deeply. That's real."

"Fuck off."

That hits him hard.

I almost feel bad.

Almost.

He's a monster. He's lied to me and manipulated me. So what if he had a point about our parents making us do things that we don't want to do? He still came so freaking close to ruining not only my life but also that of my whole family.

My family wouldn't go to prison.

They just wouldn't.

They'd fight the cops with everything they have. They'd die before they let the cops win.

He'd know this if he talked to me.

He also would've been dooming me to an incredibly painful

death. If word got out that I was the one who told the son of a cop the secrets of my family, then I would've been hunted down. Nowhere would be safe, as I'd be my family's biggest target. The whole criminal underworld would want me dead.

No matter where I ran, one day, they'd find me.

I know men like Vince save their worst tortures for snitches.

Jason came within seconds of dooming me to that fate. Of practically killing my entire family. Of dooming me to a short life on the run, then an incredibly painful death. I came within seconds of that reality coming true.

It doesn't matter that he stopped.

I can never forgive him.

"Do you hate me?" he asks.

"You don't want to know."

Which, honestly, is an answer.

"This is so fucked," he says.

He's started crying, which surprises me. I never really thought of Jason as the sort of guy who'd cry.

But he is now.

Good, I think. *He should feel bad about this.*

"Well," I say. "I better head home. Um, what are we going to do about the flights?"

He wipes his eyes. "What do you mean?"

"Obviously I'm not going to hang out with you anymore. I think getting on a flight together would be so unbearably awkward."

"Right. Take your ticket. I'll move my flight to later on tonight."

He picks up his phone. He can do that from here. He emailed my ticket to me earlier, so I already have it on my phone.

This sounds like a good plan.

"So you really don't want to see me again?" he asks.

Not bloody likely.

I think back to when I first met him. When I ran into him in the bathroom. It wasn't a random meeting. He was in there, on purpose. To pick a target.

He chose me.

I get why, but it still hurts.

"I don't think I can. I can barely even look at you right now."

He nods. "Okay. Well, for the record, I want you to know that, for me, this friendship is real. I know you might not believe that, and you have no reason to ever trust me again. But I really do consider you a friend of mine. If you ever decide you want to be friends again, you can always message me. Okay?"

"How would that even work?" I ask.

"What do you mean?"

"You're the son of a cop. I'm the son of a criminal. I'm sorry if I'm being too on the nose, but that's a horror show waiting to happen if I've ever heard one."

"You've thought we were on opposite sides before, and you made it work."

Yeah, but I honestly feel like the cops are a step further than his being a Donovan. Sure, we've been at war with them for the past year, and it's been tense since the fifties. But people like me have been fighting with cops forever. It's been nonstop. There is no circumstance where we will totally get along.

"This is different. We can't be friends. We're fundamentally incompatible."

His face falls.

I think that's a good note to end on, so I pick up my backpack. He just watches me.

I sort of hate this. But for some reason, a part of me is hoping he'll stop me. That he has more to say.

He doesn't, though. He just sits there, looking crestfallen.

That's where I leave him.

I walk away and don't look back.

* * *

I didn't cry until I was seated on the plane.

It's funny, the smallest thing set me off. I boarded and got my seat. I'd already returned to the hotel, gathered my things, and then got an Uber to the airport. The whole while I was thinking about what went down, obviously. But I managed to keep it together.

And then, once we were in the air, I looked at the seat beside me.

It was empty.

I guess in the time since he moved his flight, they weren't able to sell a new ticket.

Seeing it made me start to cry. Jason was supposed to be there.

There was a man in a suit seated in the aisle seat, so I didn't have much privacy. I turned and pretended I was looking out the window. As quietly as I could, I cried, mourning what I had with him.

I told myself it would be the first and only time I would cry about this.

I think I knew, even then, that I was lying to myself.

I just finished crying for the second time. I'm back in the city now, in my car. The airport parking lot around me is massive and totally still.

I can't stop crying.

I've never felt anything this painful.

It's over.

My friendship, or whatever I had with Jason . . . it's over.

I can never see him again. I just can't. For one thing, I know I'll never be able to trust him.

He's bad news for me.

Pull it together.

I wipe my eyes. Oh man, my cheeks are so wet. This is so embarrassing, I'm very glad nobody can see me right now. Above me, a plane flies overhead, just taking off. It's loud.

It's time.

I need to head home.

I turn the engine on, and pull out of the lot.

I feel . . . weird. I'm completely devastated by what happened with Jason. Still, under that, though, I feel this undercurrent of confidence I haven't felt in a long time. Maybe ever. I don't know what it is, or why I feel this way.

Maybe it's because I know how much I can survive now.

Or maybe this is just the leftovers of my time with Jason before his big reveal. Because I was feeling better from basically the second I left this accursed city. Maybe it'll take a few days for it to drag my mood back down.

Or it's something else. Something unexplainable.

Whatever it is, I don't feel as beaten down as I normally do.

I drive through the city. Eventually, I reach home and park. I check out my reflection in the rearview mirror. Yikes. I look like a hot mess. But there's not much I can do about that. I glance at my house.

The lights are on in the living room.

Dad's home.

But wait.

Luke said he was crashing at a friend's place all weekend so Dad would buy our story about us going away together for the weekend.

And yet, Luke's car is parked in the driveway.

He's home.

Maybe it's nothing. Maybe I'm just overthinking this, like I over-think everything.

I climb out of my car and close the door behind me. I lock it with my fob and then go up to the front door. I can hear Eddie scratching his paws against the wood. I unlock the door and open it.

Eddie is right there, expecting pats.

I give them to him, obviously.

"Hey, buddy," I say. "Miss me?"

"Matthew."

I look up. Dad is in the kitchen, wearing a dark purple shirt and slacks. His arms are crossed.

"Hey."

Luke appears, rounding the corner of the hallway. He freezes, sensing the tension. He looks like Eddie does when he gets scolded.

"I'm sorry," he says. "He was onto me, I had to tell him."

That's when I notice it. Dad's wide stance, and the throbbing vein in his neck. He's *furious*.

And Luke told him that I lied.

Oh man.

I'm so fucked.

CHAPTER TWENTY-NINE

Dad knows I lied to him.

For the first time, he knows.

"Who were you really with this weekend?" he asks. "And don't you dare lie."

It's hard to focus. I'm still so devastated after what happened that I'm not thinking straight.

If I get this wrong, it's game over for me.

And I have only seconds to come up with a convincing lie.

What can I do? How can I answer him?

Then it hits me. It's perfect.

Or, at least it's as close to perfect as I can hope for right now.

"I was with Cass; we planned a trip together," I say. "Are you happy now? You know my big secret; I officially have no space."

His eyebrows narrow. "Cassidy Strickland?"

"Yeah."

"But I told you not to see her!"

I glance at Luke. It all hangs on him.

If he somehow knows that Cassidy wasn't hanging out with me this weekend, then my plan is totally ruined.

But maybe . . .

"You sly dog," says Luke, grinning. "You told me you were just friends, that the girl was someone else. You swore on it."

"No I didn't."

"What's going on?" asks Dad.

"Isn't it obvious?" says Luke. "They're, you know . . ."

He makes an obscene gesture with his hands, the exact same one Cassidy made when we went to dinner.

Dad stares at me. "You've got a girlfriend?"

I cross my arms. "No. But we're seeing each other, I guess, and it's getting serious. I didn't tell you because I didn't think it was any of your business."

I hate dragging Cassidy into this. But it's my only option. I think I'll be able to explain things to her. It's another lie . . . But I just need to get through this conversation. If she helps me, I'll owe her forever.

Dad's still watching me. I'm not out of the woods yet. "How could you do this? She could be trying to learn your secrets! *Our* secrets!"

"Jesus, Dad," says Luke. "You can't seriously think Cass is a secret Donovan. This is just normal teenage sneakery, not some whole big plot."

"Don't question me. You know better than that."

"I'm not! But we have photos of us as kids. You really think the Donovans have been going for *that* deep a heist? Vince said it, we need to be wary of anyone *new* in our lives. Old friends are fine. I hate to say it, but you're being paranoid."

They stare each other down.

Dad finally relents.

Luke officially might be my hero. Even if he did kind of get me into this mess in the first place.

"Show me this photo," says Dad. "And, Matt, if this is true, I still don't understand why you didn't tell us you were dating her."

"I . . . um . . ."

"Dad," says Luke as he searches his phone. "He already said it, he just wanted to get to know her without us breathing down his neck. Do you want me to tell you every time I hook up with a girl?"

Dad's stare flicks between us. He's being ganged up on, and he knows it. I can't believe Luke is doing this. He's spending some of the capital he's built up by being so good at helping me out. But if he wanted to help me, why wouldn't he just follow through with the original plan?

"We're going to the bar," says Dad with a huff. "Get ready. Suzanne will be able to tell me if Cassidy was with Matt this weekend. We're leaving at nine." He walks away. A few moments later, his office door slams.

I expected this. Suzanne is Cassidy's mom, and Dad and her have been allies for years.

Now I need to get to part two of my plan.

Luke is still looking at me, grinning.

"What?" I say.

"I'm just proud of you, man. Cassidy. Nice work."

He claps me on the shoulder. I wonder if he'd act like this if he knew I'd hooked up with a guy. I hope he would, Luke is pretty chill about this sort of thing. I know he knows a few LGBTQ+ people, and he's never made a big deal about it. But I think it's different when it's family.

"Want to talk about it?" he asks.

"God no."

He laughs. "Fair."

I chew my bottom lip. "Are you mad?"

"About what?"

"That I lied? I'm sorry I did, I just . . ."

"Hey, no, I totally get it. But when you're ready to talk about it, I'm here, all right? There's so much I wish I knew about girls when I was your age. So if you want advice from someone who's been through it, I'm around."

It's actually really sweet of him.

Who knew he could be so wholesome?

"Thanks, man." I step closer. "But, dude, what happened?"

"I guess Dad pays more attention than I thought. If it was just me, I probably would've gotten away with it. But because it's you . . ."

Ah.

That does check.

"Dad's been different lately, ever since . . ."

He got shot.

"He's way harder to predict now."

Well, that's pretty terrifying.

"Anyway," he says. "We got away with it, so don't stress. I expect you to hold up your end of the deal, by the way."

"Yeah, sure."

I walk past him, back to my room. I close my door behind me, and then pull my phone from my pocket and open my messages to Cassidy. There's one last piece of the puzzle I need to sort out.

Hey, I have a HUGE favor I need to ask of you. I'm seeing this guy, and we went on a weekend away. Anyway, Dad found out, and asked me who I was hanging out with. Long story short, I said I was with you all weekend. He said he's going to double-check this tonight at the bar. Is there any chance you could cover for me? I'm not ready for him to know yet.

I hit send.

I stare at the message, like that will make her respond faster. While I wait, my thoughts return to Jason.

I fall backward onto my bed.

My room feels really still.

I rest my hands on my stomach and watch my fan spin. It's really over.

This is it.

After everything, it ended. Now I'm never going to see him again.

I mean, I can't, right?

He's the son of a cop.

This is going to be painful, but I need to do it. I open Instagram and unfollow him. For good measure I block him. Then I go through every single app I have him on and delete him. Unfriend, unfollow, the whole shebang.

I get sick of thinking about how much this sucks, so I scroll my phone, looking for the right song. Nothing feels right. I end up settling on this band I like called With Confidence. I hit play on one of their sad breakup songs.

But the song doesn't distract me. I can barely focus.

Then my phone buzzes. Cassidy.

So you want me to be your beard? Lol.

I mean, yeah? Is that okay?

It's totally fine dude . . . what are friends for? ☺

What are friends for? There's so much I can pull from her saying that.

First, that we're actually friends now. Which is pretty amazing. Also, that she's willing to cover for me to my dad, the head of the Miller empire. I don't want to underappreciate how massive that is.

She's a true friend.

* * *

When Dad, Luke, and I reach Jimmy's, I'm actually less nervous than I expected I'd be when we left the house. I don't think Cassidy is going to stab me in the back. The bad part about that, though, is it leaves some mental space to think about Jason.

And I really don't want to do that right now.

I can just see Sunshine Diner in the distance.

I picture us eating waffle fries and talking about video games. It was maybe the best night of my life. I keep thinking that, even though I know the whole truth now. I still don't even know how deliberate he was. Was he just acting like that, so I'd befriend him? How much did I actually get to know him?

Dad gets out of the car, and so does Luke. I take a second to breathe in and out, and then I step out, too.

Time to face the music.

Inside the bar, I see Cassidy is already here, with her mom, Suzanne.

Maybe I *should* be worried. Now my nerves surge. If Cassidy decides, she could ruin me.

Dad approaches Cassidy and Suzanne, who are seated at a booth.

"Can I have a word?" he asks.

Suzanne nods, and the pair go upstairs.

Luke and I sit down in Cassidy's booth.

I want to make sure she told her mom that we were hanging out earlier, but Luke is right here.

It's kind of awkward.

"So, Cass," says Luke. "I heard you two were . . ."

He makes the sexual finger gesture.

"Are you jealous?" she asks.

"Pfft, no. I ended things with *you*, remember?"

"Oh, sweetie, it's so cute that you think that." She pats him on the cheek. "Come on, Matt, let's get a drink, in private."

I mouth the word "sorry" to Luke, and then follow Cassidy across the bar. A lot of people watch us. A few guys even nod approvingly at me. I feel like Little Matty has finally stepped up and finally done good.

In their eyes, anyway.

Success is so often defined by heterosexual life-goal posts. Get a girlfriend, get married, have kids, etc. . . .

I hate that.

We sit down in a quiet section of the bar.

"I owe you big-time," I say, keeping my voice down so I know nobody can hear me. "Seriously, thank you. You're a lifesaver."

She waves a hand. "Don't worry about it. Like I said, what are friends for?" She leans forward. "Now, tell me about this guy you're seeing! You must be serious, if you went on a trip with him! I can't believe you didn't tell me."

Again, I wish Jason were just an ordinary guy.

That way I could talk to her about him.

I shrug. "He's just a guy."

"How'd you meet?"

"Grindr."

She snorts. "How romantic."

"Right?"

"Come on, dude, don't be coy. Tell me about him! If you met on Grindr, does that mean you're, like, hooking up?"

"Um."

I feel my cheeks warm.

"Oh my God, you are! What was it like?"

"It was *so* good. Have you ever done something and then, like, then after you do it, it becomes the only thing you *ever* want to do? It was very that."

I hope she doesn't ask me which position I was. I feel like that'd be really invasive. Not that I'm ashamed, but like, I'd never ask her which position she was in if I found out she'd had sex. I can't see why for gay dudes some people think asking is okay. We started out doing lighter things, and when that stopped being enough for us, I went into the bathroom and got ready. Then I came back out, and after we both decided we were sure we wanted to, we went all the way.

"I haven't, no," she says. "But I'm so glad you've found that."

"I mean, yeah."

"Tell me about him."

"He's, like . . . so sweet. And nice, too. And he just sort of knows exactly what to say to make me feel good about myself. I don't know how he does it. And he's really weird, but in this, like, cool way. Plus he really likes video games, too, which is cool. I dunno, we just click, it's hard to explain."

And I'm never going to see him again.

"It doesn't matter, though," I say. "Things actually ended between us."

"What, why?" She watches me for a moment. "Dude. I feel like you should have cartoon hearts above your head right now. You'd be a total fool to let someone like that go. And you, my friend, have never struck me as a fool."

She has a point. I can't even talk about him without turning into a gushing mess.

"We just don't see eye to eye," I say. "On, like, anything."

"I think that's normal, sometimes. How long have you been seeing him?"

"A couple of months. But it's been so difficult. To be honest it's never been easy, so maybe this is a good thing."

"Easy is *so* overrated. I don't know why people are so scared of things that are hard. It means you care, and the end result is going to be better than something easy."

I feel like that might be a slightly problematic viewpoint, and I'm not sure I agree with it.

"I just don't think you should give up," she says. "You clearly like him a lot."

"Yeah. But I feel like I shouldn't."

"As long as you're not hurting anyone, you should just feel what you feel. I . . ."

She freezes. Dad and Suzanne have reappeared back in the bar.

I guess I'm going to find out if I've managed to bluff my way through this.

The pair make their way up to us.

"And?" says Cassidy, like she's ready to fight.

"You're off the hook," says Dad, who is staring right at me. "I'm sorry that I was so nosy, Matt. I'll give you more space from now on.

Sometimes I forget that you're a young man now and I shouldn't be so domineering."

"It's fine," I say.

"You know, I always thought I'd never act like my own father. Yet here I am, acting just like him. He never gave me any space when I was your age, especially when I started dating. I can't believe I did the same thing to you."

"Time'll do that to you," says Suzanne. "Want to have a drink and work through it?"

"I think I need more than one."

"That can be arranged."

The two head to the bar.

"Oh God," says Cassidy. "If they get together because of this, I'm never going to forgive you."

She pretends to gag.

"I'd understand fully."

She smiles.

And then something comes flying in through the front window.

There's a crunch sound, and then a fiery explosion.

I can't move.

It was a Molotov.

We're under attack.

Another Molotov flies in. It explodes through the other window this time. It hits the bar, and there's a whoosh, and suddenly . . .

The bar goes up in flames.

CHAPTER THIRTY

THE BAR IS ON FIRE.

Everything caught so fast, and now the whole place is burning. It's like something out of a nightmare. Huge orange flames snake up the walls. People are screaming. Smoke is already pooling at the ceiling.

It's chaos.

I'm frozen. It's like my feet are stuck to the floor. All I can do is watch as it all unfolds. I can barely even breathe.

I feel scorching heat.

People are shouting, but I can see only dark shapes.

Another Molotov flies in through the shattered window. It hits the far wall, crunches, and explodes in a huge orange fireball. Through the flames and smoke, I can just see the wall of glass bottles behind the bar. It's all alcohol.

If that gets hit . . .

Something pulls on my wrist, yanking me to the ground.

It's Cassidy.

"What are you doing?" she shouts. "Move!"

She army-crawls along the ground, cutting a path through the bar, dodging anything that's aflame. The ground is hot, and I think I'm starting to breathe in smoke. I'm coughing, and feel light-headed. I know that's bad.

Up ahead, I see the back door.

Someone is standing in front of it, holding it open, shepherding people out.

I'm nearly there.

Once I get outside, I'll be safe.

We go around a burning table and then finally reach the exit. Cassidy sprints out. I follow her and make it outside, into the cool night air. I cough, hacking up my lungs. Through watering eyes I check and see that she's fine. Thank God.

I'm safe.

Then it hits me.

Luke. And Dad.

I rush around, checking all the people who are huddled outside. I spot Cassidy talking to her mom, along with Vince and his family. I see Tony and Grandma and almost everyone else in my family.

But Luke and Dad aren't here.

My stomach plummets.

They're still in there.

I need to go back. I have to.

I can't lose them.

I move toward the door. It's like I'm on autopilot. Someone grabs me and pulls me back. They hold me so tight I can't move.

"What are you doing?"

I turn and see that it's Vince, holding me.

"They're still in there!" My throat hurts, and my voice sounds hoarse. "They didn't get out!"

"Matt, if you go in, you'll die, too. Do you think they want that?"

But I can't just stand here. So I fight against him as hard as I can. He manages to hold me tight.

I wish I were stronger.

We watch the bar burn. The flames are towering, and a pillar of thick black smoke is rising up into the sky. *Please*, I think. I'm not religious, but I pray sometimes. I think it's a leftover from the Catholic masses Dad used to make us go to before he gave up on trying to make Luke and me religious. So I don't know if anyone is listening, but now feels like the right time to pray.

Smoke is billowing out of the doorway. I think it's getting thicker. As a group, we move down the alley, away from the burning building.

I can't lose my family tonight. I just can't.

Two figures appear in the doorway.

It's Luke. And Dad.

Luke's dragging Dad out. He's limp. They reach safety, and both of them collapse against the alley wall. I run over to them. Luke's clothes are steaming, and he's coughing a lot. But I check his body, and he seems uninjured.

Dad's mostly okay, too. He looks like he might be in shock, as he's not moving much, and his stare is fixed on a single point on the ground.

I've never seen him look like this.

I wonder if he got hit by the same shock that I did, before Cassidy pulled me out of it.

"Dad, are you okay?" I ask.

"He got trapped in the bathroom," says Luke. "I had to put out a fire by the door. There was an extinguisher under the bar."

Luke's an actual hero.

I turn my focus back to Dad. He still looks out of it.

"Just breathe," I say, trying to keep my voice as even as possible.

He takes in a few deep breaths. That seems to break him out of his daze, and he faces me. I'm expecting him to be mad, but honestly, it's relief I can see in his features.

He waves a hand. "Stop crowding me."

He's going to be fine.

We got so lucky.

And then it hits me. The Donovans. They're the reason I almost lost my father and my brother. Now that I know Jason isn't a member of the family, I have no sympathy left for them.

I think I might hate them.

"Everybody down!" shouts Vince.

Just as he says that, I notice headlights at the end of the alley farthest from us. It's a sleek silver car, blocking our path.

The headlights turn off.

What are they doing?

Has someone come to help us? If so, why are they blocking the alleyway? And why would Vince tell us to get down?

"Run!" shouts Vince.

Everything goes still.

The window lowers. It happens in slow motion.

Other people figure it out a second before I do.

Everyone around us scatters. I see the nozzle of a gun poke out of the window.

Luke grabs my wrist and pulls me into a stumbling run toward the other end of the alley. We go as fast as we can, running close to the wall. I turn back and see Dad right behind us.

I hear the gun first.

Then I feel it.

Bullets rain down around us. It's so dark, but I can hear them hitting the dumpsters around us. I see sparks, and hear bullets hitting the metal. A body to my right falls, but it's too dark to tell who it is. Luke is still holding on to my wrist, pulling me forward, his grip like a vise.

I swear I feel a bullet skim over the top of my head.

Luke and I manage to make it out of the alley. We round the corner and press our backs against the wall, so we're protected. Dad joins us a heartbeat later.

My relief is immense.

But we aren't safe yet.

Some family members return fire.

Down the street to my left, in the parking lot, is Dad's car. Cassidy and her mom made it to theirs.

"Where's Vince?" asks Dad, but I can tell in his voice he already knows.

The dark shape we saw fall.

Hatred fills Dad's features, and he pulls a gun from a holster on his hip. He takes a step toward the alley.

I glance at Luke.

We each grab one of Dad's arms. He fights us, but we manage to hold him still. I'm glad he's still weak, as we manage to overpower him.

"Dad, stop!" I shout.

"Get off me!"

"It's too late!" shouts Luke. "They'll kill you, too. Please!"

He stares at us for a second.

"Killing yourself won't do anything," I say. "If you want revenge, you need to be smart. Make them pay some other way."

It's the only thing I can think of to say that'll make him stop.

He nods. "You're right. Let's go."

He's being really scary. He just, like, switched. From furious enough to murder, to cool and collected, all in a heartbeat.

How can he do that?

If it was Luke in the alley, then, well, I don't know what I'd do.

The gunfire has stopped.

Keeping our heads low, we run over to the parking lot.

I get into the back seat, and Luke climbs into the passenger side. Dad steps on the gas, and we speed out of the lot. I glance at the burning bar, and feel something I never have.

I hate the Donovans.

CHAPTER THIRTY-ONE

VINCE'S FUNERAL IS ONE OF THE MOST ELABORATE SPECTACLES I've ever seen.

I think he'd like it.

The service is taking place in this grand churchlike building. There's a priest, apparently a high-ranking one, if clergy have ranks. He's a big deal in the community, is what I mean. He greets the family before the service with a smile, like today was just another day.

At least his eulogy is good. It's epic and sad.

I glance around. Maybe a hundred people have shown up, and each one is wearing beautiful clothes. Which is good. If someone showed up in jeans I might've lost it.

It's about respect.

To my left is my aunt Sara and her two daughters. She's a widow now, and my cousins no longer have a father. All because of the Donovans.

I've never seen three people look more ruined.

I know my uncle was a torturer. He did unspeakable things and never really seemed to care about it. But looking at his grieving family, I know he didn't deserve this.

I also can't help but think how easily this could be Luke's funeral.

Or Dad's.

Or mine.

We three got lucky.

Vince, and others, didn't.

There were numerous injuries from the fire, and two others died in the shooting. It'd be all over the news if our family didn't have control over the local media. We've kept it quiet and explained the fire as the result of a gas leak. The bar burning down made headlines, but nobody knows what really happened.

People tell us we got lucky. But that's the thing about luck. It runs out eventually.

If nothing changes, one day, maybe soon, I'll be at one of these things for Luke or Dad.

Or they'll be at mine.

*　*　*

Receptions are weird.

I mean, some people are smiling and laughing and acting like this is just an ordinary gathering. Other people are inconsolable.

"There you are," says a voice, and I turn.

Cassidy.

She sits down beside me. She's wearing a black dress. Her makeup is perfect. Either it's waterproof, because I'm pretty sure that's a thing, or she never really cared about Vince. For some reason, that thought really bothers me.

"How are you?" I ask.

She shrugs. "Shitty. How are you?"

"I don't even know, to be honest. I don't think it's hit me yet."

It's a lie.

I'm angry.

I just don't know how I feel about feeling that. It feels like the sort of thing I shouldn't admit.

She nods. "Were you close?"

I don't feel like lying.

"Not really. I guess it feels weird because now I'm never going to be."

"I get that. Death is so hard because people are built to want what they can't have. Now he's always going to be the one who got away. Sorry if that's weird to say, I've just been thinking about it a lot."

I let that sink in for a second. It brings Jason to my thoughts. Even here.

What's wrong with me?

"Hey, I was just wondering, did you talk to your dad?" she asks.

"About what?"

"My theory about the Friend Scheme."

That feels like a lifetime ago.

"Oh, yeah. I did."

"And?"

"He didn't listen to me. You shouldn't be offended; he never does."

"Oh." She frowns.

Now she knows I'm not worth her time. I'm never going to be in charge, and now that I've shown that I'm a dead end, she's going to bail.

"I'm going to do a lap," she says. "All right? And you should try the cookies over there, they're weirdly good."

"'Kay."

She stands up and walks away.

I'm probably overreacting. It's a funeral reception, everyone is acting weird, because we aren't taught how we should act at one of these things. Cassidy isn't going to drop me over this.

I pull my phone from my pocket. I turned it off during the service. No new messages.

I squeeze my phone case for a second, so hard I'm worried the screen might crack, then put it back into my pocket.

* * *

After the reception, we all went to our place.

People are drinking, but nobody is having a good time. Obviously.

Barely anyone is even talking. What could we even talk about? Talking about anything else would be disrespectful, and I don't think any of us need to vocalize just how awful this is.

Luke makes his way up to me.

He's wobbling all over the place, and his eyes are red.

He collapses onto me. I've never seen him this drunk. He stinks like bourbon.

"So this girl—I know it's not Cass," he says. "Is she hot?"

His face is so dazed it's like he isn't even listening.

"Yeah," I say. "She's smoking."

"Show me pics."

"Dude, no."

"Why?"

"Because I don't want to."

He leans in close. "What are you hiding?"

"I . . ."

"You think I don't know," he says. "But I do. I've known the whole time."

"Known what?"

He closes his eyes, for like a few seconds. Then he finally opens them.

"What?" he asks. "Why are you looking at me like that?"

"You're *drunk*."

He raises a finger to his lip. Like this is a secret, not the most obvious thing on the planet. I do think, though: What does he think he knows?

Dad makes his way up to us.

"Can you two fetch a wineglass for everyone?" he asks. "We're having a meeting."

Luke does a very wonky salute. "Yes, sir!"

Dad turns to me. "How much has he had?"

"I'm guessing a lot."

"I'm not drunk, you two are drunk."

"Christ. Luke, go sleep this off. Matt, set the table."

Luke is now leaning most of his weight against me. He's really heavy.

"Sure," I say.

I help Luke to his room. Eddie trots after us.

"Sorry," says Luke. "I'm such a mess."

"Just don't throw up on me."

We reach Luke's room. He takes off his jacket and throws it onto the floor. Then he walks around and collapses onto his bed.

"Would you say I'm a good brother?" he asks. "I try, you know."

"The best. Now lie still."

I grab his trash can, take the lid off it, and then put it beside his bed. Last, I fetch him a glass of water. When I get back to his room, he's passed out, with his arm around Eddie, who looks up at me, like: *I've got this.*

"Good boy," I say.

I leave Luke's room and then set about putting wineglasses on the table.

Dad's got a few expensive bottles of white in the fridge, so I bring those out, too. When I'm done, people start taking their seats. It's only the adults, though, along with Vince's daughters, because nobody is going to tell them what they can and can't do right now. I'm not sure if I'm supposed to join or not.

"Did you get one for yourself?" asks Dad.

I hadn't.

I go back and fetch myself a wineglass.

And I join the table. Sara pours. I take a sip, and it's actually nice. It's rich and tastes decadent.

Maybe I can get used to this.

I do hate the Donovans now.

And this is what my life is. There's no escaping it. I may as well just get on board.

Sara is here, along with her two daughters. Vince's usual seat, next to her, is empty. I guess everyone thinks sitting in it would be too weird. Becca, his oldest daughter, is holding his switchblade. I wonder if that means she's taken up his mantle. That's a fucking terrifying thought.

"Now," says Dad, and everyone falls silent. "Has everyone got a drink?"

I'm surprised Dad's not making me pour wine for everyone. A bottle is passed around, and the few people who don't have wine fill their glasses. Becca tries to pour herself one, but Sara shuts that down.

"Where's Luke?" she asks as she passes the wine bottle down the table.

"He had a little too much."

"A *little*," says Tony. "The boy was staggering all over the place."

Cruel laughter breaks out.

"Shut up," I say.

Everyone turns to watch me.

"Don't talk about my brother like that," I say. "Have some respect."

It's so quiet. But then Dad smiles.

"Well, look at you," says Tony. "Finally grown a pair, eh?"

"Bigger than yours."

Tony's eyes widen, but he, too, is smiling.

Everyone seems to be on board with this new version of me. If I ever wanted it, in this moment, I have that ever-elusive thing.

The respect of my family.

"Enough," says Dad. "We have a lot to discuss. This war needs to stop. If we had done what I suggested, my brother would still be alive and our allies wouldn't have been burned. Jimmy's has been in business since the thirties, and they took that from us, too."

Oh no.

I have an idea about Dad's plan.

Vince was one of the very few people who wanted to do it back when it was first brought up. But now Vince is dead.

Things are different.

The family will greenlight now. For him.

And if I know it, I'm sure Dad figured it out ages ago.

"I suggest we go through with my original plan," says Dad.

No, I think. *This can't be happening.*

I hate the Donovans . . . but this is mass murder.

"I suggest once again to call a peace meeting and then eliminate any Donovan who shows up. All opposed, raise your hands now."

I am opposed.

Obviously.

But nobody else is responding. Grandma is still, her expression hard to read. So I keep my hand down.

"Good," says Dad. "All those in favor?"

Grandma raises her hand, then every single hand in the room but mine raises.

We can't do this.

It's evil.

Still, I know I have no choice, and I know it doesn't really matter. It's clearly going ahead no matter which way I vote.

So I raise my hand.

Dad's lips twitch up into a small smile. "Good, it's settled, then."

I hope I find a way to forgive myself for this.

CHAPTER THIRTY-TWO

THE MEETING IS HAPPENING THIS WEEKEND.

The school bell rings. I'm in final period, calc, but I've spent the entire class staring out the window, thinking about the meeting. Dad has hired contract killers. Every Miller who goes to the meeting is supposed to be armed, too.

Even though this is a double cross, Dad's expecting a firefight. One last battle for the city.

I'm expected to go.

I pack up my books and head to my locker.

I'm feeling mostly like myself again. I still hate the Donovans, but . . .

I don't want them all to die.

I need to find a way to stop the meeting. To make Dad, and the rest of my family, see reason.

That feels impossible. I'm just one guy. And what I'm going up against is massive. I need to stop the wheels turning on a business that has successfully run the underbelly of this city for decades. It's something not even a well-equipped police force with heaps of funding has been able to do.

I head out to my car and drive home.

When I get there, I go straight to my room. I toss my backpack onto the ground and then fall onto my bed. I try to zone out my thoughts with an episode of *My Favorite Murder*, but it doesn't work.

I can't just sit by and let my family do something I know in my gut is wrong.

Jason didn't.

His family wanted him to betray me. But he stood up to them. He knew what he was doing to me was wrong, so he stopped. My situation is more complicated than his, though. And way harder to escape.

Or maybe I just feel that way.

I know it was a big deal that he stood up to his parents. It terrified him, like what I'm facing now terrifies me.

Yet he did it.

I need to see him. I can't do this alone.

I'm hoping that maybe, just maybe, he will have some sort of idea as to how I can stop all of this.

I unfollowed him on everything, though, and deleted his number. I load Instagram, and search for his profile. Huh. He's switched it to private, so I can no longer see his photos. I wonder if that has anything to do with me.

I tap the follow button.

Request sent.

I turn my phone upside down and stare up at the ceiling.

I think this is the right move. On my own, I have no chance of dealing with this. I can't tell Jason any of the details about what is going to happen. I'm just hoping that he will be able to give me some perspective and maybe some advice.

That's all I need from him.

I check my phone.

Nothing.

I get up and go about my usual routine. I play with Eddie for a while. I make myself pasta for dinner. I play some *Fortnite* with Luke.

I keep checking my phone.

It's quarter past midnight, and I'm about to call it a night. That's when my phone lights up.

He's followed me back.

Hey. ☺

Hey. Thanks for being in touch.

I didn't know if I should. What's going on?

I need your help. Is there any chance we can meet?

I don't know, man. You might be leading me into a trap.

I'm not, I promise. We could meet somewhere public? Dude, I swear, all I want is some advice. This isn't a trap. And yes, I know that's what someone who was setting a trap would say.

Haha. This might be the dumbest thing I've ever done, but okay. How about Bayshore Park, after school tomorrow? And it's public, so don't try anything.

Bayshore Park is Donovan territory.

Yet another risk. That's Jason in a nutshell, though.

Endless risk.

Sounds good. I'll be there.

* * *

The park is super pretty.

There's a row of palm trees, and in the middle of those, evenly spaced, are wooden park benches. I watch as a couple, two women, walk down the pathway in front of the ocean, holding hands.

Jason chose a great spot, is all I'm saying.

Still, what am I doing?

Maybe I should leave.

But then I see him in the distance, and it all makes sense. He's wearing a light blue dress shirt and slacks. Honestly, I can't believe I didn't see who he really is before.

He looks *just* like a rookie cop.

He stands. His mouth is hanging open, and he looks at me like he hasn't seen me in decades.

My heart goes wild.

He slowly walks toward me.

"Hey," he says.

"Hi."

He throws his arms around me.

He holds me tight, and my first thought is that I should push him off.

Instead, I sink into the hug.

God, how did I survive without this? How was I strong enough?

We hold each other. I rest my cheek on his shoulder and close my eyes. He smooths down the hair on the back of my head. For the first time in a while, everything feels somewhat okay.

I'm exactly where I want to be. With him.

We break apart.

"You look so good," he says. "I knew coming here was a risk, but I've never been able to resist a handsome man. It's my Achilles' heel."

I mean. That helps. He's not totally off the hook, but it definitely helps.

"Thanks."

I smooth down my shirt. I'm wearing a white shirt and my tailored black slacks. I wanted him to see me like this, as a reminder of who I really am.

A Miller.

I'm done pretending.

He narrows his eyes. "Are you okay?"

I shrug and stick my hands into my pockets. "How much do you know about what's happened?"

"Just that the bar burned down. That's all I know, I promise."

I picture the open window of the car blocking our path. Then the sound of gunfire.

"Were you there that night?" he asks.

"I was."

"I'm guessing it was more than a gas leak?"

"That would be correct."

He nods.

"You aren't going to tell anyone I said that, are you?" I ask.

"Not if you don't want me to."

"Good. I don't. You can't."

"I get it, Matt. Should we sit down?"

"Yeah."

We both sit down on the park bench. I keep a comfortable amount of space between us.

"You know," he says. "If you need to frisk me, you could. But I promise I'm not wearing a wire."

I blink.

"Sorry, that sounded way more sexual than I meant it to."

"No. I think it's a good idea. Can you, please?"

"Sure."

He quickly unbuttons his shirt, and then opens it. His chest is totally smooth.

"Thanks," I say as he buttons it back up. "This is weird."

"What, me stripping in public?"

"No. Just being here, with you. Your mom's a cop."

"Yeah."

"Is your dad a cop, too?"

"Nah, he's in software. Cops don't make mansion money."

"Right. So what happened with you, after . . ."

He lets out a puff of air. "Well, Mom lost her shit. She knew how close I was to finally cracking you. The only thing she wants to do is take down your family, and I blew it."

"Did she take away your trust?"

"Yeah. And my college fund. I'm hoping Dad might be able to get her to change her mind about that. Maybe I'll get a scholarship, but if not, my college plans are, well, I don't really have college plans. I was betting on that trust, honestly."

"You're smart; you'll find a way, with or without it."

He smiles. "So what do you need?"

"Advice."

"About what?"

"Well, some things are going down with my family and the Donovans. People's lives are in danger. And I can't sit by and let it happen anymore. I need to stop it. But I can't think of anything I can do to stop them. They're too powerful."

"Okay."

I wait. I'm hoping he'll have some idea that'll fix this whole mess.

"So what do you want to do?" he asks.

"Stop the war. Prevent any further bloodshed. Keep my brother and my dad safe."

"That's a lot."

"I know. That's why I need your help."

He thinks about it for a while.

"I don't think you can do anything," he says.

"Not good enough. There has to be *something* I can do. I can't just let them do this."

"I know it's hard. Trust me, I know."

"You stood up to your parents, though."

"I did. For so long I tried so hard to bend myself into someone okay with what she wanted from me. I've spent hours at baseball because it's what she wants. She thinks it's the mark of a successful young man."

"I know," I say. "I think it's why we get along so well."

"Yeah. But that's the thing. I've stopped. After I told her I couldn't follow through with the scheme, something flipped. It's like, I realized I don't actually have to do everything she says. I can live my own life. You could do the same thing."

"What are you saying?"

"I'm saying you should tell them you quit. You can't stop them, but that doesn't mean you have to be a part of it."

I've never thought about it this way. Instead of changing them . . . I could change my destiny. I could stop putting up with this life.

I could tap out.

"My dad wouldn't let me," I say. "There's no way."

"Then don't ask him. Just tell him what you're doing."

"I can't. He's . . . he's someone who always gets his way."

"Would he really go against his own son? I thought family was everything?"

"It is, but only if you play by the rules. He has expectations of me. I'm not who he wants me to be, but it doesn't matter. He's going to keep pushing me to live up to being his son."

"That's an assumption. Have you ever told him that you're unhappy?"

"No."

"Then maybe that's worth a shot."

"But what about everything that's going on? People are in danger. I can't just walk away from them. I can't let my family kill people."

"Sure you can."

"How? What kind of person would do that?"

"Matt, you don't need to be the one who solves this problem. Leave it to people who signed up for it, people like my mom. You never asked to be born into your family. Seriously, man, you don't need to be the one responsible for stopping them."

I see it now. But can I really let myself off the hook?

I have no idea how my father will react if I tell him what's going on with me. But it can't be that much worse than it is now.

Jason is right: It's worth a shot.

"You might be the smartest person I've ever met," I say.

"You need to meet more people then. But thank you. You're very sweet."

Silence falls.

"I'm guessing this is still it for us, though?" he asks. "You aren't going to see me again after this, are you?"

"I mean, never say never, but . . ."

He is still linked with the cops. This is so risky.

"Well," he says. "Then I'm hoping for a kiss goodbye . . . ? Maybe it'd help with closure. One last kiss, and then . . ."

"You don't need to explain," I say. "I get it."

I lean across and put my hand on his chest. The material of his shirt feels silky, and I can feel his firm muscles underneath. I close my eyes and kiss him like my life depends on it.

Honestly?

It is, by far, the best kiss we've ever had. It feels so good. I know I need to stop right now, or I'm never going to be able to stop myself from seeing him.

I move away.

"There you go," he says, smiling. "Was that cinematic enough for you?"

"Definitely."

"One last thing," he says. "I got you something, actually."

"Oh, okay."

He reaches into his pocket and pulls out a leather wristband.

"What's this?" I ask.

"It's a bracelet. I bought it a while ago, because I thought you'd like it. Then I realized I never gave it to you. I thought I'd give it to you now, as, like, a thanks-for-the-memories thing."

I take it from him. My first thought is that it might have some sort of recording tech in it. It's thin, just a strip of leather. But still.

"This is a friendship bracelet," I say.

"Exactly. I knew you'd get it."

"Well, thank you. I love it. But, dude, I really need to go. The longer I stay here, the more I want to keep you around. But I can't. If my dad finds out . . ."

"I know. I don't want to be sappy or anything, but I want you to know something."

"What?" I ask.

"I think we're always going to be friends."

"What do you mean?"

"We got so close and have gone through so much together. That's never going away. So, like . . . no matter what, we're going to be friends. Till the end."

I want to believe him. The thought gives me a strange comfort. Friends till the end.

CHAPTER THIRTY-THREE

I need to tell Luke first.

Well, I don't *need* to.

But I think it's the best strategy. If telling Dad about who I really am, and what I really want out of my life, is an epically bad idea, then he'll be able to tell me.

I could just walk into his room and do it.

Rip the Band-Aid and all that.

But it's Luke. And as much as we don't see eye to eye on stuff, I love him. I don't want that to change. If Dad pushes me away, I think I could deal. But if Luke starts to hate me, that would completely and utterly crush me.

I guess that's the risk I need to take.

It's been only a day since I met up with Jason, but this is the first time ever where who I am is working. As terrifying as it is to show Luke and Dad who I really am.

I can finish school and then apply for film school in California.

Then I'll be gone for good.

Until then, though, I want Dad to know I'm stepping away from the family business.

I can't stop them. Jason was right about that. I can ask Dad to try to make peace with them, but that's all I can do.

I try to muster up the courage to go to Luke's room. I'm shaking, it's that bad. I tell myself that Luke already knows.

He must. Everyone else just thinks I'm bad at the family business, but Luke knows me.

I check the time on my phone. It's ten to eight.

I'll do it at eight.

I have ten minutes.

I close my eyes, just thinking. This isn't something I can ever take back. Once this is out, this will always be out.

Eight minutes left.

Now six. Now two.

Now one.

It's time.

I sit up. Maybe I don't need to do this right now. Maybe I could just wait. Maybe . . .

I stand up and leave my room. I made a deal with myself, and my deals mean something.

Luke's door is open.

He's seated at his computer, playing *Dota*.

"Hey," I say.

He keeps playing. "What's up? I'm mid-game, dude, make it quick."

I can't do this here, when he's so distracted.

"I was wondering if you wanted to get burgers?"

"Yeah, order them."

"No, I mean, do you want to go out and get them?"

"Oh. Um, sure. Just give me ten minutes to destroy these clowns."

"Sure."

The next ten minutes pass so slowly.

Finally, Luke rounds the corner and steps into my room.

"Your car or mine?"

"I mean, yours, obviously."

I do like my car, but there's a reason he upgraded.

"Shake Shack?" he asks.

"Yes."

I practically worship at the altar of Shake Shack. So does he.

We drive out onto the highway, and he puts the top down.

I glance at him.

Time feels like it's sped up. All too quickly, we've gone to Shake Shack and ordered our food. Now we're parked in front of the beach, eating.

"So," I say. "I want to tell you something."

"I know."

"Okay . . . like, I don't really need to know where to start. I . . ."

"You're gay," he says.

I nearly drop my shake.

"What?"

"Or are you bi? I can totally see you being bi."

"I . . . I mean, I am gay, but that's not what I wanted to talk to you about."

"Oh." He grins. "I knew it."

"Did you?" I ask. "I mean, you've always been on my case about girls."

He eats a french fry. "It's not a big deal for me, I hope you know that."

"No, I do."

"So why'd you make such a big deal about it? You could've just been like, 'Yo, man, I like dudes.' And I would've been like, cool."

"I know. And if all I was doing is coming out, then I probably would've. But there's more."

"Oh," he says, his smile fading. "Okay. What is it?"

"It's really hard to say. I . . ."

"Come on, it's me. You can tell me anything. You saw how well I dealt with you coming out, right?"

I stare forward, out at the ocean. To the side is the city.

"I can't do this anymore."

"Do what anymore?"

"This life. The family business. I hate it so much, you have no idea."

He just nods.

"Say something," I say.

"I mean, I get it. Well, I don't exactly get it, but we're different. This is the life for me; I've always known that."

"I've always known it's not," I say. "I don't want to live this way."

"I get that."

"You do?"

"Yeah, man. Sometimes things just don't work. If you know it, you know it."

"But I don't want you to think that I don't love you and Dad. That's not what this is about at all. But what we do . . . I hate it."

"Okay," he says. "I didn't know it was this bad."

"It is. This whole time I've just wanted it to stop. And I think I've realized that it's never going to."

"But what about Dad's plan?"

"What? Mass murder? You don't think that's going to have ram-ifications?"

"Yeah, but—"

"I need to get out. Then maybe apply to school in California. I should go as far away as I can."

My brother's eyes spark. "I think you should tell Dad that. If you do, I bet he'll let you go. Like, right away, too."

"Really? Why?"

"Just trust me."

"You don't think he'll be mad?"

"Oh, he'll be furious. But he's different now, after the shooting. I don't know—just be honest."

"Okay, I will."

Luke puts his burger aside and starts up the engine.

"What are you doing?" I ask.

"Driving you home so you can do this."

"There's no rush, man. I sort of feel like this is nice, hanging out with you. Plus, you know all my secrets now."

"Huh, I guess that's true."

He turns off the engine.

There's slightly awkward silence.

"So," he says pointedly. He wants things to go back to normal between us.

I take a bite of my burger. There's this warm feeling in my chest.

I let Luke know who I really am. If I knew it'd feel this good, I would've done it ages ago.

CHAPTER THIRTY-FOUR

LUKE AND I ARE PARKED OUT FRONT OF OUR PLACE. DAD'S car is still here, so I know that he's home.

"What are you waiting for?" he asks.

Good question. Courage, I guess?

There's never going to be a perfect time for these hard conversations. It's better to just get it over with.

"You sure he's not going to lose his shit?" I ask.

"No, I'm not. But tell him about school in California."

I have no idea how school will make a difference. But whatever.

"You've got this," says Luke. "Just do what you did with me, and you'll be fine."

On that note, we both get out of the car.

Inside, Dad is behind the closed door of his office.

I rap my knuckles against the wood.

"I'm working."

"I know. Can I come in? I'll be quick."

He mumbles something that sounds like an agreement.

I open the door. The walls of his office are dark wood. The floor is cream carpet, and there's a lattice window at the back. He's seated at a desk facing the window. On his desk are a laptop, a notebook, expensive pens, a clipboard, and a few stacks of paper. To his left is a lazily stacked bookshelf.

I hardly ever come in here. It's always been implied that Luke and I are not allowed.

"What do you need?" he asks.

"A word, if now's a good time."

"It's not, but you're already here. So go on."

"Um," I say.

This is definitely way harder than telling Luke. I can barely get myself to form a sentence.

"I've been meaning to tell you something for a while," I say.

"Tell me what?"

"I, um . . ."

I just need to say it.

"I've tried my best," I say. "I swear, I really have. But what you do . . . I can't do it. I've never been able to. I'm not built like you and like Luke. I need to tap out."

Dad watches me for a second.

"You want out?"

"Yeah."

"Of what?"

"Everything," I say. "This." I gesture around his office. "I love you guys, but I can't . . . I've tried so hard to make it work so you'd be happy. But, Dad, I'm miserable. I barely sleep, and most of the time I'm an anxious wreck. I keep hoping these feelings will pass, but they never do."

He nods.

"Well?" I ask.

"You've totally blindsided me. I thought you were happy."

"I'm not. And I'm really sorry."

"How can it not be for you?" he says, the anger in his voice rising. "Our family has been in this business for generations. It's what we do."

"I know. But it doesn't work for me."

"So what?" he says. "You think you're the first person to spit in the face of years of tradition? Get over yourself and deal with it. I only want the best for you, and you have to trust me when I say this is the best path."

"Please, Dad—"

"And what will you do? I hope you aren't coming to me without a plan for your future."

"I'm not. I'd stay here until the end the year and work my ass off to get a scholarship. Then I'd move out west for college, and you'd never have to see me again, if you don't want to."

His brow creases. "Why west?"

"I've always wanted to try living there. I've never told you, but I have. It's what I've wanted for years. I hate it here."

He leans back in his chair and stares at me. But I see in his gaze something like a spark.

"I've suspected this for a while. One son takes after me. The other . . ."

Oh.

Mom.

He shakes his head. "Matt, I have something I need to tell you, too."

I freeze. *What's going on?*

"Your mom. Diane. You two were always incredibly close. From the time you were little, she wanted a different life for you."

My breath goes shallow, and my eyes fill with tears.

"You remind me of her in so many ways. It's possible I took some of my anger at losing her out on you."

He twists the silver ring on his finger.

"But that was wrong. You take after her. She was right. She loved you so much, Matt, and so do I. I hope you know that. I want what's best for you."

I can't believe it. My father has never spoken with me so openly. I feel shell-shocked.

"Dad, I don't know what to say."

"Son, I want you to be happy. No matter how complicated this gets, never forget that."

I won't.

CHAPTER THIRTY-FIVE

IT'S TAKEN ME A FEW WEEKS TO WORK EVERYTHING OUT. My applications are submitted, and now I'm ready for this change.

There have been a lot of family meetings, none of which I attended. Being done means being done all the way. Luke has kept me posted, and the biggest news is that the meeting with the Donovans was an actual meeting. Not a massacre.

Dad is slowly coming around to the idea that bloodshed just leads to more bloodshed.

I like to think I have something to do with that.

Millers may never be friends with Donovans, but that doesn't mean they need to be enemies.

I look around. My room is so barren now that I've taken down all my posters. Dad has said I can keep my room as is, in case I decide to visit, but I know Luke already has his eyes on it. I think he wants it to be a home gym.

Luke appears in my doorway. Eddie is beside him, his ears pressed down.

I think he can tell something is up, as he's been sulking all day. I've been giving him so much attention and a lot of treats, but he's too smart to fall for that.

"Is there anything left?" asks Luke.

"Nope, I think that's it."

He nods.

"This is really happening, huh?" he says.

"Yeah. It's not like I'm dying, though. You can always come visit."

He crosses his arms, and leans back a little. "Will you ever come back?"

"I don't know. Probably not for a while, at least."

"That's fair."

Together, we go down to the living room. Dad's in the kitchen.

"Ready?" he asks.

"Yeah."

Eddie seriously looks so sad.

I bend down. "Buddy, stop making that face. This isn't for good, I'll come back."

I'm not even sure if it's true. I pet him, and he licks my hand. I'll miss him, but I'm not going to miss how much he slobbers. I scratch the top of his head one last time, then go to wash my hands in the sink.

* * *

The drive across the city is uneventful. But still, I notice so much about it. Like how truly pretty it is, even during the day.

I know I've made the right decision, though.

We reach the airport and go through the motions. Soon, my bag is checked in, and all I have left to do is go through security.

And you know.

Say goodbye to Dad and Luke.

"You still sure about this?" asks Dad.

"I am," I say.

"As long as you're sure."

He offers his hand. I shake it.

It makes me feel so adult.

"Text me when you land," he says.

"Will do."

Luke grabs me in a big hug. "I'm going to miss you, man."

"I'll miss you, too."

We break apart. So this is it.

I wave at them and then head to security. I unzip my backpack and take off my shoes, and then go through the metal detector. Once I'm through, I turn back and look for Luke and Dad.

They're gone.

ONE YEAR LATER

CHAPTER THIRTY-SIX

I NEVER WANTED TO BE A CRIMINAL.

And now I'm not.

I'm just an ordinary guy. There's nothing special about me anymore.

But I'm the happiest I've ever been. By far.

Right now, I'm at my job at the movie theater in the mall closest to my house. I'm behind the counter, waiting to sell some tickets. I've been working here for nearly six months now, and unfortunately . . .

I'm starting to get over it.

As much as I love film, this job involves a lot of cleaning. And dealing with annoying customers.

Then more cleaning. And more dealing with annoying customers.

Rinse and repeat.

I still have no idea how people spill so much stuff. It's like they've never been taught to eat properly. Or that as soon as they walk into a theater, they completely forget and feel totally fine leaving their crap everywhere.

Also: Why are people such assholes?

Anyway.

There are a lot of things I could be doing that are way worse.

I know that for sure.

"Matt!" calls a voice.

It's my manager.

She's actually pretty great. I think she likes me because I plan on sticking around for a while. The staff turnover is high here, and showing someone new the ropes gets annoying if you have to do it every month. I've made it clear I'm here for the long haul, if she wants me. Which means at least through college, and she seems happy about that.

Plus, she loves David Lynch as much as I do.

"Can you clean cinema five?" my manager asks.

Damn. They were showing a kids' movie in there earlier. It's bound to be a shit show.

"Sure."

I grab the cleaning stuff, head inside, and sigh.

Like I suspected, it's a damn mess.

I get to work, starting in the back row. Maybe I'm being too negative. I really do like this job. Even if it isn't totally perfect, I feel as if I'm on the right track when I'm doing it. Being here just sits well with me, in a way my old life never used to.

I'm surrounded by movies.

More important, though, I'm never going to hurt anyone doing this.

I'm happy.

I won't lie, though, I still think about Dad and Luke all the time.

I miss them.

I know I made the right decision to get out, though.

As I bend to scoop up some spilled candy, I see someone walk in from the corner of my eye.

God.

People are so dumb.

I look up.

"Hey, you," Jason says.

He looks . . . different. He's more tanned than last time, and his hair is way longer, now tousled on top. He's just as good a dresser, though, and he's clearly kept on working out.

He looks down. I'm wearing the bracelet he got me. I've never taken it off.

"Dude," he says. "I missed you."

I can barely find my voice.

"I missed you, too," I say.

We smile at each other.

"So, *Matthew*," he says, looking at my name tag.

"Yeah?"

"Are you seeing anyone?"

"Nope. Are you?"

"Nope." He grins. "I guess my question now is: How would you feel about being friends again?"

I step closer to him and decide to go for it.

"Fuck friends," I say.

And I kiss him.

EPILOGUE

JASON IS COMING OVER TODAY.

I can't wait.

It's been nearly two weeks since I saw him at work, and we've spent basically every spare minute together. Now that I'm out, there's nothing stopping us from hanging out as much as we want.

He's never actually been to my house, though, which is why I'm excited. I want him to see what my new life is like.

I'm in my room now, trying to make sure it's as clean as possible. I know I've cleaned a bunch, and I can't see any mess, but still, I feel like there's more I should be doing. This moment has been a long time coming, and I want it to be totally perfect.

"Look at you," says Miriam, my roommate, and she stops in my doorway. "What's got you all stress-y?"

I turn and face her.

"Nothing," I say. "But I look good, right?"

"You look great. But if you want to impress whoever is coming over, why don't you wear that shirt I like?"

"The red one?"

"Yeah."

"It's not too dressy?"

She shakes her head. "Wear it with jeans, you'll be fine."

She's in school for fashion design, so I figure she knows this stuff.

"Okay. Noted. Thanks."

She smiles and then heads off down the hall.

I pull off my shirt and switch into the red shirt. I button it up and then check myself out in the mirror.

She was right.

I roll the sleeves up so it's a little less formal. And then I fix my hair.

The doorbell rings.

Okay.

He's here.

I jog down the steps, and see Ashley, Miriam's partner, open the door. Miriam stands beside her, grinning eagerly.

"Hi," he says. He scratches the back of the neck. It's so adorable.

"You must be the boyfriend," says Miriam. "Matt's told us a lot about you."

Er.

So, I have talked with them about Jason. But I've never called him my boyfriend. Because he's *not* my boyfriend.

Why would she say that?

"We're just friends," I say, saving Jason from this epic shit storm of awkwardness.

"Yeah," he says.

"Oh," she says. "I thought . . ."

"Just stop," I say, and I grab Jason by the wrist. "You've done enough."

I throw her an eyeroll, and she smiles. She's kind of known for talking a lot and making things awkward accidentally. I know if we stick around, she'll just make it worse.

We reach my bedroom, and I shut the door behind us. I lock it for good measure.

Jason is grinning.

"Shut up," I say. "Seriously, not a word."

He smiles and looks around. My room is pretty similar to my old one. He walks up to my *Mulholland Drive* poster.

"Your roommate seems nice."

I nod. "I got lucky, that's for sure."

It's the truth.

"Well, I'm glad," he says. "You deserve the best."

"Thanks. So, what's new?"

It's a joke, as we've been basically inseparable.

He looks up. "Mom called."

"Oh shit, what'd she say?"

"Same as always. She thinks studying game design is a waste of time, and I'm ruining my life. I think she's just mad I'm not in Florida anymore so she can't control my every move."

"And what do you think?"

"I think I'm exactly where I should be."

He smiles. "Anyway, I think we should circle back to your roommate thinking we're boyfriends."

I start blushing. "It's ridiculous, right?"

"I mean, I wouldn't say that." His voice is shaking.

"It's complicated," I say.

He looks into my eyes. "Does it have to be?"

He touches my arm.

"Does it?" I ask. My voice has gone thick. "Because . . . because I've thought about it a *lot*. And I . . . I think I'd really like it. I just didn't think you wanted that. It'd be really *complicated*."

"It would be," he says, laughing. "But I think it's worth a shot."

I can't believe this is happening.

It's so perfect.

I want this moment captured on film.

"So, boyfriends?" he asks.

"Boyfriends."